BETTY JOHANSEN

Lilli's Song

First edition

This book was professionally typeset on Reedsy.
Find out more at reedsy.com

This book is dedicated with adoration and praise to Jesus Christ, the Lord of Glory,
Who loves me and gave Himself for me.

Contents

Foreword	ii
Chapter 1: Mr. Fletcher's Experiment	1
Chapter 2: Lunchtime Colloquies	10
Chapter 3: Lilli's Decision	17
Chapter 4: Friday at Skyport High School (SHS)	27
Chapter 5: Falcon's Threat	36
Chapter 6: UFO Theology	50
Chapter 7: Tumbling Grades	60
Chapter 8: Calm Before the Storm	67
Chapter 9: The Longest Weekend	73
Chapter 10: Hubble's Fate	89
Chapter 11: Anna and Malcolm	95
Chapter 12: Falcon's Story – Fact or Fiction?	107
Chapter 13: Doomed Experiment	118
Chapter 14: Alibis	129
Chapter 15: End of the Search	137
Chapter 16: Revised Approach	145
Chapter 17: Stolen Gun	155
Chapter 18: Coach's Story	162
Chapter 19: Showdown	174
Chapter 20: Final Farewell	190
Epilogue	201
Author's Note to the Reader	208
Acknowledgments	210

Foreword

Named Characters in Approximate Order of Mention

Kip Fletcher - World History teacher at Skyport High School and author of historical novels

Named members of Mr. Fletcher's second-period World History class of freshmen:

- Zion (pronounced **Zee**-awn) Johnson
- Nobu (Nobby) Tanaka
- Palmer Evans - quarterback and captain of freshman football team
- Camilla Rodriguez
- Lilli Park
- Jasmine Clark
- Marion Rogers - science nerd

Coaches and named members of Skyport's varsity basketball team

- Shad Harris – head coach
- Len Josephs – assistant coach
- Elroy (Royal) Douglas - junior
- Morton (Hyper)Hooper - junior, point guard
- Titus Murphy – sophomore, student trainer
- Kent Spencer – senior

Hubble - Lilli's zebra

Adolf - Royal's Doberman Pinscher

Aziz (pronounced uh-**zēz**) - leader of the Soterians

Named teachers in Mr. Fletcher's lunch bunch:

- Sadie Sharp - World History teacher
- Len Josephs- U.S. History teacher (and assistant varsity basketball coach)
- Tulsa Grant - English teacher
- Laurel Tanner - Biology teacher

Bryce Douglas - Royal's father, a prison warden

Anna Park - Lilli's mother, a certified nurse-midwife

Treena Wood - high school senior, treasurer of Student Council

Darron Vance - one of Mrs. Sharp's students

Myles(Falcon) Dyer - ex-con whose brothers, Condor and Hawk, are still in prison

DeDe Fletcher - Kip's wife who manages his book sales

Riley Wood - Treena's Dad, youth pastor at their church (Community of Faith)

Donte Rhodes - wide receiver on freshman football team, Palmer Evans's best friend

Members of the SWH (Sowers, Waterers, Harvesters) prayer group:

- Andrew Paxton, senior
- LaDawn Hardy, junior
- Jarred Norman, junior
- (Also, Treena Wood, Nobby Tanaka, LilliPark, and Jasmine Clark - already listed above)

Caleb Carson - detective for Skyport Police Department

Judson Wheeler - owner of farm close to the Douglas farm, a search team leader

Shawna Douglas - Royal's missing mother

Irene, Judith, and Karon - Anna's grown daughters

Malcolm Park - Anna's ex-husband, a petrochemical engineer

Asa Latimer (Doc) - Skyport veterinarian

Lucas Moreno - county sheriff

Abe Blanchard - farmer north of Skyport

Kandi Park - Malcolm's wife

Diego Calderon - owner of garage where Falcon works

Tandy Koch - real estate agent

Kasi Mann - accountant

Peyton Starr – defense attorney

Peg Norman - Skyport P.D.'s internet guru

Maisie Spencer - Kent's mother

Lillianna - Anna's granddaughter

Wade Lambert – well-known Texas defense attorney

Mason Atkins - Texas state senator

Molly Atkins - Mason's deceased first wife

Kolton, 10 years old, and Kraig, 8 years old – sons of Malcolm and Kandi Park

Chapter 1: Mr. Fletcher's Experiment

"Welcome to 2020 at Skyport High School," said Mr. Fletcher to his second-period World History class. His words were friendly, but the tone of his voice was uncharacteristically stern. "I hope you got the monkeyshines out of your systems over the holiday and are now ready to learn some history."

Twenty-three students glued their gazes to his face. They did not react with grins as they usually did at his use of an old-timey word. "Monkeyshines" was part of what their teacher called his "historical vocabulary," words rarely heard in modern America. He loved to use these words, and his students loved to hear them and later spring them on their family and friends.

Today, the teacher's tone did not invite levity. What was his problem anyway? It was the first day back from the Christmas/New Year vacation. Snow covered the ground. The day was crisp and bright. Why would anybody be interested in studying history when there were snow wars to strategize? And why did their easy-going teacher sound so serious?

"Last semester, my freshman students had the most disgraceful grades I have seen in my entire career," Mr. Fletcher continued, "and I've decided to do something about it. It will be like an experiment this six-weeks."

Some of the students exchanged curious frowns. Others kept their focus on their teacher. He was tall and lean with short brown hair that had a natural wave. When he felt especially happy or goofy, he wore a green bow tie with yellow and orange polka dots. Most days, he wore no tie. Today, he was wearing a light blue dress shirt and dark blue slacks. His necktie was perfectly prim - dark blue with light blue diagonal stripes. It matched both his shirt and his slacks. The upgrade in his attire seemed ominous to the students who noticed.

"Here's how it's going to work," Mr. Fletcher continued. "Those of you who make very high grades will share with those who make very low grades. Some of my best students are in this class - students who can afford to give away a few points to your needy neighbors. If you all work very hard, I believe we can get a 100 percent passing rate this cycle. Are there any questions?"

Zion Johnson raised his hand. "That doesn't sound exactly fair." Zion's sharp, black eyes were fixed on the teacher. He wore an uncharacteristically serious expression, as he considered Mr. Fletcher's plan.

"Is that a question, Zion?" asked Mr. Fletcher.

Zion's mobile face creased into a frown. "Okay. Here's my question. Is that fair?" His cheerful red and white sweatshirt contrasted with the serious expression on his face.

Mr. Fletcher shrugged. "Why not?"

"Well…," Zion hesitated as he searched for the right words to convey his confusion. "Well, it's just that…well, some people work harder. So they make better grades. Shouldn't they make better grades if they work harder?"

Mr. Fletcher was nodding. "Of course they should. But maybe you didn't hear what I said. I said, 'If *all* of you work very hard…' If you're *all* working equally hard, don't you *all* deserve to make passing grades?"

"I… I guess so," said Zion.

"Very good, Zion." Mr. Fletcher looked around. Nobu Tanaka was scowling. "Nobby, what are you thinking?" he asked. "You don't look happy." He smiled at the small, energetic Japanese boy.

"It's not right," said Nobby. "I need all my points so I can go to my best college."

Mr. Fletcher saw Nobby's quick glance at Lilli Park. "Losing a few points in World History this six weeks won't keep you out of the college of your choice, Nobby. And since Lilli is in here, she'll be sharing points too, so you don't have to worry about her getting ahead of you."

"I am not worried!" said Nobby, blushing and sinking lower in his seat. He and Lilli had been rivals for top-class standing every year since 6th grade when the Tanaka family had arrived in Skyport from Japan.

"Well, I think it's a smashing idea, Mr. Fletcher!" called Palmer Evans from the back of the room. He didn't bother raising his hand to be recognized. "Congratulations on being probably the most brilliant teacher in this school!"

Mr. Fletcher's gaze went to the back of the room where the russet-haired quarterback of the freshman football team was framed by the teacher's pride and joy – a map of the world that covered the entire wall. Everyone in the room knew that Palmer struggled to keep his grades up to passing. And all of them probably knew that his hearty praise for Mr. Fletcher's plan was Palmer's typical ingratiating flattery.

Mr. Fletcher gave Palmer a little smirk, then turned his attention to Camilla Rodriguez. Camilla was smiling and waving a hand. The dark-haired girl had dreamy eyes and a cute little nose that gave her a piquant appearance. Today she was wearing a bright green pullover sweater adorned with an image of a fluffy white cat. The animal was seated on a golden pillow, looking huggable. Below the cat, the name "Cuddlesberry" was stitched. Undoubtedly a Christmas present, Mr. Fletcher thought. "What do you say, Camilla?" he asked.

Her smile turned into a grin. "I know what you're doing," she said.

"What am I doing?"

"You're showing us how socialism works," she said. "It's the same thing, except with grades instead of money."

Mr. Fletcher smiled. "Thank you for the compliment, Camilla. But what I'm trying to do is keep my job. If my students start failing left and right, I'll get booted out of here, and no other school will want me."

"Of course, they will," Palmer said. "Are you kidding? You're the famous novelist of Skyport High School. Every school in Texas would be fighting over you if you decided to leave."

"I don't think so," said Mr. Fletcher. "Getting published is a big deal for college professors. It's not exactly an endorsement for high school teachers."

He looked around the room, and his gaze settled on Lilli Park. She had a slender, still-girlish figure and an open, trusting face. Although she never flaunted her intelligence, she also never hid her love of learning. Today, Mr. Fletcher suspected, she, too, was wearing a Christmas gift - a white sweater with black stripes around the middle and down the arms. "What about you, Lilli? Are you willing to share some of your points with your classmates?" he asked.

Lilli ducked her head shyly, and her limp, blond tresses hid her face. "I guess so," she said softly, "if they really need them." Suddenly she looked up eagerly. "What is your next book going to be about? Are you nearly through with it?"

Kip Fletcher smiled at her fondly. He was fond of anyone who appreciated his historical novels. He'd had three published so far and was working on Number Four at night and on weekends. "This one is about the Russian Revolution," he said, "and I hope to finish it next summer."

Lilli returned his smile. She liked Mr. Fletcher. She liked all her teachers. She liked school. And books. And studying. Someday, she hoped, she would be studying the stars as an astronomer.

"Any more questions?" asked Mr. Fletcher. He glanced around quickly, then added, "Okay, let's learn some history."

This time, Palmer raised his hand, although he still didn't wait to be recognized. "Mr. Fletcher," he said, "if we're going to learn some history, I have a question."

Mr. Fletcher nodded. "Very good. I like questions, especially questions about history."

"Okay, well, I've been wondering. Why is this town called Skyport? It's a weird name. Maybe everybody else knows why, but I've only lived here a year and a half, and I've been wondering…"

Mr. Fletcher hid his smile. Of course, Palmer wanted to send him off on a rabbit trail. It was the age-old ploy to delay the evil moment when the class would actually have to get down to work. "We'll allow your question two minutes, Palmer," he said, giving the clock on the wall a good, long stare. "Then we're moving on. As you may know, I haven't lived here as long as you have. I've heard a few stories, but I can't verify their accuracy. Does anybody know the answer to Palmer's question? Perhaps you've had parents or grandparents living here for a long time. Anybody?"

The students looked at each other. Some poked others. But no one spoke.

"I guess we'll have to take up the question another day…" began Mr. Fletcher.

"Wait!" said Palmer. "I've heard something. A lot of people say it's named Skyport because it's a landing place for UFOs. Other folks say it's a Christian name because when somebody dies, they take off for the sky. I want to know the real…"

Zion interrupted him. "Jasmine knows," he said.

All eyes turned to Jasmine Clark, who was glaring at Zion. She was one of the beauties of the freshman class with crimped hair that reached to her waist and framed a lovely face. Her dark eyes were intense and shrewd. Although she often dressed like her classmates in blue jeans and a tee shirt, today she had dressed up for the first school day of 2020 in a hot pink blouse tucked into gray slacks.

"What about it, Jasmine?" asked Mr. Fletcher.

Jasmine's voice was hesitant at first, but it gained strength as she talked. "Well…my family has lived around here since…before the Civil War. Of course, they were slaves then. After the war, the rancher who had owned my great-, great-, greats gave my family some land and helped them buy some cattle. We've been here ever since."

"And what stories have you heard from your parents and grandparents?" asked Mr. Fletcher when she paused.

"I don't like to say because it sounds crazy," said Jasmine.

"Come on, spit it out," Palmer commanded. As captain and quarterback of a football team, he was used to giving orders.

Jasmine searched Mr. Fletcher's face. "I don't think I can tell it in two minutes," she said.

He returned to his desk and sat down. "Go ahead, and take your time. I'd like to hear the story myself."

Jasmine took a deep, tremulous breath before she began. "Well, back then

- before this area was a town - there were only some ranches around here. One of them was owned by a young man from Dallas. He moved here with his beautiful young wife. I think their names were…um…Gordon and Ginny. Ginny didn't want to leave Dallas and her family, so she told Gordon the only way she would move to some God-forsaken ranch in the 'outback' of Texas was if he would get her a zebra…"

"A zebra?" several voices gasped. And Palmer got in his two cents worth, saying, "A camel would have been better. At least it could carry things and wouldn't mind the heat."

Nobody noticed Lilli's confused expression or heard her whisper to herself, "A zebra?"

Jasmine shrugged. "I guess she thought zebras were pretty - all black and white striped. I don't know. I'm just telling you what I heard."

"You're doing fine," said Mr. Fletcher. "Go on."

Jasmine took a deep breath. "Well, Gordon got a zebra somehow. Nobody seems to know where it came from. Did they have circuses back in those days?" she asked, looking at Mr. Fletcher.

He nodded. "Yes, but I doubt that they came to this part of Texas."

"Sure, but if some circus brought a zebra to this side of the ocean, ol' Gordo could have gotten one," said Palmer excitedly.

"Right. Go on, Jasmine," said Mr. Fletcher.

"So, Gordon and Ginny moved here with their zebra. They were kind of like those 'Green Acres' folks. You know that old TV show? They didn't know what they were doing. So, the other ranchers and their wives had to teach them everything. It kind of made them popular, you know, because Gordon and Ginny made everybody else feel smart. The ranchers and their wives really liked helping those two greenhorns from the city."

Jasmine glanced around and saw a few heads nodding in understanding before she continued. "Well, it took them about five years to feel like they were fitting in. People didn't much like the zebra. But since they liked Gordon and Ginny, they were okay with it. And by then, they had a three-year-old son, named Luke, and everybody in the county was wild about Luke.

"It was about a month after Luke's third birthday that the tragedy happened. Luke was playing in the yard, and the zebra kicked him in the head. He died two days later. The zebra disappeared the next week. And Ginny disappeared two weeks later."

Camilla gasped. "Where did they go?" she asked. "Nobody knew," said Jasmine.

"Well, I know where that zebra went!" Palmer called out. "Ol' Gordy kicked *him* in the head and knocked his lights out!"

"No," said Jasmine, "Gordon said zebras are wild animals and can't be blamed for acting like wild animals. He wouldn't let anybody touch the zebra."

"What about Ginny? Where did she go?" asked Camilla.

"She disappeared," said Jasmine. "The whole county searched for her, and when they couldn't find her, Gordon went to Dallas to see if she had gone back there on her own. She was so sad about Luke that she couldn't do anything but cry. Gordon had offered to take her back to Dallas to see her folks, but she said no. It was spring, and he was really busy. She said he couldn't be leaving the ranch at such a busy time. But he could hardly work for grieving over Luke and worrying about Ginny. So, he might as well have taken her to Dallas."

"Was she there?" asked Lilli. "In Dallas?"

"No, nobody ever found out what happened to her," said Jasmine. "But when Gordon got back from Dallas, he said he was sure that Ginny and the zebra had both been abducted by invaders from outer space."

"That's stupid," pronounced Zion.

Jasmine looked crestfallen. "I didn't say I believed it," she retorted. "I'm just telling you what Gordon said."

"Go on," encouraged Mr. Fletcher. "We're fascinated."

Jasmine smiled. "Okay, well, nobody was too surprised. There had been reports of UFOs at night around here for years, and ranchers in the area started saying creatures from distant galaxies must be visiting Texas. They always said, 'Of course, the aliens would choose Texas because it's the best place on Earth. They're probably jealous of us and want to take our land for themselves.' Then everybody would laugh and agree, but nobody exactly believed it."

"Did Gordon believe it?" asked Lilli thoughtfully.

"Yes, he got sort of…fanatical, I guess you would say," Jasmine replied. "And when the people in the area wanted to get a post office and become a town, Gordon insisted that they name it Skyport. He said it was only fair to give it a name that warned people their loved ones could be carried off into the sky without a word of warning. And the Christians liked it because they said they were going to a heavenly home someday, and Skyport sounded like a good 'taking-off' place. So, they named the town Skyport."

Jasmine stopped and looked around. "I guess that's about all. You hear all kinds of stories, but that's the one my grandma told me."

"I think ol' Gordo was right," Palmer offered. "Aliens carried Ginny off to some distant planet. They did it because they couldn't bear to see her suffering. They were going to do experiments on her to see if they could find a way to make her forget Lu…"

"That's enough, Palmer," said Mr. Fletcher. "We're through with this rabbit trail." He smiled at Jasmine. "Thank you for that intriguing story, Jasmine. It certainly gives us something to think about."

He moved to the front of the room and began the day's lesson. "Now, class, you may have noticed," he waved a hand at his whiteboard where the day's learning objective was written, "that we're going to be talking about the Scientific Revolution today. I know, I know, this is a history class, not a science class. But how many of you know that science has affected our lives in thousands of ways throughout history?"

Most of the class put up a hand half-heartedly. But Marion Rogers, the science geek on the front row, said, "Millions!"

"Of course," Mr. Fletcher agreed. "So, let's begin. Who has ever heard of a guy named Copernicus?" Three hands went up. "Okay, what about Galileo?" A few more hands went up. "Not very encouraging, but I'll ask my question, anyway. Can anyone tell me a radical scientific belief that Copernicus and Galileo had in common?"

He looked at Lilli. She blushed but raised her hand. "Yes, Lilli?"

"Copernicus and Galileo were two of the first scientists who said our solar system is heliocentric rather than geocentric. It got Galileo in trouble with the Catholic Church."

Mr. Fletcher beamed. "Excellent, Lilli. I don't know why I bother to teach. I should just turn you and Nobby loose and let you take over. Nobby, why don't you explain what 'heliocentric' and 'geocentric' mean?"

Nobby's face lit up. "Heliocentric means the sun is at the center of the solar system. Geocentric means the Earth is."

"Perfect!" cried Mr. Fletcher. He almost gave his two star pupils a standing ovation. But that wouldn't be appropriate. It was going to hurt him to take points from their grades to boost the grades of the lay-about bums in the class. He would have to find another way to reward them. He had no way of knowing that one of them wouldn't be around long enough to donate points to anyone.

Chapter 2: Lunchtime Colloquies

"I am da bomb!" Seated at a long lunch table surrounded by his friends, Royal Douglas was musing to himself, remembering the way the new redhead in his English class had given him a coy smile. Tall, with sandy blond hair and a confident air, he was used to being noticed by the prettiest girls. Now, he reproduced the sly grin he had offered back to the new girl. Around him, his basketball teammates were laying bets on the spread in tonight's game. Of course, everyone on the team expected to win. The only issue was - by how much? They didn't notice Royal smiling to himself.

He wondered if he should invite the enchanting redhead to the next home game as his date. But, no, that wouldn't be a good first date. He would have to arrive early and leave late. She would not be impressed if she had to wait hours for him or if he asked someone else to pick her up. He could tell that much by looking at her. Anyway, he didn't remember her name.

"Hey, Royal, how much ya' in for?" someone yelled over the lunchroom clatter.

He looked up and shrugged. "Ask me tomorrow."

His teammates howled and hurled insults at him. But he didn't have time to hurl his own salvo back at them. Someone was trying to rip his shoulder out of its joint.

"Hey!" he yelled, pulling away. Frowning, he glared up into the dark, troubled eyes of Lilli Park. "What is it?" he asked irritably. "I need that shoulder. Don't take it off!"

Lilli released her frantic grasp. "I have to talk to you," she whispered.

"So talk," he growled. "Not here. Outside."

Royal sighed. He glanced at his half-eaten lunch. It looked wilted. "Who wants this?" he shouted, holding it up.

Hyper Hooper, the fastest, skinniest kid on the team, reached for the tray.

"Come on." Royal stood up. He pulled his jacket on, took Lilli's hand, and led her through the lunchroom throng. "Is your mom okay?" he yelled over the clamor.

"She's fine. Everybody's fine. It's not that," said Lilli.

Royal didn't try to pump her for any more information. He just led her to the parking lot and clicked the locks on his red Dodge Ram pickup. While Lilli clambered up, Royal started the engine. "It will only take it a minute to get warm," he told her. "So, what's the problem?"

Quickly, Lilli told him the story of Gordon, Ginny, and their zebra. Then she asked, "Royal, do you think…?" She hesitated. "Do you think…*they* took Ginny's zebra?"

"Lilli, quit calling them '*they*' like that. They have a name. They're from the planet Soteria. So, they're…I guess they're Soterians like we're Earthlings, and people from Mars would be Martians. It's insulting to them if you don't use their name."

Lilli nodded. "I know. I try. But what do you think?"

"Do I think the Soterians took Ginny's zebra?"

"Yes. Do you?"

"What kind of question is that? Why would I think such a thing?"

"Well, Hubble disappeared. Maybe they took him too," Lilli whispered. Then suddenly she was crying. "He always goes in the barn when it's cold. But you said he wasn't there during the whole snowstorm. Where can he be? I *have* to find him!"

Royal hid his exasperation and made his voice gentle. "Y'know, Lilli. Hubble was probably old. He may have gone off somewhere to die."

"But…but…if they like zebras…," Lilli's sobs were heartbreaking.

Reaching across the console, Royal held her while she wept.

"That blasted zebra!" he thought. Nobody knew where it came from. It had just wandered into the yard a few months ago, and Lilli had fallen in love with it. She named it Hubble after some telescope or some astronomer or some astronaut she liked. But it had disappeared shortly before the snowstorm of the previous weekend.

"Royal?" Lilli was regaining control of herself. She sat up and dried her eyes on the lapel of her jacket. "Royal, do you think it's the same zebra?"

He frowned. "The same zebra as what?"

"Hubble and Ginny's zebra. Do you think they're the same one?" "How could they be?" he scoffed. "Zebras don't live hundreds of years."

"But if *they*…if the Soterians took him into space…I mean, they would have to travel at the speed of light or something. Wouldn't that keep Hubble from aging?"

Royal just shook his head. How could Lilli be so smart and so dumb at the same time? "That's sci-fi bunk. Anyway, nobody can travel at the speed of light."

Lilli sniffled. "They would have to. They couldn't travel so far in a lifetime if they couldn't travel at the speed of light."

"Really? How long is a lifetime for them?" Royal asked.

Lilli's mouth formed an "O." She shook her head. "I don't know. Do you?"

"Not a clue," said Royal. "Listen, I'll tell you what we'll do. We'll take Adolf out and see if he can find Hubble. How about that?"

Lilli shivered at the thought of Royal's big, black Doberman Pinscher. "I don't think it's a good idea," she said. "Hubble is afraid of Adolf."

Royal sighed. "Okay, then, what do you want me to do?"

Lilli hesitated before she asked, "Have you seen…*them*…lately?"

"Last week," said Royal. "Why?"

"Well, if you saw them, you could ask them…well, ask them if they know where Hubble is."

"You mean ask them if they stole your zebra? Why would they want that old nag anyway?"

"To study him, I guess," mumbled Lilli. "Isn't that what they do? Study the…animals and the…humans on Earth?"

Royal suddenly grew earnest. "They're here to help us, not to study our wildlife, remember?"

He sighed deeply. He could remember, like yesterday, his earliest encounter with the Soterians. He had been ten years old, spending the night with Hyper Hooper. The boys had been camped out in the Hooper's basement, experimenting with Hyper's brother's Ouija board. Then they watched a scary movie about aliens taking over the Earth. Royal had fallen asleep with the television set still flickering in the dark room.

As he slept, a strange little gray creature appeared in his dreams and announced, "I am from the planet Soteria. Here is a story I want you to know." Then, still dreamlike, Royal had watched on the screen of his mind a movie about a beautiful garden planet that had existed for thousands of years under the leadership of wise and caring rulers. But as the story began, an evil king named Zyquobe manipulated his way to power. He pretended to be as kind and intelligent as his predecessors.

Yet, unbeknownst to his people, Zyquobe had allied himself with invaders from an alien world who wanted to take over their planet. His diabolical plan unfolded on the screen of Royal's sleeping mind. He was literally trembling in his sleep.

But just in the nick of time, a teenage boy named Tojo managed to contact aliens from another distant world. They showed Tojo how he could save his planet from the villainous invaders. The plan was ingenious. Zyquobe was soundly defeated and destroyed. The grateful people of the garden planet made Tojo their new king.

Royal would never forget that night and that dream. It was the road map of his future. And Tojo was his hero. But he could not seem to make Lilli understand the implications of the dream for himself. For the Earth. And for herself, too. With her brains and his athletic abilities, the two of them could be the human allies the Soterians needed to turn planet Earth into a garden planet just like Tojo's. He desperately wanted her to catch the dream and to long for it as much as he did.

"I know they say they want to help us," Lilli was saying. "But they're so scary. And so weird!" She tried to smile. She knew Royal admired and believed in the Soterians. But she wasn't convinced.

Royal patted her shoulder. "Okay. Next time I see one of them, I'll see what I can find out. But don't get your hopes up, kiddo. I don't think they're interested in zebras."

"Thank you, Royal." Lilli beamed at him. "When do you think you'll see them again?"

"I can't answer that one," said Royal. "It could be a week, a month, or a year. You know that. They can't be hanging around some old, weed-infested town in the Texas Panhandle. So, I never know when they'll be back."

Lilli nodded. "Okay," she said.

Royal waited several long moments before he added, "I think Aziz would be pleased if you were the one to ask."

Lilli's eyes flew to his face, and her whole body trembled. "No," she whispered. "Please, not me."

Royal shrugged. "It's your Hubble."

★★★

While the students gathered in the school cafeteria for lunch, many of the teachers gathered in the teachers' lounges. Kip Fletcher and some of the other social studies teachers generally joined English teachers and a few science teachers in the lounge closest to the history department. Other teachers frequented a lounge on the other end of the school.

Mr. Fletcher had just taken a bite of his tuna sandwich when Sadie Sharp descended on him in full attack mode. She was a dumpy little woman with long brown hair pulled into a ponytail at the nape of her neck. She was the other World History teacher at Skyport High School and a constant source of amusement for Mr. Fletcher.

"What do you think you're doing?" she demanded. *"Have you lost your mind?"*

He swallowed, then answered, "Lost it… Found it later… But thanks for asking."

"Kip Fletcher," Mrs. Sharp said severely, glaring into his twinkling eyes, "this is no joke. You cannot take points from one student and give them to another student. That is patently unfair!"

Mr. Fletcher shrugged. "I don't remember seeing that rule in the handbook." He didn't have to glance around to know that every eye in the room was now on Mrs. Sharp and himself.

"Of course, it's not in the handbook. Nobody else on this planet would be ignorant enough to do such a thing."

"Ignorant, is it?" asked Mr. Fletcher. "Well, now, I believe you're getting the point."

"What point?"

Mr. Fletcher smiled. "The point that socialism is *ignorant*."

Mrs. Sharp paused. "Socialism?" she repeated. "What does socialism have to do with it?"

"Think about it," said Mr. Fletcher. "Camilla Rodriguez was smart enough to figure it out. I bet you are, too."

Mrs. Sharp looked around the room at the rapt faces turned toward her. Blushing, she flopped into an empty chair and took a long breath. "You're doing this…this…"

"Experiment," Mr. Fletcher supplied.

"You're doing this experiment to show the students how socialism works?"

"I'm doing this experiment to show the students that socialism is *codswallop*!" Most of the teachers grinned at his "codswallop." They were familiar with his historical vocabulary. "So, what are you telling me - that you're a fan of socialism?" asked Mr. Fletcher.

"Of course not!" Mrs. Sharp was indignant. "I'm not an idiot. But that doesn't change the fact that you can't be manipulating grades like that. Why, you're *stealing* grades from one student and giving them to another student!"

"My point exactly!" Mr. Fletcher's voice was triumphant. "Socialists steal *money* from one person and give it to another. Supposedly. We all know they actually give it to themselves. Don't you think our students should know what a flawed system it is? Not just know it in their heads." He pointed to his head. "But *feel* it in their guts?" He gave his abdomen a resounding whack.

"But it's corrupt. You can't do it to our children," Mrs. Sharp maintained. "Don't you think the parents are going to raise the roof? And go to the administration? It's going to be a fiasco!"

Mr. Fletcher laughed. "Sounds like fun. Anybody else got an opinion?"

"Undoubtedly a brilliant idea," said Len Josephs, a U.S. History teacher. He was a fan of Kip Fletcher's, always supporting him in his verbal skirmishes with Mrs. Sharp.

Ironically, Mr. Josephs resembled Mrs. Sharp. At least, the broad strokes were similar. He was taller than she was, but he had a roundish shape and long, graying brown hair that he gathered in a rubber band at the nape of his neck. Even their eyeglasses were similar - rimless lenses and narrow, gold-colored arms. He was jolly and easy-going, a favorite among the teachers. Privately, Mr. Fletcher couldn't help being amused at the similarity in the appearance of his two colleagues, but he kept this opinion to himself.

"Thank you, Len," he said. "Okay, who else wants to vote?"

A quick poll of the room revealed that the other teachers had found the argument between Mr. Fletcher and Mrs. Sharp very entertaining, and all wanted to be told how Mr. Fletcher's experiment turned out. With that bit of business out of the way, the teachers returned to their private conversations.

Mr. Fletcher looked at Mrs. Sharp. She was sitting upright in the chair across from him, a defiant expression on her face. "I don't see any lunch," he observed. "Aren't you eating?" Mrs. Sharp always ate.

"I'm fasting," she said.

Mr. Fletcher's eyebrows went up. "Another one of your spiritual exercises?" he asked.

"No, a health exercise," Mrs. Sharp replied primly, "and I don't believe I want to discuss it with *you*." She rose and marched out of the room.

"Won't hurt her to miss a few meals," an English teacher observed as soon as the door was shut. And the rest of the teachers chuckled.

"Still...it's odd," said Mr. Fletcher thoughtfully.

Chapter 3: Lilli's Decision

That week, Lilli spent two evenings tramping over the Douglas farm, hunting for Hubble. Royal searched with her one evening, but his heart wasn't in it. He thought Hubble was a nuisance and, besides, what was a zebra doing in the Texas Panhandle anyway? It should go back to Africa, where it belonged.

It was Thursday, and he didn't have a basketball game the next night. "Look," he said, "this is a 'bye' week for us. Why don't you come for the weekend? We'll take Adolf with us and see if he can find the thing." Seeing Lilli's confused expression, he backtracked. "A 'bye' week means no basketball game tomorrow night."

"Oh." Lilli nodded. "Okay, but where will we look? We've been everywhere. At least, I have."

"I know you think it's useless because Hubble doesn't like to go there, but we might as well check out the A.G."

Lilli nodded her agreement. The A.G. was the automobile graveyard, a field where Mr. Douglas made a few extra dollars by collecting wrecked vehicles and selling their used parts - the parts that weren't worn out or rusted. Not much vegetation grew up between the closely packed old wrecks, and Hubble avoided the place. But in the winter, there wasn't much vegetation anywhere. Maybe the zebra had gone into that field in search of a snack and tripped over one of the rusted hulks. If he had broken a leg, he wouldn't be able to get back to the barn.

"Thank you, Royal. That's a good idea," she said.

He nodded. "Okay. Right now, I have to head back and practice my free throws before it gets any darker."

He strode off, his long legs leaving Lilli far behind because she was picking her way back to the Douglas farmhouse carefully. All the snow had melted, but plenty of mud remained. And she had foolishly gone with Royal immediately after school while there were still a couple of hours of daylight left. Now, she regretted not changing her shoes. She would hate it if she ruined the new white Nikes she had gotten for Christmas.

As she approached the farmhouse, Lilli admired it. Made of cream-colored brick with a dark gray roof, she thought it might be the prettiest home in the world. Tall pecan trees growing in both side yards were bare now, but the stark, graceful limbs had their own charm.

Royal was shooting baskets on a concrete slab his dad had laid for that purpose. Normally, Lilli would have joined him and retrieved the basketball for him each time it swished through the basket. Her help saved him a lot of steps and increased the number of practice shots he could make. Plus, he always let her shoot some baskets and helped her improve her accuracy. When he had time, they would play some one-on-one.

But this evening, Lilli had noticed smoke rising from the chimney. She loved a fire in the fireplace on a cold day. So, instead of stopping, she hurried to the house and burst through the door. Heading straight for the den, she found Bryce Douglas arranging wieners, buns, mustard, and marshmallows on a rolling cart next to the blaze.

"Goody!" cried Lilli. "Hot dogs! I'm starving!"

Bryce laughed. "You should be. Look at you – you're not as big as a minute."

Lilli drew herself up to full height. "I've grown an inch and gained five pounds in just six months. I must be bigger than a minute by now!"

Bryce grinned. "Okay. A minute and a half," he conceded. "Go ahead and roast a dog for yourself. I've got hot chocolate warming on the stove. I'll bring you a cup."

"With marshmallows?" she asked eagerly.

Bryce pointed to the full bag of marshmallows on the cart. "You can have all you want for roasting *and* for hot chocolate." He started toward the kitchen but paused at the door. "Your mom called. I told her Royal will bring you home in an hour."

Lilli nodded. She gave a sigh of contentment as she skewered a wiener. She had enjoyed searching for Hubble with Royal. She hadn't been nearly as frightened of an encounter with the Soterians while he was with her. On Tuesday, when she had searched alone, she trembled at every strange sound and searched the skies for an alien spacecraft more than she had searched for Hubble.

With Royal's promise to help, Lilli felt more hopeful. But she barely slept that night. And when she did, her nightmares were populated with spindly little gray creatures that ogled her with huge blue, diamond-shaped eyes. She had seen them only once, but she would never forget them. Especially Aziz, their stern leader. And she relived the terror every time she thought of them.

Royal had seen the Soterians at least ten times. And they excited him. Excited him to a fever pitch. If they would take him, he would travel with them to that planet of theirs - Soteria. In fact, he told her they had taken him to Mars once. He described the planet as a reddish plain dotted with craters. She did envy him that space cruise. Astronomy was her passion, and if it were actually possible to visit Mars… Well, maybe she would be brave enough to spend some time with the creepy little monsters if she could visit another planet.

The next morning, Lilli was pale and quiet. She picked at her breakfast and drank only a few swallows of orange juice. Anna Park, her mother, watched her with a worried frown.

Finally, she asked, "Lilli, are you ill?"

Lilli started. "No, Mom, why?"

"You look pale and tired. You're not eating. Are you hurting anywhere? Throat? Head? Ears?"

Anna, at 55, looked ten years younger. Her thick brown hair, worn short and curly, showed only a spattering of gray. Her mild middle-age spread was carefully concealed under tailored clothing. And her brown eyes, perceptive and sympathetic, matched Lilli's.

Lilli shook her head and spoke firmly. "I'm fine, Mom!" If there were a single ailing cell in her body, her nurse-practitioner mother would ferret it out and fix it. Cell! Her mother would find a single, sickly mitochondrion and cure it!

"Are you worried about that experiment of your teacher's?" asked Anna.

"Experiment?" Lilli frowned. Then she remembered. She had told her mother about Mr. Fletcher's announcement the evening before, and her mother had just nodded distractedly. "Oh, you mean Mr. Fletcher sharing our grades?"

"Right. If that's worrying you, I'll talk to him today."

Lilli had to smile, remembering Tuesday's World History class. "No, Mom. He can take all the points he wants. It's only for this six- weeks. Nobby's the one who doesn't like it."

Anna smiled, too. "He wouldn't." She glanced at her watch. "Okay. Well, if you're not sick, let's move. Get your teeth brushed and be in the car in five minutes."

Lilli put on her best cheerful act during the ride to school. Her mom didn't know about the Soterians, and Lilli knew it would be best to keep it that way. She hopped out of the car at the school, waved goodbye, and walked jauntily inside. But as soon as her mother was out of sight, she sagged. Weariness was a weight on her shoulders, and the thought that she might have to face Aziz in order to find Hubble terrified her.

The lobby of the school was empty. It was still 45 minutes until first period. Lilli headed for the library, her usual morning hangout.

The library was even quieter than the lobby. Lilli walked straight to her favorite table and sat down. Usually, she had assignments to work on or a book to read. Today, she couldn't even remember if she had any unfinished homework or not. As for the quiz in World History second period, she wasn't ready. Usually, she made 100 on quizzes and tests, but she had been distracted all week. Too distracted to give her classes her full attention. She knew she wasn't ready for this quiz, but what did it matter? Mr. Fletcher wasn't going to let her keep all her points anyway. Well, that was why she should do even better, so her grade wouldn't be *so* low. She would just have to make it up next time.

With a shuddering sigh, she buried her face in her arms and tried not to imagine Hubble lying injured in some ravine. Or frozen to death. Or in a spaceship headed for the planet Soteria.

"Lilli?" someone said softly, putting a hand on her shoulder.

Lilli gasped in surprise at the unexpected presence. Looking up, she saw Treena Wood bending over her. How did Treena Wood know her name? Treena was a senior. Lilli only knew who Treena was because she was the treasurer of the Student Council.

"Yes ma'am," Lilli quavered.

"Ma'am?" Treena laughed. "I don't think anybody ever called me 'ma'am' before."

"I'm sorry," Lilli whispered.

"Don't be sorry! It's *my bad* for scaring you," Treena said. "May I sit here?" She touched the chair next to Lilli's.

Lilli nodded, her pale hair screening her face, as usual.

Treena seated herself. She was a pretty girl with shoulder-length brown hair and gentle brown eyes. "Please tell me if I'm disturbing you," she said. "I don't want to keep you from your work."

Lilli shook her head shyly. She was obviously not working. "It's okay," she said.

"Oh good. Well, I was just wondering what's wrong. You looked so sad sitting over here, almost like you were about to cry. I wanted to see if I could help."

"I'm okay," said Lilli. "You're not about to cry?"

Lilli's lip quivered. "I was trying not to."

"Is there anything I can do to help?" Treena asked, and her voice was so sympathetic that Lilli suddenly longed to tell her all about Hubble and the horrible Soterians.

Lilli shook her head and whispered, "I can't tell you. It's *crazy!*"

"Really?" Treena sounded intrigued. "Crazy sounds interesting. Tell you what..." She looked around. "Let's go into that carrel over there where we can talk without disturbing anybody." She pointed toward the back of the library.

Lilli had to smile. "Disturbing who?"

Treena returned her smile. "I know there's nobody else in here now, but somebody could walk in any time. And we don't want them to overhear us, do we?"

Lilli had to agree with that. She shook her head. "No."

"Come on." Treena stood up and led the way into the little study room at the back of the library. Lilli hastily gathered her things and followed.

Once the two girls were settled in the carrel with the door shut, Treena said, "Okay. Now tell me all about it. I promise I won't think you're crazy. And I won't tell a soul what you tell me." Her eyes were intense, and her concern unmistakable.

Lilli took a deep breath. "Well, you see, there are these… these aliens…these extraterrestrials that come to the Douglas's farm sometimes. I saw them there once. And Royal has seen them ten or 12 times. Maybe more. They're really scary."

Treena's eyes were wide with surprise. "E.T.'s?" she gasped.

Lilli nodded. "I know. It's crazy, but I saw them myself."

Treena swallowed her surprise and composed her face. "And why do they upset you so much?" she asked.

"Well, see, there's this zebra, Hubble. I named him Hubble. He's a pet. He stays in the Douglas's barn when it's cold. But he disappeared last weekend. You know, right before the big snowstorm. I've looked everywhere for him, and I can't find him."

Treena was nodding and listening carefully.

"So, Tuesday in my World History class, Jasmine was telling us how Skyport got its name, and in her story, there were some aliens that stole a zebra. So, I thought maybe it was the same aliens, and they took Hubble." Lilli paused. "Do you want me to tell you Jasmine's story?"

Treena shook her head. "That's okay. Nobby Tanaka told me."

Lilli was surprised. How did this popular senior girl know a couple of obscure freshmen? But she didn't ask. She just continued her story.

"Well, anyway, I wanted Royal to ask the Soterians - they're from the planet Soteria - whether they took Hubble. He said they would like it better if I asked them myself." Lilli's hands, resting on the table, began to quiver. She lowered them to her lap, clasping them tightly to stop the trembling.

Treena put a warm hand over Lilli's cold ones. "And you're afraid of the Soterians?" she asked.

Lilli nodded. "They're like monsters. They're little gray people with big blue eyes. And they just stare at you. They don't talk with their mouths, but it's like they put their words in your mind. Then you have to answer them out loud because you can't put your words in their minds. It's creepy."

Lilli's trembling had increased, and Treena put both her hands around Lilli's icy ones. "Lilli," she said urgently, "listen to me. You don't have to be afraid. They're not aliens. They just want you to think they are."

Lilli looked into her eyes with wonder. "You believe me?"

"Of course I do," said Treena firmly. "But they're not aliens. Now, prepare yourself. What I'm going to tell you will sound scary, but it's really not. Are you ready?"

Lilli was confused, but she nodded.

"Okay, here's the deal," said Treena. "They're demons. Do you know what demons are? Do you believe in the Bible? Do you know who Jesus is?"

It was a lot of questions to answer at once, but Lilli's answer was the same for all three. "Sort of," she said.

"Okay," Treena said. "I want to start by telling you how I know Nobby and how I know who you are. Didn't you wonder about that?"

Lilli nodded.

"I belong to a group of Christians here at the school. We call ourselves God's Harvesters, and our only purpose is to pray for our friends who don't know Jesus and try to encourage them to be born again. Do you know what that means? Being born again?"

Lilli shook her head.

"Being born again is how you become a Christian. We say we're 'born again' because it's a whole new life. And it's a whole new life because we become part of Jesus's family. So, we – the Harvesters, I mean - we meet once a week, during lunch, to pray for our friends. Nobby is in our group, and he asked us to pray for you to come to know Jesus. We've been praying for you since last September, and Nobby pointed you out to me one time."

"Nobby did that?" Lilli asked wonderingly. She smiled, and tears came to her eyes at the same time. "I thought we were just…well, not enemies. Rivals, I guess."

Treena shook her head. "Not at all. Nobby thinks you're wonderful."

A tear escaped from Lilli's eye and rolled down her cheek. "I think he's kind of wonderful too."

"Me too," Treena agreed. "Anyway, I have to hurry before the bell rings because I want you to know that you don't have to be afraid. See, Jesus is God, and He's the Champion of the whole universe. He defeated the devil and all his demons. If you want to be born again so that Jesus lives in your heart, those demons will have to turn tail and run from you!"

Lilli's eyes sparkled. "They will?"

Treena held up three fingers. "Scout's honor."

A cloud passed over Lilli's face. "But I don't understand. What do I have to do to make them run away from me?"

Treena nodded. "You have to give your life to Jesus and ask Him to come live in your heart. But you don't have to do it right now. You can think about it and maybe ask your mom what she thinks."

Lilli was shaking her head. She could be very shy, but she could also be decisive. "I want to do it," she said. "I've been afraid all week. I don't want to be afraid anymore."

"Okay," Treena said. "Here's the deal. God is perfect and holy. He made people, and He loves us, but we're all sinners, and we can't go live with Him in Heaven when we die unless we're righteous like He is. But there's only one way for us to get righteous. We have to confess our sins and ask Jesus to forgive us. See, Jesus died as a sacrifice for our sins because He's perfect. So, if we believe in Him and ask Him to live in our hearts and be our Lord, He will. Do you think you can do that?"

Lilli was listening closely. "Yes," she said, "I can do that."

"Then we'll bow our heads. I'll pray a sentence, and you'll pray it after me. Then I'll pray another sentence, and you'll say that sentence. We'll keep going until we finish. Are you ready?"

Lilli nodded and bowed her head.

"Dear Lord Jesus, I confess to You that I'm a sinner," prayed Treena.

"Dear Lord Jesus, I confess to You that I'm a sinner," Lille prayed.

"I believe You died on the Cross so that I can be saved," Treena continued.

"I believe You died on the Cross so that I can be saved," said Lilli.

"And right now, I'm making You my Lord and asking You to live in my heart," Treena said.

"And right now, I'm making You my Lord and asking You to live in my heart," Lilli repeated.

"Thank You for loving me. Amen," Treena finished.

"Thank You for loving me. Amen," Lilli said, and there was a triumphant tone in her shy voice. When she looked into Treena's face, her eyes were damp. "Is that all?" she asked.

"Not hardly," Treena laughed. "That's just the beginning. But here's what you need to know for now. If you see those Soterians again, say something like this: 'I rebuke you in Jesus's Name. Now go away!' The main thing is to use Jesus's Name. They're afraid of Him."

Lilli nodded, and her face reflected the calm that had settled in her heart. "I'll remember," she said.

"Okay, now, let's talk about church," said Treena. "Would you like to go to church with me and my family on Sunday? It's the best place to learn more about Jesus."

The girls quickly made plans for the weekend. When the first-period bell rang, it had been arranged that Treena's family would pick Lilli up on Sunday morning. After church, she was invited to go home with them for dinner.

Treena gave Lilli a hug. "You're my sister, now," she said. "I'm so glad!"

"I am, too," Lilli said shyly. She gathered her things, and they headed in opposite directions for their classes.

Just before second period, when Lilli spied Nobby in the hall, she beckoned urgently. "Nobby, come here!" she called. "I have to tell you something."

"Hi, Lilli," Nobby said. "Are you ready for the quiz?"

25

Lilli shook her head. "No, but listen. Treena Wood talked to me today. She told me about Jesus."

Nobby's eyes widened. "Lilli!" he cried. "For real?"

"Yes, and I asked Him to come live in my heart!" Lilli exclaimed. Nobby's mouth fell open. Then his whole face lit up. "Lilli, that's the best news ever," he said eagerly. "Will you tell me about it sometime?"

Lilli nodded. "Maybe at noon," she said. "And Nobby, Treena said I'm her sister now. Am I your sister, too?"

Nobby nodded. "I guess you are," he said.

They beamed at each other until someone gave both of them a push toward the classroom. It was Camilla. "Come on, you two," she said. "The bell's about to ring."

Chapter 4: Friday at Skyport High School (SHS)

By the time Lilli finished the quiz in World History, she was distraught again. She had never made less than 95 on one of Mr. Fletcher's quizzes, and she didn't think she had even passed this one. Mr. Fletcher would think she had failed it because of his experiment. He would be *so* disappointed in her!

She was fighting back tears when she turned in her quiz. Mr. Fletcher gave her his usual bright grin, but she couldn't even smile at him. She returned to her desk, opened her textbook, and began reading the next section. The words swam on the page, and she could not understand a single sentence.

At noon, she sat with Nobby, Zion, Jasmine, and Camilla in the lunchroom. They were all moaning over the quiz. They always moaned about quizzes and tests. This time, Lilli was as mournful as the rest of them.

"Did you make a hundred, as usual?" Zion asked her.

"No, I think I failed it," Lilli said. "I didn't exactly study for it." She looked at Nobby. "Did you make a hundred?"

Nobby's face took on a defiant expression. "Not me," he said. "Why should I work hard to give my points to Palmer Evans?"

"You shouldn't!" said Zion emphatically. "Let him make his own grades!"

The five of them laughed, and Nobby changed the subject. "Now tell me about this morning, Lilli," he said urgently. Then, remembering his manners, he added, "Lilli got born again this morning."

"Oh, Lilli, I'm so happy for you," said Jasmine. "Righto!" agreed Zion.

Camilla smiled. "That's nice," she said. "Okay, now tell us about it," said Nobby.

"Well, I was in the library crying," said Lilli, choosing her words carefully. She didn't want the whole world to know she'd thought a bunch of demons were space aliens. "Treena Wood came in and asked why I was upset, so I told her about Hubble being lost."

"What's a hubble?" asked Camilla.

"He's my zebra," said Lilli, blushing a bit. Having a zebra was almost as strange as having close encounters with UFO crews.

"Are you serious? You have a zebra?" asked Zion.

"Well, he just wandered up to the Douglas's farm one day," Lilli explained. "Nobody else cares much about him, but I love him. I named him Hubble. After the astronomer, you know."

"So, what happened to Hubble?" Nobby asked sympathetically.

"I don't know," said Lilli. "We haven't seen him for a week. At first, he wandered off all the time, but not so much lately. I think he's getting pretty old."

"Well, that's it, then," said Zion. "He probably died of old age." "But if he did, why can't I find him?" asked Lilli.

No one had an answer, so she returned to Treena and the library. "Anyway, Treena told me about Jesus. She said He would live in my heart and that I'm part of His family. She said I'm her sister now. And I'm Nobby's sister, too."

"Me too," said Jasmine, beaming at Lilli.

"Me three," said Zion.

They all looked at Camilla, but she just shrugged and stood. "I need to go find…um…my cousin," she said. "Mom said I was to find out if her dad is still in the hospital." She smiled and waved goodbye.

"We should put her on our list," said Nobby.

"What list?" asked Zion.

"Well, I'm in this group called the Harvesters," said Nobby. "Actually, it's Sowers, Waterers, Harvesters or SWH. But we usually call ourselves God's

Harvesters or just the Harvesters. We pray for people to get saved. Lilli was on our list until this morning," he added, smiling at her.

"I never heard of that group," said Jasmine.

"All we do is pray," said Nobby. "It is not a group many people want to be in. But you can come. We meet every Wednesday at lunch in Mrs. Tanner's room."

"I'll come," said Jasmine.

"Me too," said Lilli.

Zion shrugged. "Not me. I'll be too busy eating."

The group laughed, and talk turned to the Martin Luther King holiday coming up in only a week.

★★★

Meanwhile, in the teacher's lounge, Mrs. Sharp was angry with Mr. Fletcher again. She stormed into the room and marched straight to his chair. She flung her lunch bag onto the table, placed her hands on her hips, and addressed him in her haughtiest voice. "I had to write up Darron Vance today, and it's your fault."

"Who is Darron Vance?" asked Mr. Fletcher.

"A boy with a filthy mouth. He says if you can use swear words in your novels, he can use them in the classroom."

"He said that?"

"That's exactly what he said!"

Mr. Fletcher shrugged and sighed. "How many times do we have to go over this, Sadie? He's just using me as an excuse. He talks the way he talks because he hears it at home."

"Of course he does," Mr. Josephs said. "Some of these poor kids come from dreadful environments."

Mrs. Sharp sat down and opened her lunch. "I know that! And that's why we should be setting a better example for them here at school."

"I don't use smutty language in my classroom," said Mr. Fletcher wearily. They'd had this conversation before. "I always set a wonderful example for my little darlings."

Mrs. Sharp popped her lunch into the microwave. "But you don't have to use profanity in your books," she insisted. "You're a role model here at the high school."

"You write your books your way. I'll write my books my way," said Mr. Fletcher. "And I'm tired of being blamed for all the ills of the world. Can't you find somebody else to blame for *something*?"

"So, how's your experiment going, Kip?" Mr. Josephs asked before Mrs. Sharp had time to reply.

"Better than I could have hoped," said Mr. Fletcher heartily. "Both of my star pupils made bad grades today. The worst they've ever made on one of my quizzes."

Mrs. Sharp put her lunch down on the table and took a seat. "Your best students are making bad grades, and you're pleased?" she asked, her voice drenched with sarcasm.

"They're just proving my point," said Mr. Fletcher, eying Mrs. Sharp's plastic dish of roast beef. "Where are the potatoes and carrots?" he asked. "And besides, what happened to the fast?"

Mrs. Sharp took a bite, then hopped up to heat her tepid meal again. "I don't fast *every* meal," she said. "But when I do eat, I try to reduce carbohydrates."

Tulsa Grant, an English teacher, looked interested. Like Mrs. Sharp, she needed to lose some weight. "Are you on a keto diet?" she asked. "Does it work?"

"No, I wouldn't say I'm on a keto diet," said Mrs. Sharp. "But I am trying to reduce my carbs."

"Why carbs?" asked Mr. Fletcher.

"Haven't you heard? Carbs are the enemy," said Mrs. Sharp, returning to the table. "They stimulate insulin the most of all the nutrients, and insulin keeps fat molecules in our cells, so they can't be used for energy. They just sit in our cells, keeping us fat."

"Carbs are the enemy?" Mrs. Grant asked. "So, it's bad to eat carbs?"

"No, no, not all carbs, I guess," said Mrs. Sharp. "Vegetables are good and some fruits. But anything with sugar added to it is bad, especially candies, cakes, cookies - all the good stuff! And flour seems to be a problem, too."

"So, you're still fasting sometimes?" Mr. Fletcher asked.

"Yes, I fast twice a week. It's good for my health, and I've already lost five pounds."

Mr. Fletcher whistled. "Well, now that sounds promising! Where are all these ideas coming from? And what makes you think not eating is good for your health?"

Mrs. Sharp sighed. "Actually, it's all over the internet. I don't know why it took me so long to find it. I got some books and learned that fasting has a lot of health benefits."

"Like what?"

"Well, for starters, it seems like fasting is a good treatment for type 2 diabetes, and…" Mrs. Sharp stopped to dab at a drop of moisture forming in her right eye. She sighed again, a deep shuddering sigh. "… and my doctor just told me that I'm pre-diabetic. He says I have to start taking medicine for it if I don't get my blood sugar down."

"Whoa, bummer!" said Mrs. Grant.

The room took on a sad air as the other teachers made sympathetic comments.

★★★

That afternoon, eighth period, Mr. Fletcher was in his classroom gathering up the things he was taking home for the weekend. As the school's tennis coach, he was usually out on the courts eighth period, yelling corrections and encouragements to his young players. But on Fridays, he often left them early to practice on their own while he prepared to make a quick exit as soon as the final bell rang.

Anyway, with the snow earlier in the week leaving the tennis courts soggy, his students were in the gym, mixed in with the P.E. students. Nobody would know or care that he had disappeared a few minutes early.

That's why he was seated at his desk, rummaging through a drawer, when someone knocked on the door. He looked up with a frown. Now what?

The man standing in his open doorway was a stranger. A *strange* stranger. His garb was pretty standard for the area - a dark felt western hat, blue jean jacket, blue jeans, and black western boots. But his shoulder-length hair was stringy, his five o'clock shadow was unkempt, and the fringes of his tattoos crawled up his neck. A silver earring dangling from his right ear lobe had the shape of some kind of bird with wings spread in flight.

"Yes," said Mr. Fletcher, "can I help you?"

"You Kip Fletcher?" asked the caricature.

"That's right. And who might you be?"

"Name's Myles Dyer. Call me Falcon."

"Okay, Mr. Falcon, how can I help you?"

"No 'mister' to it. Name's Falcon. And I'm here to stake my claim."

Mr. Fletcher's eyebrows rose. "Your claim to what?"

"Not a what. A who," said Falcon.

"Okay. Stake your claim to whom?" This nut was preposterous, but Mr. Fletcher was ready to get home for the weekend. So, he played along. Until he heard Falcon's next word.

"Dede."

Mr. Fletcher scowled. "My wife?"

"Dede Fletcher. That your wife?" asked Falcon.

"Yes. What exactly do you mean by 'stake your claim'?"

"Well, ya' see, it's like this." Falcon's expression softened. "Her and me. We want to be together."

Mr. Fletcher looked him up and down. "Hogwash!" he muttered.

"Oh, it's true!" said Falcon. "We're one of those, what you call soul mates."

"You want my wife?" asked Mr. Fletcher. "Is that what you're telling me? That you want my wife?"

Falcon beamed. "Now you got it!" he exclaimed. "I want your wife. We want to be together."

Mr. Fletcher was certain there was not one chance in a hundred trillion that Dede would give this character a second glance. So, his main objective was to get the guy out of his classroom. "Well," he said with a shrug, "that's entirely up to her. Now, if you'll please excuse me, I was just…"

"Oh…," said a small voice at the doorway.

Both men turned to see Lilli Park standing there. Neither of them had noticed when the final bell rang, dismissing classes for the weekend.

"I'm sorry," Lilli said. "I didn't know you were busy." She turned to go.

"Wait, Lilli," Mr. Fletcher called. "Mr. Dyer was just leaving."

Lilli stopped, and Mr. Fletcher turned back to Falcon. "It has been a real trip meeting you, Falcon," he said. "But I'm going to have to ask you to move on now."

Falcon looked flustered. "But what about what I said?" he asked. "Don't you want to talk about it?"

"Thank you so much," said Mr. Fletcher courteously. "I don't have the time right now, but I will discuss it with Dede. And, as I said, it's entirely up to her. You have a wonderful weekend!"

He escorted Falcon out and gestured to Lilli to come in. Then he shut the door in Falcon's face.

"Who was that guy?" asked Lilli. "He's weird looking."

"He's *very* weird looking," agreed Mr. Fletcher. "Do you want to sit down or did you just come to find out what grade you made on the quiz?"

Lilli blushed. "I came to apologize about your experiment," she said shyly. "I didn't mean to do so bad. But I've been worried all week about...about a... personal problem. And I didn't study much. Or listen in class much. I'm sorry. It wasn't because of your experiment. It was just all my fault..." Her voice faded away, and she looked up at her teacher with penitent eyes.

Mr. Fletcher laughed. He actually laughed. "I'm sorry you're having a personal problem, Lilli," he said, "but don't apologize. Please don't tell the rest of the class, but Camilla was right. I'm only doing this experiment to help my students understand that socialism is pure *humbuggery*. So, if you made a bad grade, that's fine. It just helps prove my point."

Lilli's eyes opened wide. "Then you're not mad at me?" she asked.

"Of course not! Lilli, I'm always so proud of you I could bust. You and Nobby are my best students, and if you both make horrible grades this cycle, I'll be even prouder of you!"

"Oh." Lilli gave a tentative smile. She studied Mr. Fletcher's face a moment and saw that he meant what he said. "Oh, well, then, I'm glad I failed."

He laughed again. "You didn't fail. You made 75. Come on, let's turn off the lights and get out of here."

In the nearly empty hallway, Mr. Fletcher asked, "Which way are you headed?"

Lilli pointed toward the stairwell at the far end of the hall.

"All right, then, I'll go that way too," he said, "and you can tell me – what is the most exciting or interesting or fun thing you learned this week?"

Lilli grinned. "It wasn't in any of my classes."

Mr. Fletcher grinned, too. "That doesn't surprise me. So, what was it?"

Lilli's face was alight, and she spoke with a sense of awe. "I learned that God's name is Jesus, and He loves me. Isn't that wonderful?"

Mr. Fletcher hid his surprise at this answer as he replied, "That does sound like wonderful news. Why don't you tell me about it?"

His expression was tender as he listened to the story of Lilli's very personal and private experience with God. Lilli's upturned face was radiant. Both were so engrossed in their discussion that neither noticed Palmer Evans, standing alone on the opposite side of the hall, watching them.

Mr. Josephs, trying to come out of his classroom a few moments later, found his door blocked by Palmer's body. As a coach, he was familiar with all the athletes, whether they played his sport or another. So, he addressed Palmer by name. "What are you doing, Evans?" he growled. "Why are you blocking my door?"

Palmer didn't answer the question. Instead, he jabbed a finger in the direction of Mr. Fletcher and Lilli. "That explains a lot," he asserted. "No wonder little Miss Wonderful is teacher's pet!"

At the end of the hall, Mr. Fletcher was politely holding the door for Lilli. Mr. Josephs watched them disappear from view, then he turned to Palmer. "What are you talking about, Evans?"

"Didn't you see them?" cried Palmer. "They're a pair of love birds! First, they were in his room with the door shut. Then they came out and walked right past me all goo-goo-eyed. They didn't even see me standing here because they couldn't take their eyes off each other."

Scowling, Mr. Josephs took Palmer's arm in an iron grip. "Don't you ever let me hear you talking like that again!" he snarled. "Do you hear me, Evans? Never!"

Palmer jerked his arm out of Mr. Josephs's grasp. "Yeah, that just about figures. All you teachers stick together. You think you can protect each other. But I know what I saw, and you can't do anything about that!" He glared at Mr. Josephs, then strode off down the hall.

Mr. Josephs rolled his eyes. He would have to talk to the football coaches about Palmer Evans. The boy was getting too big for his britches. Way too big. But it was Friday. Finally! And he didn't have to worry about Palmer or any other students for two whole days. He buttoned his coat and headed out, trying to decide which of the town's restaurants would get his business that evening.

Chapter 5: Falcon's Threat

That afternoon, it took Lilli only a few minutes to slide out of Royal's pickup, dash into her home, retrieve her overnight bag, and climb back into the big red Ram. Knowing she planned to spend the weekend at the Douglases', she had packed her bag the previous evening and left it by the front door that morning.

"You got everything?" Royal asked. "I think so," said Lilli.

"No! Think again and be sure," Royal insisted.

Lilli waited three seconds and said, "Yes. I have everything." Royal put the pickup into gear and headed for the Douglas farm. "I have really exciting news!" Lilli said, her eyes bright with excitement.

"'Oh yeah? What's that?" What Lilli found exciting rarely interested him, but he usually pretended.

"I got born again today," exclaimed Lilli. "Now I don't have to be afraid of the Soterians anymore! They're not even aliens. They're demons!"

"You got what?" Royal slammed on the brakes, throwing his passenger into the dashboard.

Lilli, who hadn't fastened her seatbelt yet, pulled it out and snapped it shut before she turned to look at Royal. "I got born again. I'm a Christian now," she said. Then, seeing the horrified expression on his face, she asked, "Why? What's wrong?"

"Oh, Lilli, you're probably the smartest kid in your class, but you can be *so* dumb!" Royal glared at her. "Besides that, what are you talking about?

36

You don't have to be afraid of the Soterians. You make it sound like they're trying to hurt you. They came to this planet to save us. Not to hurt us."

"I know," Lilli said meekly, "but they're scary."

"And what do you mean - they're demons? That's insulting! Where did you get such a stupid idea?"

"Treena Wood told me," said Lilli. "She told me I could ask Jesus to come live in my heart, and I wouldn't have to be afraid of them anymore."

Royal was glaring at her, and Lilli shrank away from him. Finally, he shook his head and took his foot off the brake. Pounding his fist on the steering wheel two times, he said urgently, "I don't know what Aziz is going to do when he hears this. Lilli, you have to be smarter about things. It's not time to tell people about the Soterians yet. Look, Jesus has been dead thousands of years. He doesn't live *anywhere*. Why would you believe such garbage?"

A tear was trickling down Lilli's cheek. "I thought…it…sounded true," she mumbled.

"Come on, kid, you don't want to be one of those uptight, bigoted Christians," said Royal urgently. "They're the ones trying to ruin things for everyone else."

Lilli looked up in surprise and wiped away the tear. "Who's trying to ruin anything? Treena is very nice, and she helped me feel better when I was really sad!"

"Don't you get it? That's all an act," said Royal with the tone of a patient teacher. "They want to turn everybody into clones, make everybody just like *them*. They think we should all be wearing black clothes, going around with stone faces, afraid to do anything fun for fear it might make somebody happy!"

"Treena doesn't wear black clothes," said Lilli, sounding stubborn. "Neither do Nobby and Jasmine and Zion."

"Oh, man! You mean there are more of them?" moaned Royal. "Look, you'll have to forget Hubble today. I need to think about this. Maybe I can contact Aziz and ask him what to do about it. You can't just turn your back on everything we're trying to accomplish."

Lilli's eyes widened in dismay. "You're going to talk to Aziz about me?"

she gasped.

Royal nodded thoughtfully. "Yes. I think I'd better. You know, Lilli, you can't go around telling people about the Soterians. The time has *got* to be right, and it's not right yet. I don't know what kind of damage you might have done. The Soterians have to know so they can deal with it. Look, we'll try to find Hubble another time."

The rest of the drive passed in silence. When they reached the Douglas farm, Royal parked and strode off across a field alone. Lilli went to the barn, as she always did, to see if Hubble might have returned. As soon as she disappeared into the big red building, Royal pulled out his phone and made a call.

"Hey, Coach," he said when the call was answered, "I need to talk to Aziz *now*. Is it okay?" Two minutes later, he was back in his pickup and headed for town.

Coach Len Josephs, the U.S. History teacher and assistant varsity basketball coach, lived in Skyport's haunted house. It was a weathered, old, two-story building with peeling gray paint and sagging windows. At least, so it appeared from the front. The old house had a history that Coach Josephs didn't want to lose.

Built over a hundred years earlier, it had once housed a wealthy ranch family, the Baileys. They owned the best pastureland in the area. Then, a prairie fire wiped out more than half their herd. Within ten years, every member of the family had died or moved away except the lone son of the family, Ambrose, and his grandfather.

Ambrose worked during his high school years for an old Comanche shaman who owned a local drug store. He left Skyport long enough to be trained as a pharmacist, then returned and bought the drug store from his former mentor, who was eager to retire.

By the age of 30, Ambrose was managing the Bailey ranch and running his own drug store. Prompt, efficient, and polite, he was generally respected and, over time, became one of the wealthiest men in the county.

Still, Ambrose was a loner and was considered an "odd duck." Twice a year, he sponsored a mesmerist in his home for a week. He promoted these occasions as opportunities for people with various ailments to be cured through hypnosis. The more reputable citizens of the county expressed horror at such goings-on. Only Ambrose knew how many of those horrified citizens plopped down good money to purchase a hypnotic cure.

Gossips claimed that Ambrose participated in various questionable activities, such as séances, wizardry, and astrology. However, he and his companions were very secretive. Eventually, it was the gossips who were discredited, not Ambrose.

Around the age of 50, at the height of his career and respectability, Ambrose made a fatal mistake. Among his pharmacy clients were an elderly husband and wife in poor health. The wife suffered from crippling arthritis, and the husband had a brain tumor. When the couple were discovered dead one morning, the blame was eventually traced to Ambrose, who had given them an unauthorized painkiller developed secretly in a lab in the basement of his home.

The town was divided. Many were outraged that Ambrose had given an untested, unproven drug to a desperate couple. Ambrose's supporters said their pharmacist was just too soft-hearted. He couldn't bear to see the couple's suffering, and if they hadn't overdosed themselves, they would have been fine.

When the police arrived to arrest Ambrose for involuntary manslaughter, he was gone. Efforts to locate him were fruitless. And the old Bailey place had stood empty for over 20 years. When Len Josephs moved to town eight years earlier, he had fallen in love with the house and its history. He bought it for a bargain price.

Contractors, hired to remodel the inside of the house and make sure it was structurally sound, shook their heads when he insisted that the "face" of the place must stay the same. He liked its haunted house appearance.

"The old coot is as crazy as Ambrose," they muttered to each other. But his money was as good as Ambrose's had been. They were happy to do his bidding and pocket their wages.

Royal, who at age six had explored the haunted house with some older boys, loved the old place too. But this night, he ignored the front of the house.

Instead, he drove up the alley and pulled into the backyard between the coach's car and his hothouse. The plastic-covered Quonset-style hothouse took up half the yard. The structure and its contents fascinated Royal, but tonight, he barely gave it a glance. He bounded past the shiny barbecue grill and the dark green picnic table on the patio. After giving the door a quick, perfunctory knock, he pushed it open and entered Coach Josephs's kitchen.

The tidy kitchen had an unused look. No dishes in the sink. No stray paper wrappers. Even the trash can was empty. Royal pulled the door shut and locked it. He moved to his left, where a door in the corner stood ajar.

Royal walked through this door with something akin to reverence. Stepping onto a dark flight of stairs, he began a slow, solemn descent. He could not have explained the sense of awe he felt when he entered Coach Josephs's basement, but it captured him every time.

The subterranean room was a wondrous cavern. Three black walls twinkled with tiny lights arranged as constellations and planets in the inkiest of night skies. The chamber, in fact, resembled a small planetarium. The only illumination, other than the flickering lights on the walls, was a red glow from a lamp in the corner.

A carpeted platform facing the stairway held a large, plush armchair upholstered in gold fabric. It was a throne. Coach Josephs, seated on it, wasn't wearing a crown, but he was king. He watched Royal's slow, respectful entrance with pleasure. The boy always curbed his natural cockiness in this hallowed grotto. It spoke well for him and his future with the Soterians.

The coach didn't have to instruct Royal. Facing the stage were three comfortable, red velvet armchairs. Royal crossed the room and sank down into the middle one. It was positioned directly in front of the five stairs leading onto the platform.

Coach Josephs studied Royal. "What's the emergency?"

Royal sat straight and tall. "It's Lilli," he said urgently. "She's decided she's a Christian. She's turning her back on everything we're trying to do."

Josephs shrugged. "She's young. What? A freshman?" Royal nodded.

"Well, she'll learn. In fact, she'll probably be back with us before she graduates," Josephs said. "Why should I summon Aziz over it?"

Royal took a deep breath. He didn't like to rat Lilli out, but his gut told him the issue was serious. "She's telling people about the Soterians. She's saying she's afraid of them. And Treena Wood told her they're demons. So now, Lilli is going around saying they're demons, and she doesn't have to be afraid of them because she has Jesus living inside her."

Royal paused for another gulp of air, then continued. "Look, Coach, I know it may not sound like much to you, but Aziz has told us over and over not to be talking about the Soterians and our future plans. Now, Lilli has defied him. He's going to be furious! And we need her. She's *so* smart. She knows all about stars and galaxies. Black holes. Supernovas. Quasars. All of it! We have to stop her before she goes too far, and Aziz kicks her out for good. I need to make him understand that she's just mixed up. He can help me save her. I know he can. If he knows how to save a whole planet, he should be able to save one little kid!"

Royal ran down.

Coach Josephs was nodding. "Okay. I get it," he said. He leaned back in his chair with his eyes closed. "Master Aziz," he said, speaking into the air as if the Soterian were an invisible presence, "Young Cadet Royal has urgent need of your attention. Can you communicate now?"

He stopped, and the two listeners waited in silence. Royal knew that the Soterians had implanted a tiny, futuristic transponder in the coach's throat. Through it, Josephs could contact the Soterians no matter where they were, and they could use his vocal organs to respond.

The hush following Josephs's request stretched into a minute. Then, two minutes. The tension growing in Royal's body since Lilli made her announcement began to dissipate. He relaxed in the comfortable chair and relived his first time in this basement sanctuary...

He had been a seventh grader then, and Josephs was head coach of his basketball team. The breaking news in Skyport at the time was the recent sightings of whole flotillas of UFOs in the night skies. At least, many residents asserted fiercely that the lights represented UFOs. Others argued with equal fervor that the lights were just lights – reflections or Earth-based aircraft or something equally terrestrial.

During basketball practice one afternoon, Royal and Kent Spencer, an eighth grader, had almost come to blows in defense of their opposing positions. Royal claimed that extraterrestrial forces were scouting the area for landing sites and command posts. He insisted that Skyport was honored by their presence. Kent Spencer said Royal should have his head examined.

Kent and Royal were the highest scorers on their respective teams. They competed constantly to outscore each other. Their rivalry smoldered just below the surface in every practice and every game. The coaches stoked that competitive fire. It was one of the reasons the two teams were not only undefeated but also ran up lopsided scores. Still, the coaches didn't need two of their players to be at war. So, they made the boys apologize to each other and run extra laps.

After practice, the coach called Royal into his office, and they talked "space aliens." Royal had seen the Soterians for the first time three years earlier. He had met Aziz the following year. And the next summer the Soterians had taken Royal into outer space to see Mars and to discuss the future of Earth. That experience had altered the entire trajectory of his life.

As for Coach Josephs, he referred to himself as a "lieutenant" in Aziz's squadron. He had made contact with the aliens six years earlier. An alien medic had implanted the transponder in his throat two years later. Now, he was one of the most trusted members of the force.

The same week that Royal and the coach realized they had this star-studded connection through the Soterians, Josephs invited Royal to his home for a session in the basement. It was an astonishing experience! Royal was actually able to hear Aziz's loud, guttural voice, which was nothing like Coach Josephs's soft, smooth voice.

They discussed Aziz's home planet, Soteria, and the Soterians' dreams for the future of Earth. Aziz said that since Coach Josephs was already 60 years old, he would not have time to work his way up to a leadership position in the organization. He would always be a respected officer, but he would not be able to reach the highest echelons of power.

Royal, on the other hand, was young and ambitious. He was committed to devoting his youthful energies to the project. He would undoubtedly become a world leader on his home planet Earth. A world leader!

In his mind, Royal wandered back to the garden planet he had dreamed about when the Soterians first contacted him. He wondered if Earth could ever be so beautiful and so lush. He knew that if he could help bring such a wonderland to pass, he would be honored and admired all around the globe.

Aziz's harsh voice suddenly filled the room. "Yes, Royal. What is your need?"

Royal jerked to attention. "It's Lilli Park. Do you remember her?"

"I remember."

Royal nodded. "Well, someone at school has persuaded her that she's a Christian. Now she's saying that Jesus lives inside her and that you are a demon. Master Aziz, Lilli is the smartest person I know. We need her on our side, but I can't make her understand how important our mission is. Can you help me? What can I say to her to save her from this foolishness?"

A long silence followed Royal's speech. Finally, Aziz said calmly, "If Lilli is foolish enough to believe this myth, how smart can she be? Why should we spend time and energy on one who is so easily duped?"

"It's just that she's very bright about most things," said Royal. "I think she can be especially effective in helping us to accomplish our goals."

"Hmmm," said Aziz, but the sound came out as a growl through Coach Josephs's throat. "Perhaps this development has come to pass for your sake, Cadet Royal. Perhaps this is your first great opportunity to prove your own effectiveness in our mission. Show us how wise and wily you can be in wooing Lilli back to our side. Can you do it?"

Royal shivered. *Could* he do it? "Master Aziz, can you give me some pointers? How would you suggest that I win Lilli back?" he asked. "I tried to talk to her, but she was resistant. That's why I've come to you for help."

"As it happens," Aziz said, "I am very busy elsewhere just now. But look forward. Do you see your Coach Josephs before you? He is wise, and he is faithful. Look to him for your help."

With that, Josephs sagged in his throne-like chair. Aziz was gone.

It always took the coach about ten minutes to recover from one of these experiences. He would be drained and unaware of the substance of the conversation. This fact puzzled Royal. How could Coach Josephs be in the room - actually be the mouthpiece for one of the speakers - and not know what was said? But he never did.

Royal could not help wondering if the coach's ignorance was a scam. Maybe the coach pretended not to be aware of the conversation so he could see whether Royal reported it truthfully.

And then, there was the puzzle of the coach's exhaustion after the sessions. What was it about a simple discussion that sapped his energy? When Royal had posed this question, the coach replied that he didn't have an answer, but he was glad for the change in his strength and energy. Otherwise, couldn't Aziz and the Soterians eavesdrop without his even being aware of it? "I would not like it if they could overhear my conversations, and I didn't know they were listening," the coach had said.

Royal agreed. He didn't want anybody eavesdropping on him either.

Coach Josephs stood and stretched. "Well, what did you learn?" he asked. "Let's go upstairs. It's always as hot as blazes down here when Aziz visits."

Royal followed the coach up the stairs to the kitchen. The coach pulled two beers out of the refrigerator and handed one to Royal. They seated themselves at the table, and Royal recounted the conversation. The coach was gulping his beer thirstily. Royal was sipping his.

"So, Aziz put the onus on me, did he?" asked the coach when Royal finished reporting.

"The what?"

"The burden. The load. The problem," Josephs clarified.

Royal nodded. "I guess so." He paused before adding, "On both of us, actually. I have to prove myself."

"So you do," said the coach. "So you do."

Suddenly, Royal's eyes were wet with tears. "Please help me, Coach," he whispered brokenly. "Lilli is my best friend. I kind of forget that sometimes, but I've always imagined us working together to save our world."

Coach Josephs patted Royal's shoulder. "Don't worry, son," he said. "We'll figure something out."

★★★

Bryce Douglas arrived home at 6:00 that evening. He was tall - six feet, three inches - and muscular. His blond hair was the same sandy shade as Royal's, and, at 48, it was still as thick as it had been 20 years earlier.

He found Royal gone and Lilli sitting on the bed in the guest bedroom. Her arms were around Adolf's neck, and her cheek rested on the dog's head. Lilli looked sad, and Adolf looked sympathetic. When Bryce appeared in the doorway, Adolf looked at him, and his tail thumped once. But the big black dog didn't move a muscle that would disturb Lilli.

Bryce was the warden at a federal prison in a neighboring town. He had been too busy to eat lunch that day and was ravenous, so he wasn't sorry to see that Royal and Lilli weren't out hunting for Hubble. He was ready for food. And he didn't even ask Lilli why she was sad. He knew why. She was worried about Hubble.

"Hey, Chickadee," he greeted her. "What did you do with Royal?"

Lilli jumped up and came to hug him. "I made him mad, and he left," she said sadly.

"Uh oh. How did you make him mad?" Bryce asked.

"I got born again," said Lilli.

"Born again?" Bryce repeated. "You got born again? Now, that's a new one. And why did it make Royal mad?"

Lilli sighed. "He said I was causing trouble for Aziz and the Soterians." Lilli looked up pitifully. "I didn't mean to make trouble for anybody."

Bryce laughed. "Don't worry about it. Let's go get a pizza, and you can tell me all about it. I'm starving! What about you?"

Lilli nodded. "Me too!"

"Did you or Royal feed the chickens and gather the eggs?"

"I did," said Lilli. She loved taking care of the chickens and collecting their eggs. It was like having Easter every day.

"Good deal!" said Bryce. "Why don't you text Royal and tell him to meet us there while I change clothes?"

By the time their large pepperoni pizza arrived, Lille had told Bryce the whole story. Bryce was torn. He halfway agreed with Royal. But he had been in the prison system for a long time. He had seen a few lives changed dramatically by this experience they called being "born again." Maybe there really was something to it. But he wasn't in any mood to deal with the issue at the moment. It was Friday evening. Time to kick back and enjoy some R&R.

"Tell you what, Chickadee-dee," he said, "let's talk about all this another time. I'm too tired tonight. And don't worry about Royal or Aziz or the Soterians. It's all going to come out in the wash. In the meantime, why don't you tell me about your week?"

With a sigh, Lilli told him about Mr. Fletcher's experiment and how she had made the humiliating grade of only 75 on today's quiz. "But Nobby said he didn't do so well either," she finished, "and Mr. Fletcher wasn't upset with us, so I guess it's okay."

She studied Bryce's face to judge his reaction. He opened his mouth to reassure her, but a shadow suddenly fell on their table.

"Well, if it's not Top Cop!" came a sneering voice.

Bryce and Lilli looked up to see Falcon standing over them.

Bryce glared, and Lilli gasped. Falcon turned his attention to Lilli.

"Well, well, well. Who do we have here?" he asked. Now his voice was oily, his eyes narrowed.

Lilli hopped up and went to stand in the circle of Bryce's arm. "Do you know Falcon?" Bryce asked her.

Nodding, Lilli quavered, "He was talking to Mr. Fletcher today." Bryce pulled Lilli closer, then looked at Falcon again.

"What do you want, Dyer?" he asked.

"I want to know how long you fascists are plannin' to keep my brother in that cage of yours."

"Would you be referring to Condor or Hawk?" asked Bryce.

"You know Condor's in for life," snarled Falcon. "What about Hawk?"

"I think he has at least two more years on his sentence, doesn't he?" Bryce asked.

"Yeah, well, what about good behavior?" "Good behavior?! Hawk?"

Falcon studied Bryce's face and finally asked, "He's not gettin' out early?"

"Not hardly," said Bryce. "Look, Dyer, we're trying to eat here. Why don't you get lost?"

"Go ahead and eat. I'm not stoppin' ya'," said Falcon. "I want to know what ya' can do for my brother. I bet ya' can make those doors swing open for him."

Bryce shook his head. "I'm just a warden. The courts are the ones that make the doors swing."

"But if ya' wanted to, ya' could do something about it, couldn't ya'?" asked Falcon.

"Falcon, blow, or I'll call the cops," Bryce said.

Falcon stared at Bryce long and hard, then turned his gaze on Lilli. "That's a real pretty little girl ya' got there. Ya' wouldn't want anything bad to happen to her, would ya'?"

Bryce took out his cell phone and punched in 9-1-1. But Falcon was out the door before the call was answered. Bryce broke the connection and returned the phone to his pocket.

Lilli went back to her chair. "What did Mr. Falcon mean?" she asked. "Is he going to hurt me?"

"Of course not!" Bryce exclaimed. "Just let him try! Go on now; eat your pizza."

"I don't like him," Lilli said, "and I don't think Mr. Fletcher likes him either."

Bryce snorted. "Nobody likes him."

"Nobody likes who?" asked Royal, flopping onto an empty chair. "A lowlife that calls himself 'Falcon'," said Bryce. "He used to be an inmate himself."

"You mean the guy that just left?" asked Royal, gazing out the window where he could see Falcon leaning against an old, black pickup, smoking a cigarette.

"That's right," said Bryce. "Falcon's a two-time loser. One more strike, and he's out."

Royal picked up a slice of pizza. "Pepperoni again?" he grumbled. "Don't you two have any imagination at all?"

"Hey, if you don't like it, don't eat it. Yours will be here in a few minutes. They put it in the oven when you walked through the door," said Bryce.

"Okay! That's more like it," said Royal, tossing the slice back onto the tray.

"So, did Lilli tell you what she did today?"

"Yes, she told me all about it," said Bryce. "And it was pretty rude of you not to help her hunt for Hubble."

"I told her we'd do it another time," said Royal. "I had to think about this born-again stuff. It sounds pretty lame to me." He frowned at Lilli, then picked up the slice of pizza he had tossed down and began eating it. He did not mention the discussion in Coach Josephs's basement. Those sessions were strictly secret.

Bryce turned his attention back to Lilli. "Did you say Falcon was talking to your teacher today?" he asked.

Lilli nodded. "What about?"

He waited until Lilli had finished chewing and swallowing her bite. Then she said, "I don't know. I think it was something about Mr. Fletcher's wife, but they stopped talking when they saw me. I don't know what it was about."

"Nothing good if Falcon is involved. That's for sure," Bryce said. "So, son, what about the game Tuesday? Are we going to win?"

While Bryce and Royal discussed basketball and Lilli thought about Jesus, Myles "Falcon" Dyer was the topic of conversation in a home on the other side of town.

"You ever hear of a sleaze that goes by the name of 'Falcon'?" Kip Fletcher asked his pretty, young wife. He was washing dishes, and she was drying.

Dede Fletcher looked up in surprise. "How do you know Falcon?" she asked.

"How do *I* know him? The question is - how do *you* know him?"

Dede grinned. "I asked first."

Kip chuckled. "I guess you've got me there. He came by my classroom this afternoon to stake his claim."

"To stake his claim?" Dede repeated.

"That's what he said."

"His claim to what?"

Kip studied her face. "You. He said you're soul mates, and you want to be together."

Dede gasped. "No, he didn't!" Suddenly, she gave her husband a mischievous look and added, "That's piffle!"

"Claptrap!" he responded.

"Poppycock!" said Dede.

"How about flapdoodle and fiddle-faddle?" asked Kip.

Both were laughing uproariously by now. They collapsed into each other's arms.

Dede had met Kip Fletcher at a book signing a few months after his first wife left him, taking their two children and moving to Fort Worth. She considered herself his biggest fan and told him so the day she met him. Their romance had proceeded from there without a backward glance. Now, Dede handled the business and publicity for Kip's historical novels. She was still his biggest fan and loved his historical vocabulary, which she also used, but only in private conversations with him.

When Kip finished laughing, he asked. "How do you know this Falcon dude?"

"I see him sometimes at the YMCA. We both use the weight room and some of the cardio equipment. He's asked me to go for a drink twice. I turned him down, of course."

"Sounds like a pest," said Kip.

"He's starting to sound like a stalker," said Dede. "Why would he look you up and 'stake his claim' like that?"

Kip grinned suddenly. "I think he had the idea I might pay him to 'unstake' his claim. So, I just shrugged and told him you're free to do whatever you want."

Dede grinned, too. "How did that go over?"

"About like the classical lead balloon. Fortunately, Lilli Park came along, so I was able to hustle him out. But I don't like his looks. Shall we call the police?"

Dede shook her head. "Not yet. Let me give him a warning first."

Kip wrung out the dish rag and tossed it onto the counter. He dried his hands and took Dede into his arms. "It's your call," he said, "but watch out for any jiggery-pokery from that one. I have an idea he'd be right at home under a rattlesnake's belly."

Chapter 6: UFO Theology

Since Lilli was planning to go to church with Treena on Sunday, she didn't spend the whole weekend at the Douglas farm as she had first planned. Instead, her mother picked her up before lunch on Saturday morning, and she spent the afternoon doing homework.

Anyway, Royal was still angry with her and clearly had no intention of helping her hunt for Hubble. He spent all of Saturday at school, working out and practicing with the basketball team. Bryce was at the prison. So, she had no reason to stay on the farm, although she did spend an hour Saturday morning with Adolf, wandering around the automobile graveyard. They found no sign of Hubble.

At 9:15 Sunday morning, Treena Wood dashed up to the front door of Lilli's home. She raised her hand to ring the bell, but the door suddenly flew open.

"Don't ring it!" Lilli commanded. "Mom worked last night, and you'll wake her up."

Treena pulled her hand away as if it had been burned. "I didn't touch it," she said earnestly.

Lilli smiled. "I know you didn't. I'm ready." She was pulling on a fleecy white coat as she spoke.

Treena's dad, Riley Wood, was standing by a silver mini-van waiting for them. "Welcome to the family, Lilli!" he exclaimed as the girls approached.

"Lilli, this is my dad. He's the youth pastor at my church," Treena said.

"You can call him Riley or Mr. Wood or Mr. Riley."

"Or 'hey you,'" Mr. Wood added with a grin. He was a slender man with sparkling dark eyes and a mostly bald head. His grin was wide and friendly.

Lilli returned his grin. "I'm happy to meet you, Mr. Hey You," she said.

"If it's okay with you, we'll sit in the back, and Treena will drive," Mr. Wood said. "I'd like to talk to you and ask you something very important."

Lilli glanced at Treena, who smiled and jangled the keys. "Okay, Mr. Wood," she said.

It wasn't far to the church, and Mr. Wood got right down to business. "I know I'm asking a lot," he said, "but I was wondering if you would be willing to share your story with my class today. You know, about the aliens?"

Lilli went white. And still.

Treena had called Friday evening and received permission to tell her dad about Lilli's experience with the Soterians. But Lilli had not imagined he might want to tell the story to anyone else. Especially a whole class full of her peers!

Seeing her distress, Mr. Wood hurried on. "Well, you see, it's an important subject. I wanted to talk to you about it, and it occurred to me that it would help all the kids to hear your story and then hear what I have to say."

Lilli was trembling now. "It makes me feel stupid that I thought demons were people from another planet," she quavered.

Mr. Wood was very intense. "There's no reason to feel stupid," he said. "Older folks with decades more experience have made the same mistake. Think about all the movies being made these days about freaks and monsters from distant galaxies. The idea is getting so common that hundreds of people are falling for the lies these creatures tell. You would be doing a great service to our students if you would let us discuss your experience."

Lilli studied his face wonderingly. "I… I like to help people," she said shyly.

"Then you'll do it?" he asked. "I won't try to tell your story. You'll tell it yourself. That way, you can share only those things you want to share and leave out anything that makes you uncomfortable."

Lilli was nodding. "Okay," she said.

From "Okay" to sitting in a circle with fifteen pairs of eyes staring at her passed in a fuzzy flurry. Lilli gulped in a huge helping of air when she heard Mr. Wood say, "Okay, Lilli. Tell us your story."

Lilli looked at all the eyes aimed at her. She recognized a few faces from school, but besides Treena, the only person she knew was Kent Spencer, a member of the varsity basketball team. She had been introduced to everyone, of course, but the names had floated through her frantic mind without lodging. She knew Mr. Wood had greeted the class and prayed and said something about her, but those words, too, had floated past her. "Um...," she said. "Mmmmm...I don't know where to start."

"Would you like me to ask you questions?" Mr. Wood asked kindly. "You could answer if you want to, and you can decline to answer any question you don't like."

Lilli nodded eagerly. "Yes, that would be the best."

"Okay. Have you ever seen a UFO?"

Lilli nodded.

"How many times?"

"Three for sure. Sometimes I think I'm seeing one, then I decide I'm not...so I'm not too sure."

"Tell us about the first time."

"Well, I was nine or ten. It was dark, and I had been playing with a friend. My Mom called and told me to get home to dinner. I was running through a vacant lot when suddenly, a red light surrounded me. I was so scared I nearly fainted."

Lilli paused and took a couple of deep breaths before she continued, "When I looked up, I saw this thing floating over my head. It was shaped like a boomerang...and it had...I don't know, something like portholes along the front. Probably six or seven of them. My legs were weak and shaky, but I knew it was going to get me if I fainted or fell down. So, I made myself keep running. I ran as fast as I could.

"When I got home and told my mom, she said to forget it. She said it was probably just my imagination or somebody playing a stupid trick on me. I knew she was wrong, and I couldn't eat anything. That night, I was afraid to go to sleep because I thought they had seen where I went, and the aliens might come in the night to get me."

She looked at Mr. Wood and said apologetically. "I had just seen a movie about space aliens. I don't remember what it was, but in the movie, the people got taken away to another solar system, and I thought the same thing was going to happen to me."

"Did the UFO come back that night?" a boy in the group asked.

Lilli shook her head. "No, and I didn't see another one for maybe two years. That time, I was out in a field with Royal - he says the Douglas farm is an official landing site for space vehicles because they're welcome there." She shivered.

"Anyway, we saw a red spotlight shining down out of the sky. It got brighter and brighter, then suddenly, there was the same UFO hovering over us, and I could see that the red light was coming out of it. The UFO was about as high up as a two-story house. I screamed, but Royal grabbed me and put his hand over my mouth. He said not to be afraid because they were friendly."

Lilli looked around the group to see if anyone seemed to be laughing at her. But everyone was watching her with rapt attention.

Lilli was trembling now and wiping away tears. "We just stood there for a few minutes, then it seemed like I went to sleep. When I woke up, I didn't remember anything at first. But later, I had dreams…or visions…or something. I remembered being in a room in the spaceship. There were a bunch of little gray men with big turquoise-colored eyes."

"How big were they?" someone asked.

"They were a few inches taller than I was," said Lilli. "So, they were probably about the same height I am now. One of them, the tallest one - his name was Aziz - kind of talked to me. He didn't really say anything. He just seemed to put his thoughts into my mind. And then I had to answer him out loud."

"What did he say?" asked Mr. Wood when Lilli paused.

"He said they were from the planet Soteria, and they discovered Earth a long time ago. Well, he didn't say Earth; he said 'your world.' He said it's a beautiful world, and they're worried about it. They think we're killing the Earth, so they want to help us save it."

"How did he say they were going to help?" Mr. Wood asked.

"I'm not sure. It was like a bunch of double-talk, but it seemed like they think they need to take charge of everything and run the planet. Like being the president of the Earth. Or king or something."

Lilli's face registered her confusion. "I didn't really understand what he was talking about, but Royal tried to explain it to me - how they're going to have to take over and rule the whole world to make sure people stop polluting and disrespecting the planet. He says they know how to turn deserts into tropics and polar ice caps into warm springs. They told Royal that someday he's going to be their regent. They took him to Mars once, and he's all excited about them and the good things they're going to do for the Earth."

Lilli paused, and Treena asked, "What about the third time? You said you'd seen a UFO three times."

Lilli nodded. "The third time was last summer. Something woke me up in the middle of the night, and I saw a red glow outside my window. When I looked out, the same UFO was out there. It was just hovering over the yard. I think Aziz was telling me to come outside. I didn't hear anything with my ears, but I heard him in my mind. And he kept telling me to come out."

"Did you go?" someone asked when Lilli paused.

She shook her head. "No, I went and got in bed with my mom."

Treena laughed. "That was smart!"

"Did you say the aliens took Royal to Mars?" asked Mr. Wood.

Lilli nodded.

"Can you tell us about that?" he asked.

"Not too much; I wasn't there. He told me they didn't land on Mars. They were in the Soterians' spaceship, and he saw a reddish-brown plain with lots of craters and a dry riverbed. While they were flying around, he saw a huge mountain. It was shaped like a volcano, but it wasn't giving off any smoke or lava. And he saw a dust storm; it looked like a red tornado." She shrugged. "That's about all I know."

Then she added, "Well, except that it started when he was astral projecting. Do you know what that is, Mr. Wood?"

"I've heard of it," replied Mr. Wood. "Isn't it an out-of-body experience?"

"I think so," said Lilli. "I've never done it, but Royal loves it. He does it when he wants to see the Soterians."

"So, he's not afraid of them?" asked Treena.

Lilli shook her head. "No, they're his heroes. He thinks they're going to save the world someday. And he's going to help them." A tear trickled down her cheek. "If they're demons, then…" She paused and pulled her sleeve across her eyes.

She looked up at Mr. Wood. "If they're demons, what are they going to do to Royal?"

Mr. Wood, who had been sitting in the chair next to Lilli, rose and moved to the front of the room. "That's a very good question," he said. "And so is this one - what do they want to do to *all* of us?"

He smiled at Lilli. "Thank you so much for sharing your story with us. Let's leave it for now and talk about the UFO plague that's stalking our planet these days. How many of you have ever seen a UFO or an alien or know someone else who has?"

Everyone in the room raised their hands.

Mr. Wood nodded. "Okay. Here's the first thing you need to know. Most of the UFO sightings that are reported are not visitors from another planet. What do you think they are?"

"Some kind of weird military aircraft," one boy answered quickly.

"Hoaxes," said a girl.

"Right! Somebody playing a mean trick," agreed Treena.

"A weather balloon or some kind of scientific equipment" was another answer.

"An LSD trip," chortled one of the boys.

The answers kept coming: "A meteor." "Clouds." "A planet." "Mr. Wood's bald head" was the last suggestion. It was received with hoots of laughter.

"With that rude remark, we'll move on," said Mr. Wood, grinning. "I think you've covered the field. Good job! As a matter of fact, one physicist has stated that 95 percent of UFO sightings can be identified as natural phenomena. It's the remaining five percent that I, personally, believe might be attributed to demons."

"Demons?" gasped a boy sitting behind Lilli. "Come on! You think demons come from some distant solar system?"

"Not at all," replied Mr. Wood. "I believe demons are the spiritual beings described in the Bible. But they're liars. And they want to be worshiped as gods. Did you hear what Lilli said - they want to be world dictators. They're trying to convince Lilli and Royal that they're good guys here to save our world. Who remembers what the serpent told Eve when he was tempting her?"

"He said she could become like God," Treena answered.

"Right! And in the book of Isaiah, we learn that the fallen angel Lucifer wanted to exalt himself to a place of rulership and become like God," said Mr. Wood. "So, it sounds like the Soterians have the same agenda as the devil's. They want to be rulers and be in charge of this planet. They want to make themselves into gods.

"Okay, how many of you have a phone with you that's connected to the internet?"

Three students raised their hands. "Good," said Mr. Wood, "here's what I want you to do."

He went to a whiteboard at the front of the room and wrote, "soteria."

"We're going to break into three groups, each led by one of you who can surf the net on your phone. Put the word 'soteria' into a search engine and see what you get. Then discuss among yourselves why you think these E.T.s chose this word for the name of their planet."

Mr. Wood quickly facilitated the formation of the groups. "Don't waste time," he warned them. "No more than five minutes searching, then you'll have five minutes to talk among yourselves. I'm going to pass around pads and pencils. I want each group to write one sentence about what you've found out or what you believe it means."

Fifteen minutes later, Mr. Wood had managed to quell the excited chatter and get the following sentences written on the board:

"Soteria is a Greek word that means Salvation."

"Soteria was the Greek goddess of salvation, deliverance, and preservation from harm."

"We believe the demons chose to call their home planet Soteria because they were going to tell people they came to save the Earth, and Soteria means Salvation."

Mr. Wood looked around proudly. "Very good, students," he said. "Now, we're almost out of time, so I'm going to throw out just one more thing for you to think about. Next week, I want to hear your thoughts on it. "How many of you know what the rapture is?" Everyone raised a hand except Lilli.

"Well, Lilli, let me give you a quick definition. We believe the Bible teaches that a time will come when God will bring an end to life on this planet as we know it. But first, there will be seven years of terrible tribulation. Before that seven-year period begins, everyone who has received Jesus Christ as their Savior will be whisked up into Heaven, where we'll be safe from the gruesome times to come. We call that whisking away the 'rapture.' Not all Christians agree with that interpretation of the Bible, but most of us at this church believe there will be such an event."

He turned his attention back to the whole group. "Now think about this. What are people going to say when all the Christians in the world suddenly disappear? Will they want to believe the Bible is true and God is fulfilling prophecy?"

He paused so his listeners could consider the question. Then he said, "How about this? What if world leaders claim that extraterrestrials have removed all the Christians because we're standing in the way of progress? Do you think people would believe that?"

Some of the teenagers nodded thoughtfully.

"Perhaps there will be other explanations," said Mr. Wood, "but I think a massive alien abduction might be one explanation a lot of people will accept. So, think about it. Talk about it. Next week, I would love to hear your ideas."

After he had prayed and dismissed the group, he kept Lilli for a few minutes. Handing her a booklet, he explained, "This little book is a short - very short – synopsis of the Bible. If you choose to read it, you won't be so lost about the things you hear in church. But I hope you'll read the whole Bible over the next few years. It's the most amazing book ever written!"

Lilli smiled at him shyly. "Thank you," she said in her soft voice. "I'll read this book today. And I'll read the Bible too."

"Did you enjoy our class?" Mr. Wood asked. "I hope I didn't make you feel uncomfortable."

Lilli actually beamed at him. "I loved it!" she said. "I want to come back next week." She hesitated, then, before adding, "Mr. Wood, may I ask you something?"

"Of course, Lilli. What is it?"

Worry lines creased Lilli's forehead. "What about Royal? What's going to happen to him? And why does Royal think Aziz is a space alien when he's really a demon? How can I make him understand that Aziz is a...a liar?"

Mr. Wood's eyebrows surged upward. "That's a lot of good questions," he said, "and they're also very hard questions to answer."

He took a seat and beckoned for her to take the chair next to his. When she was seated, he said, "I wish I could tell you what you want to know, but I'm not a prophet or a mind reader. I don't know what's going to happen to Royal or how you can make him understand. But I can try to answer the 'why?' question."

He paused and gathered his thoughts. Then he said, "According to the Bible, God made two kinds of living beings. There are humans like us. And there are spiritual beings, like angels. The problem is that some of God's creations are rebellious, including some of the angels. We call those mutinous angels 'the devil' and 'demons.' It's like they've declared war on God. They can't really do anything to hurt Him directly because He's so powerful. But they know He loves people, so they can hurt Him by hurting people."

Mr. Wood paused again and smiled ruefully. "I don't want to get into deep theological issues, so I'll just say that demons want to harm people any way they can. In Royal's case, they are trying to hi-jack his life and ruin him so completely that he'll miss out on the wonderful future God has planned for him."

"So..." Lilli was frowning. "So, there are demons everywhere just waiting to pounce on everybody?"

Mr. Wood smiled. "They would like to pounce on everybody, but usually, we have to do something that gives them access to our minds."

"What kind of something?" Lilli was still frowning.

"Well, things like witchcraft or fortune telling or using a Ouija board or…" He paused to think, then his face brightened. "Or like astral projecting. You said Royal liked to do that, didn't you?"

Lilli nodded. "So, we have to kind of *invite* them to come confuse us?" she asked.

Mr. Wood nodded. "Something like that."

"Only they can cause us to think they're making us happy. Anyway, they make Royal happy," Lilli said thoughtfully.

"Yes, they're very devious," said Mr. Wood. "It's one reason they're so dangerous."

Lilli shivered. "I wish I could do something to help Royal see what they're really like."

"The best way you can help him is to pray for him. Someday, when he's ready to listen, maybe you'll get a chance to tell him about Jesus."

Lilli nodded. "I wish I could do more," she whispered.

Mr. Wood smiled. "It's enough," he assured her.

Chapter 7: Tumbling Grades

O n Monday morning, Palmer Evans was beside himself with excitement. He put his hand up as soon as the second-period tardy bell rang and asked, "Mr. Fletcher, what did I make on my quiz Friday? How many points did I get added to my grade?"

Mr. Fletcher looked grim. "Well, it seems my experiment is off to a *piddling* start. Every single student in this class, except…" He paused and consulted a paper before continuing, "…except Marion Rogers, made a lower grade on this quiz than they did on the last quiz we took in December."

He gazed around the room. "What happened to *all* of you working *very* hard?"

"Yeah!" exclaimed Palmer. "What happened to that?" He glared at Lilli Park and Nobby Tanaka. "You guys are just selfish. You don't care about anybody but yourselves."

"You're a fine one to talk!" Zion Johnson interjected. "It doesn't sound like you did so good!"

"Of course not," said Palmer. "Everybody knows I'm not as smart as *some* people in this class. Everybody knows I need help."

"But Palmer," said Mr. Fletcher gently, "even if you're not as smart as *some* people in this room, you still should have done as well on this quiz as you usually do. You didn't. Your grade was ten points lower."

"What about Lilli?" asked Palmer accusingly. "How much lower was her grade than usual?"

Everyone's gaze turned to Lilli, who blushed and ducked her head.

"It's none of your business!" cried Nobby. His eyes blazed. "It's not her job to make points for you."

Palmer was out of his seat. "Yes, it is. Mr. Fletcher made it her job!" He turned to the teacher. "Didn't you, Mr. Fletcher?"

"Sit down, Palmer," said Mr. Fletcher, taking a few steps toward the angry quarterback. "Lilli's grades are her own business. But she can tell you how she did if *she* wants to."

Instantly, the whole class was staring at Lilli. Her blush deepened. "I… I made 20 points worse," she whispered.

Palmer, who had returned to his seat, now leaped up again. "There! I only made ten points worse. She made 20 points worse because she doesn't want to give away any of her points. She's selfish!"

Lilli was crying now and trying to explain. "No, I…I…was…"

But Nobby was out of his seat and moving toward Palmer. His hands were closed in tight fists at his sides. The two squared off, and the whole class held its breath, waiting to see who would throw the first punch.

Lilli half rose from her seat, her hand extended toward Nobby as if to pull him back. Then he spoke. "Twinkle, twinkle, little star. What you say is what you are," he chanted scornfully before he turned away, muttering under his breath, "You call *Lilli* selfish…"

The other students relaxed in their chairs and laughed.

Now Palmer was turning red. He was not used to being laughed at. "Okay, shrimp," he shouted at Nobby's back, "what did *you* make on the quiz? Your usual one hundred?"

Nobby paused and turned to Lilli with a perplexed expression. "I do not know what I made," he said. "How did you know your grade, Lilli?"

"She came by last Friday to find out," Mr. Fletcher said before Lilli could respond. "Now, all of you settle down. We need to get a few things straight right now."

He strode back to the front of the room, and the class followed his progress with their eyes. "Here's how the experiment is going to work," said Mr. Fletcher sternly. "No points are going to be added or subtracted from anyone's grade until the end of the six-week cycle. You will all make what you make, and I will do the adjusting when the grades for the cycle are complete. Is that clear?"

Some of the students nodded.

"And we won't have any more discussions of this type ever again," Mr. Fletcher added. "You got that, Palmer Evans?"

Palmer was back in his desk, slumped low in his chair. "Whatever," he growled.

Mr. Fletcher rolled his eyes. "Okay, let's look at the quiz," he said. He passed the papers out and briefly discussed the correct answers before retrieving them and putting them away.

Then he looked toward the back of the room. "So, Palmer," he said, "you claim you're not as smart as some students in this class. I disagree. I've seen you on the football field. In the last game of the season, you saw that the play you called wasn't going to work, and you readjusted your plan right on the spot. Instead of being tackled for a loss, you made a first down. You can't tell me that wasn't a smart move."

Palmer sat up straighter. "That's different. That was football."

Mr. Fletcher shrugged. "It was also smart. And…" he paused dramatically, "…because you're smart, I'm going to expect you to start making better grades and donating some of your points to your classmates."

Palmer scowled. "You're nuts. If I can make good grades, I'm not going to give them away. It's too hard for me."

"Selfish!" Nobby hissed.

Mr. Fletcher ignored Nobby. "So, we talked about the Scientific Revolution last week," he said. "This week, we're going to discuss a different kind of revolution. Palmer, what can you tell us about either the American Revolution or the French Revolution?"

Palmer frowned in concentration. "I think they both happened in the 1700s," he said hesitantly.

"Gadzooks! Methinks you've got it!" Mr. Fletcher exclaimed, grinning. He looked around the room. "Okay, who else can give us a nugget of information about those two critical events in history?"

Nothing more was said about grades during class, but the topic wasn't closed for the day. At lunch, Lilli was seated, as usual, with Jasmine, Camilla, Nobby, and Zion. Suddenly, Palmer and three other members of the freshman football team took the seats surrounding them.

Nobby was the first to react. "What do you want?" he asked Palmer belligerently.

Palmer stretched lazily, "Well," he said, "I just got to thinking about the little discussion we had in class today. I thought maybe you would want to talk about it some more. Maybe explain to me how you're not selfish. How you managed to make your worst grade ever last Friday."

"Sure, I will talk about it," said Nobby. "I think you should make your own grades instead of thinking you can take mine. And Lilli's. Mr. Fletcher said you are smart enough to make your own good grades."

"But you see," said Palmer, "I shouldn't have to make my own grades. Look at it; I'm bringing glory to the school on the football field. I'll probably even play varsity next year when I'm only a sophomore. So, I don't have time to be studying day and night."

"Hey, Mr. Quarterback," said Zion, "football season is over, in case you didn't notice."

Palmer shrugged. "Doesn't matter. I have to be working on my game all year. That's my job. Making good grades is your job."

"If that is your opinion, maybe you are not as smart as Mr. Fletcher thinks you are," observed Nobby.

"That so?" drawled Donte Rhodes, Palmer's buddy and his favorite wide receiver. "And I guess your little group here has all the brains, right? What d' we got here? Let's see, one whitey." He pointed at Lilli. "Two blackies." He motioned toward Jasmine and Zion. "A brownie." He nodded at Camilla. "And, of course, this little Jap."

Palmer laughed, "Yeah, I guess this is the multicultural table where all the geniuses hang out."

As one, Zion and Nobby rose to their feet. "Get lost, Palmer, and take your brain trust with you!" Zion snarled. He and Nobby took positions on either side of Palmer. They were both on the small side. Zion had masses

63

of curly black hair and wore holey jeans. Nobby had short, straight black hair and wore a neat blue shirt tucked into chinos. They were a contrast in appearance, but they were a match in spunk.

"Or what?" laughed Palmer. He stood and stretched to his full height. Tall and athletic with muscles on top of muscles, he looked down at the two smaller boys in amusement. "You gonna' beat me up? And Donte? And the two biggest tackles on the team?" He waved toward the other three football players who had stood when Palmer did and were now advancing on Zion and Nobby.

"Zion! Nobby! Sit down and ignore them," pleaded Lilli. "They're not worth it."

"Really? We're not worth what?" Palmer asked, leaning over and putting his eyes on level with Lilli's eyes.

"Palmer Evans, get out of Lilli's face!" The voice was deep and threatening.

The whole group looked up to see Royal Douglas standing behind Palmer's two bruisers, glaring.

Palmer frowned, then he glanced toward Royal's usual table and saw the whole basketball team watching alertly - the varsity basketball team, most of them two or three years older than Palmer's band of freshmen. "Yeah, well, I guess we're about done here," he muttered. "Come on, guys."

Royal watched them leave, then turned to Lilli. "You okay?"

She nodded, but she was trembling. "I think so," she whispered. "Thank you, Royal."

"What's *his* problem?" Royal asked.

"He's a lazy bully," Nobby replied. "And a stupid one," Zion added.

Royal grinned. "Sounds like you have him pegged about right."

★★★

Meanwhile, in the teachers' lounge, Mr. Fletcher's colleagues were demanding a report on his experiment. "It's rolling along like a charm!" was Mr. Fletcher's happy assessment. "Almost every student did worse than usual on Friday's quiz."

Mrs. Sharp shook her head. "Your students are failing, and you're happy?" she asked.

"I didn't say they were failing," corrected Mr. Fletcher. "I said they did worse. Anyway," he grinned boyishly, "if they continue to prove my point so perfectly, I may just give them all bonus points at the end for their excellent support of my experiment."

"In the meantime," Mrs. Sharp observed, "there's going to be a six-week gap in their learning. And you seem to think it doesn't matter."

Mr. Fletcher sighed and changed the subject. "So, how's that keto diet of yours coming along?"

Mrs. Sharp frowned at him. "I never said I was on a keto diet. I said I was doing intermittent fasting."

"Oh, right. Well, how 'bout it?"

She smiled. "Actually, my blood sugar is falling, and so is my weight. I just might manage to stay off diabetes drugs if I can keep it up."

"Is it hard to keep up?" a science teacher asked. "I've been reading about it, and it sounds good. But I don't think I could handle fasting."

"I felt the same way before I tried it," said Mrs. Sharp. "But it's not as hard as I expected."

Having successfully removed Mrs. Sharp from his case and turned the attention of the women in the room to diets and weight loss, Mr. Fletcher and the other men looked at Len Josephs, the assistant basketball coach for the varsity team.

"How's it looking?" Mr. Fletcher asked. "Any chance of our winning district this year?"

Mr. Josephs beamed at him. "Not just a chance. I would say it's almost inevitable. This year, Skyport has the best team we've seen in decades."

The men perked up. "Well then, what about state?" asked an English teacher.

Mr. Josephs's head bobbed up and down. "It's possible. Very possible!"

When the bell rang, ending lunch, Mr. Josephs walked with Mr. Fletcher back to the Social Studies hallway. "Just wanted to give you a heads up," he said. "Palmer Evans saw you and Lilli come out of your closed classroom and walk down the hall together last Friday. He got the idea you were together."

Mr. Fletcher halted. "Together? What does that mean?"

Mr. Josephs stopped, too. "I think he's imagining a romantic involvement. Seems like he said something about you looking at each other with 'goo-goo eyes,' whatever that means."

Mr. Fletcher stared at his colleague, open-mouthed, for a few moments before he spat out, "What a load of horse pucky!" He drew a couple of deep, shaky breaths before he could ask, "Palmer Evans? For real?

Mr. Josephs nodded. "Yes, Palmer Evans. The coaching staff chewed him out, up one side and down the other, this morning. Then, he spent the rest of the period running laps. But I'm afraid he wasn't repentant. He knows I'm the one who reported him, so he gave me his best 'evil eye' on his way to class this morning."

Mr. Fletcher was beginning to regain his equilibrium. "Okay, thanks for letting me know. I'll try not to kill him, but he may have a hard time passing World History this year."

Both men knew he was kidding, so they shared a chuckle, then headed for their classrooms.

Chapter 8: Calm Before the Storm

That week was pretty typical for Lilli except for the Wednesday noon prayer group. She and Jasmine joined five regulars in Mrs. Tanner's biology classroom. Mrs. Tanner never attended, leaving the group to function on their own.

Treena greeted Lilli and Jasmine with a radiant smile and introduced them to Andrew Paxton, a senior, and Jarred Norman and LaDawn Hardy, who were juniors. Of course, Nobby was there too.

"About all we do is pray," Treena explained. "Here's a list of the people we're praying for." She handed out pages of notebook paper. "First, you can tell us if you have somebody you want added to the list. We'll all add the new names to our lists, and we use these lists every week. How about you, Lilli? Would you like us to pray for someone?"

Lilli nodded. "Yes, please pray for Royal. He got really upset when he heard I was born again."

"Okay, that's Royal Douglas," Treena said. Seven people added the name to their lists.

"And Jasmine? How about you?"

"Please add Camilla Rodriguez," said Jasmine. "That's Camilla, C-a-m-i-l-l-a, Rodriguez, R-o-d-r-i-g-u-e-z."

"Very good," said Treena. "Okay, we all pray individually." She looked at Lilli. "Praying is just talking to God the same way you would talk to a friend." She smiled. "Or a loving Daddy. You can pray silently or whisper, whichever you like better. We usually pray for 10 or 15 minutes, then eat our sack lunches. Mrs. Tanner always makes sure we have bottles of water for everybody." She pointed to a cooler on the floor beside the teacher's desk. "Any questions?"

When Lilli and Jasmine both shook their heads, the students scattered around the room and began to pray. Most of them prayed silently, but some whispered earnestly.

Lilli looked at her list. There were ten names on it. Hers was third, and it had been neatly crossed out. She smiled, but a tear trickled down her cheek. She didn't even know these people, but they had been thinking about her and praying for her all year. She leaned back in her desk, relishing the gentle spirit in the room, and spoke to her Heavenly Father about every person on the list.

★★★

Lilli determinedly refused to think about Hubble that week. Going to school and learning as much as she could was her job. She wouldn't let herself be distracted by obsessing about a lost zebra. Besides, she had a three-day weekend coming up, and she could dedicate those three days to finding Hubble.

On Thursday, walking home from school, Lilli was surprised to see Royal Douglas pull his red pickup to the curb beside her. He thrust his head out of the window and said, "Come on, Lilli. Get in, and I'll take you home. I have some wonderful news." He was glowing, and Lilli hurried to join him. She couldn't wait to hear his good news.

"What is it?" she asked as soon as she was buckled in.

Royal pulled away from the curb, then gave Lilli a dazzling smile. "I talked to Aziz last night. I was so afraid he was going to be angry with you. But he's not. He said the Soterians get that lie all the time from people thinking they're demons. It doesn't make any difference."

"It doesn't?" Lilli's voice quavered. A discussion with Aziz was not something she considered "good news."

"Not at all!" Royal enthused. "Aziz says the officials on his home planet are in a huge debate about the best way to proceed. It will take at least a year of planning and preparing on Soteria before they'll be ready to make a move here on Earth. So, it doesn't matter. People will forget by then.

"And he said you're young; everybody has to make their own mistakes. He's certain I'll be able to make you understand the importance of our mission in time for you to be part of it. It's going to be the most exciting thing that ever happened on this planet, and we'll be right in the middle of it!"

Rarely had Lilli seen Royal so happy, and she tried to mirror his excitement. "That's really something, Royal," she said. "What kind of mission is it exactly?"

"Well, that's what the debate is about on Soteria," Royal explained. "Aziz said he's proud of my loyalty, and I'll be one of the first Earthlings to hear the plan when it's revealed."

"So, you're not mad at me anymore?" Lilli asked, and she was unable to keep the tremor out of her voice.

"Of course not!" Royal exclaimed. "Look, Lil, I'm sorry I got so upset with you. You just took me by surprise. Why don't you come over Saturday afternoon? We'll take Adolf and find Hubble."

"Oh, thank you, Royal! That will be wonderful. Did you ask Aziz if he knows where Hubble is?"

Royal's face fell. "I forgot. I'm sorry. I was so worried about this 'born again' business that I just didn't think of it."

Lilli sighed. "Oh well. Maybe we'll find him Saturday."

★★★

Friday morning, instead of going to the library as usual, Lilli went into the cafeteria, where most of the students gathered before school. It didn't take her long to find Nobby. She hurried to the table where he and his friends were glued to their phones.

"Nobby, may I talk to you?" she asked urgently.

Nobby looked up, startled. "Sure," he said, smiling when he saw Lilli. "Sit down."

"Not here," she said. "Too many people."

Nobby shrugged and stood. "Okay, lead the way."

Lilli led Nobby out onto a corner of the patio. "Listen, are you ready for the history test today?" she asked when they were alone.

He frowned. "I guess I am. Why?"

"Well, are you going to make a good grade? You didn't on last week's quiz."

"What are you going to do?" Nobby asked.

"I don't know," wailed Lilli. "I've been thinking and thinking about it. I'm ready this week, but I don't think Mr. Fletcher *wants* us to make good grades. It will spoil his experiment!"

Nobby looked thoughtful. "Look, Lilli, does it make you mad to be giving away some of your points to a lazy goon like Palmer Evans?"

Lilli nodded. "A little bit. But I wouldn't mind if he would really try."

"Do you think he's going to really try?" asked Nobby.

"No. I think he's lazy," Lilli admitted.

"Hey, look at the love birds hiding in the corner!" someone shouted. Lilli and Nobby looked up to see Palmer pointing at them. "So, are you two Einsteins ready to make some decent grades for the sake of your classmates this week?"

"Of course they are!" yelled Donte Rhodes. "Look at them. The smart is just oozing out of their brains."

The two football players howled with laughter as they strutted away to join their buddies.

Nobby looked at Lilli. Lilli looked at Nobby.

Nobby spoke first. "I think I'll make about a 50 today." Lilli hesitated. Then she lifted her chin and said, "Me too."

An hour and a half later, Lilli was struggling to put wrong answers on her test. She knew every answer. She could make 100 on this test. Her fingers *itched* to write correct answers. But...

She took a deep breath and marked half the questions wrong. When she finished, she glanced at Nobby. He grinned and held his thumb up. She smiled and turned in her paper.

★★★

The Skyport Rockets basketball team had a home game that evening. Of course, Lilli and her mom went to see Royal play. As far as Lilli was concerned, Royal was the team's star player. She awarded him MVP after every game.

When they arrived in the gym just before tip-off, they spotted Bryce Douglas sitting alone. Lilli pointed him out, and they climbed to the top of the bleachers to join him.

"Evening, Bryce," Anna Park said. "I haven't seen you in a coon's age." She reached out and shook his hand.

"That's probably because you're working all the time," Bryce said. He winked at Lilli and gave her a quick hug. "Hey, Lil, Royal said to remind you to come over tomorrow about 1:00. He'll pick you up if your mom is busy. He says he's sure Adolf will be able to help you find Hubble. What do you say?"

Lilli gave a little bounce on the bleacher. "Oh, I hope he's right." She looked at her mother. "Is it okay, Mom?"

Anna nodded. "You might as well. I'll probably be called to the hospital. They're short-staffed now, and somebody always seems to get sick on weekends."

"Goody!" Lilli exclaimed. "I just know Royal's right. We'll find Hubble tomorrow!"

She looked toward the student section of the bleachers then and saw Jasmine and Camilla beckoning. "Mom! It's Jasmine and Camilla," she cried, pointing. "I'm gonna' go sit with them." Without waiting for an answer, she went to join her friends.

Anna and Bryce watched her go with indulgent smiles. Then Anna asked, "Well, who's going to win this one? Does Royal have any idea?"

Bryce laughed. "He always says the Rockets are going to win. Of course, I always agree with him."

And win they did. When the last buzzer blared, the score was Home 59, Visitors 45.

"What do you say? I think we should celebrate," said Bryce, trying not to sound like the proud papa he was. "How 'bout if we take Lilli to the Dairy Dream for an ice cream?"

"Oh, let's," Anna agreed. "Too bad Royal can't join us."

Bryce made a wry face. "Are you kidding? His team just won a big basketball game. Why should he be punished by being dragged to an ice cream joint with two old people and a little kid?" He glanced around. "Where did Lilli go? I thought she was right in front of us in the student section."

"No telling," said Anna. "Let's sit fast and let her find us."

Bryce pulled on his coat, then scanned the gym for Lilli. When his gaze reached the door, he froze. Myles "Falcon" Dyer was standing just inside the door, and Lilli - two feet from him - was talking excitedly to Jasmine, Camilla, and Nobby.

"What is that sleaze doing here?" Bryce muttered. "Come on." He grabbed Anna's hand and pulled her down the bleachers. He never took his eyes off Falcon. But Falcon looked up, saw Bryce coming, and melted into the crowd.

"What's wrong?" gasped Anna when they stopped at the door where Falcon had been.

"Shhh," Bryce whispered. "Don't let Lilli hear you. It's just one of the Texas prison system's former 'clients.' He has no business being here in a crowd of children. But he scrammed when he saw me coming."

Bryce and Anna collected Lilli and her friends and adjourned to the Dairy Dream. By the time they had all had their fill of ice cream, replayed the basketball game, and found their way to their various homes, it was nearly midnight.

Lilli collapsed into her warm bed and fell asleep. But around 2:00 A.M., Anna got a call from the hospital. A nurse had gone home ill, and the obstetrics department was desperate for help. When Anna softly kissed Lilli's forehead before heading out, Lilli's rest was ruffled. She didn't wake up immediately, but as the door closed behind her mother, she squirmed restlessly.

Ten minutes after Anna drove away, Lilli sat up in her bed. There was a red glow outside her window. She trembled. Aziz was out there!

"Lilli, Hubble needs you. Come now. Hurry!" The words were so clear it was almost as if she had heard them spoken aloud.

She climbed out of her warm bed and went to the window. She couldn't see the Soterians' spaceship, but she knew the red shimmer in the yard was coming from it. They were up there. And they knew where to find Hubble!

"Lilli, are you coming? Hubble's hurt. If you don't help him, he'll die."

Chapter 9: The Longest Weekend

Anna worked a shift and a half that Saturday. It was after 4:00 in the afternoon when she left the hospital. At home, she barely had enough energy to kick off her shoes before collapsing on her bed. She was getting too old to work these long hours!

At midnight, Anna got up, showered, ate a snack, and went back to bed. Lilli's room was still empty, and Anna was sorry she hadn't wakened sooner. She should have called to find out if Lilli and Royal had found Hubble. She sighed. She was almost certain Hubble was dead. Lilli would be devastated. Anna should have been there for her.

She wiped away a regretful tear, yawned, and fell back into a deep sleep.

Sunday morning, Anna woke at 9:00. Still groggy, she shuffled into the kitchen and made coffee. While she waited for the coffee to brew, she sat down at the kitchen table and turned on her phone to see what was happening in the world.

Suddenly, she sat bolt upright. The note she had left Lilli early Saturday morning was still leaning against the salt and pepper shakers. Surely Lilli had read it. Then why had she left it there, right where her mother had put it? Anna frowned. She couldn't remember Lilli ever doing that before. She always picked up her mom's notes, read them, then left them lying flat on the table or counter.

Before Anna's mind could process the puzzle, the doorbell rang. She pulled her robe tighter and went to see who was calling at this hour on Sunday morning.

Treena Woods's smiling face greeted Anna. But her smile disappeared as soon as the door opened.

"Oh, Mrs. Park!" Treena gasped. "Did I wake you? I'm so sorry!"

"No, no. It's okay," Anna said. "I was up. Can I help you?"

Treena looked confused. "We're here to pick up Lilli. Is she ready?"

Anna shook her head. "Didn't she tell you? She's spending the weekend at the Douglases'. She and Royal were determined to find Hubble this weekend."

"Oh! I thought she wanted to come to church with me again today," Treena said. "I'm really sorry I bothered you."

Anna smiled. "No bother. And I'm sorry Lilli didn't let you know she wouldn't be here. Thanks for coming by."

Treena nodded and turned away. Anna returned to the kitchen, poured a cup of coffee, and noticed for the first time that she had a message on the answering machine.

She took a sip of her coffee, punched "play," and heard Bryce's cheerful drawl.

"Hey, Chick-a-dee, I thought you were coming out. Was Royal supposed to pick you up? Apparently, the basketball team celebrated their win all night. He hasn't showed up home yet. If you still want to look for that zebra of yours, give me a call. Adolf and I will help you hunt. I should have gone out with you sooner. I know more secret spots around here than Royal does. Let me know!"

The call had come in at 1:42 Saturday afternoon. Why hadn't Lilli listened to it? Well, maybe she heard it as it was coming in and didn't bother to delete it. Then why didn't she answer the phone, which would have cut off the message?

Anna almost ran to Lilli's room. Lilli's cell phone was on her dresser, charging. Lilli had left without it. Why would she do that?

A quick scroll through recent calls revealed that Bryce had called Lilli's cell phone before he tried the landline. Why hadn't Lilli answered? A fearful little tremor spread through Anna's body. She returned to the kitchen, picked up the handset of her landline, scrolled to Bryce's number, and punched "send."

After the second ring, Bryce answered, "Lilli! About time you called!"

Anna nearly fainted. "Bryce, isn't Lilli *there*?" Her voice was ragged with fear.

"Here?" Anna could hear the surprise in Bryce's voice. "No. I was expecting her yesterday, but she never showed. Where is she?"

"I don't know," Anna moaned. "I thought she was *there* all this time."

"All what time?" Bryce's voice was urgent. "When did you see her last?"

Anna's breathy voice was almost too weak for him to hear. "It was…it was…about 2:45 A.M. Saturday. The hospital called, and I checked on her before I left. She was asleep. When I got home yesterday afternoon, I thought she was out at your place, hunting for Hubble."

"So, you never saw her all day Saturday?" Bryce asked.

"No. No, I just assumed she was at your place. I've been… sleeping."

A long silence followed while Anna and Bryce separately tried to unravel the mystery of Lilli's whereabouts. Finally, Bryce said, "Okay, let's start calling her friends. Somebody has to know where she is. I'll tell Royal. He can call his friends, too, in case one of them has seen her."

"I'm calling the police," Anna said. "Somebody took her out of the house. I know they did because she never read the note I left for her."

There was a long pause. Then Bryce spoke, sounding defeated. "You're right. Call the police. Then her friends."

That Sunday and Monday were two of the longest days in Skyport history.

As soon as Anna and Bryce realized that none of Lilli's friends knew where she was, the frantic alarm went out. Lilli Park, a 14-year-old Skyport High School freshman, was missing. Appeals for help went out over radio, television, telephone, and social media.

In a matter of hours, half the town of Skyport and many citizens from neighboring towns were combing the countryside, looking for Lilli. The police department and the sheriff's office headed the operation. Off-duty officers participated. Restaurants fed searchers. And Lilli became a celebrity, as her story topped every newscast in the area.

At nightfall, the hunt was called off until morning. Nobby Tanaka cried himself to sleep that night. Treena Wood prayed and worried most of the night. And Anna Park had to be hospitalized and sedated in order to - as Bryce put it - "preserve her sanity."

Through the night, the grating buzz of drones equipped with thermal cameras could be heard overhead. At daylight, zoom cameras on the drones were turned on. Weary operators, aided by local law enforcement personnel, worked doggedly to find the missing teenager.

On Monday morning, the town turned out again to look for Lilli instead of enjoying the Martin Luther King holiday. But Lilli could not be found. Not so much as a microscopic clue was uncovered. And by mid-afternoon, the brass at the police department were ready to turn the search for a lost child into a search for an abductor.

Police detective Caleb Carson headed up the investigation. He was a tall, powerful man in his mid-fifties with short, neatly combed, graying hair. His love of a good mystery made him the ideal person to oversee major crimes for the P.D. - what major crimes there were in the town.

It didn't take Carson long to set his sights on Royal Douglas as a person of interest. So, Royal was the first person brought to the police department for questioning.

Royal and Adolf had been out searching for Lilli for the past 24 hours, except for a short nap around 4:00 A.M. Now Royal was drooping. He stood in front of Carson's desk, running his fingers through his thick, sandy hair. "Are you Detective Carson?" he asked.

"That's right." Carson rose to shake Royal's hand. "Sit down. You look beat. What can I get you? A soda pop? Coffee?"

Royal shrugged and sat down. "I left my DP in the pickup. Maybe a water bottle if you have it."

Carson nodded, returned to his chair, and made a phone call. Then he turned his attention to Royal. "I can see you've been doing your share to help find Lilli. I understand you and she are very close."

"I guess so," Royal said. "I've known her all my life."

"And how long have you been dating?"

Royal's posture stiffened. "Dating? Who says we've been dating?"

Carson frowned. "You telling me you haven't been dating Lilli Park?"

"Of course not…" Royal paused as the receptionist came in and handed him a cold bottle of water. Royal sat the bottle on Carson's desk and glared at the detective. "Why? Do you date your sister?"

"Sister!" Carson couldn't hide his surprise. "Lilli is your sister?"

Royal sighed, snagged the water bottle, and twisted the lid off. He took a long drink, then answered. "Right. At least, she's my half-sister."

Carson leaned back in his chair and studied the boy. "Lilli is your half-sister," he mused. "Then why do your classmates - and hers - think she's your girlfriend?"

Royal grinned wryly. "Well, it's what you might call…sort of…a family secret. I guess Dad and Anna didn't want people to know they ever got together."

"Why not?"

Royal shook his head. "I don't know. It was always that way. Kind of like pretending you believe in Santa Claus, but you know all the time he doesn't exist. I've always known Lilli was my sister, but I was supposed to pretend she and Anna were just friends of the family."

"Well, I'll have to think about all this," said Carson. "I thought I was going to be talking to Lilli's boyfriend." He hesitated for a long moment. "But I guess it doesn't make much difference. I still have the same questions. When was the last time you saw Lilli?"

"She and her mom came to my basketball game Friday night. I saw them in the stands, but I didn't talk to them. I guess… Do you mean, when was the last time I saw her to talk to her?"

Carson nodded.

Royal had to study on his answer. Finally, he said, "I see her around school most days, but I think the last time I talked to her was last Monday when that thug Palmer Evans was giving her a hard time."

Carson's eyebrows rose. "Tell me about it."

"Do you want the long version or the short version?"

"Long."

So, Royal explained about Mr. Fletcher's experiment and Palmer's harassment of Lilli and Nobby. He concluded, "See, my sister and Nobby are the two smartest kids in their class. And Evans is a useless waste of space. He thinks just because he's a big football star - on the *freshman* team - he shouldn't have to trouble his tiny brain with schoolwork." Royal was glowering now, his eyes shooting sparks and his body tense.

"I see," said Carson. "I'll have to talk to Palmer Evans and see what he has to say. What about this - what did you call him - Nobby?"

Royal smiled and relaxed. "Sure, Nobby's been around for a few years now. I forget his real first name, but his last name is Tanaka. His family moved here a few years ago from Japan. He's real smart, and he's been giving Lilli a run for her money ever since he got here."

"So, Lilli and Nobby are enemies?" asked Carson.

"Naw. I think they like each other. In fact, I think they challenge each other. Same way we - the basketball team, I mean - like to play better teams pre-season. It helps us improve."

"I can see that," said Carson. "Well, I guess my most important question is - where do you think Lilli is?"

For a moment, Carson thought Royal was going to cry. But the boy quickly tightened his lips and cleared his throat. When he answered, his voice was almost under control. "I… I don't know. I've looked everywhere I can think of." He paused and breathed deeply. "I… can't… find her."

Carson stood and extended his hand. "Okay, thank you, son. You need to go home and get some sleep. Maybe then you'll think of something helpful she might have said."

Royal rose and shook hands with the detective. He turned to go, then stopped. "Oh wait, the last time I talked to Lilli was Thursday afternoon. I saw her walking home from school and gave her a ride. I'd forgotten that."

Carson nodded. "I see. And did she say anything about the weekend? About any plans she might have?"

"Sure. She was going to come out Saturday afternoon so we could hunt for her zebra. Do you know about Hubble?"

Carson's eyebrows rose. "Did you say her 'zebra'?" By that time, he'd heard about Lilli's lost zebra, but it wouldn't hurt to see if Royal would add anything new. So, he put on a startled expression as he said the word "zebra."

"Right. We don't know where he came from, but he wandered up one day. Lilli was crazy about him, but he disappeared a couple of weeks ago and she was worried to death about him. She's been hunting for him ever since."

"So, she was expected at your farm on Saturday afternoon?" Carson asked. "How was she going to get there?"

"I thought her mother would bring her. If not, I would have picked her up. But she never showed, and she never called for a ride."

"Okay," Carson said. "Thanks for the information." Royal nodded and walked away.

Carson watched him go. So, Bryce Douglas was Lilli's father. In that case, Douglas would be worth talking to. Carson pulled on his jacket and headed out the door. His first goal was to check on the search teams. Of course, he could call each team leader, but he'd rather check on them in person. Maybe he would run across Douglas in the process.

All the search teams were tired and discouraged. The town of Skyport had been crisscrossed over and over, as well as the surrounding farms. In the dead of winter, vegetation was sparse, and hiding places were few on the semi-arid plains of the Texas panhandle. Yet no trace of Lilli had been found.

"The kids want to start searching homes," one team leader told Carson. "Of course, I told them it couldn't be done because we don't have search warrants. But they said we could search if the occupants gave us permission. And if they refused permission, their names would go down on a list of suspects. I tried to think of a good argument against that plan, but I got nuthin'. I'm about ready to start knocking on doors myself."

Carson nodded. "Same here. Listen, it's getting late. Please make sure everybody on your team is home safe before dark. We don't want to lose anybody else."

The weary man nodded and turned away. "Oh, I almost forgot," Carson said. "Do you have Bryce Douglas's cell number?"

"I don't. Try Judson Wheeler. His place is just down the road from Bryce's."

"Thanks. He's next on my list," said Carson.

Wheeler's group was searching outside town, in the area of his farm.

Carson decided to make an exception for this group and call instead of going to them. He had entered the cell phone numbers of all his search leaders in his own phone, and it took him only a few minutes to contact Wheeler, get another disappointing search report, and obtain Bryce's number.

Like Royal, Bryce had slept only a few hours the preceding night. Now, exhausted, he was on his way home, and he invited Carson to meet him there.

Coffee was ready when Carson arrived, and the two men seated themselves at the kitchen table to talk. "Any luck?" Carson asked.

Bryce shook his head wearily. "Not a trace. I can't understand it. Lilli is so smart and so timid - I can't imagine any way she could have just disappeared." He sipped his coffee, then added. "Your men said there was no evidence of a break-in."

The detective agreed. "Not a sign. No windows loose. No damaged doors. Nada!"

"I guess you tried to trace her phone?" Bryce asked.

Carson shook his head. "Nope. It's still in her room, charging."

The two men drank their coffee in silence for a few minutes, then Carson broached the subject that had brought him to the farm. "Royal tells me you're Lilli's father."

Bryce nodded. "That's right. Anna and I were never married. Didn't even have much of a romance. Once she got pregnant, both of us lost interest." He smiled sadly. "I offered to marry her, but she'd never gotten over her ex. She wasn't interested."

"And you never claimed Lilli?" asked Carson.

"Well now, that depends on what you mean by 'claim.' I've always paid child support. And Lilli's over here all the time. Anna and I both have irregular jobs, so it took both of us to make sure she was cared for when she was little. And Anna usually kept Royal, too, when I was called out at night."

"But Royal's not her son?"

"Naw. His mother walked out on us when he was little. I think she left because she got a bad case of the baby blues. I don't know why she never came back. Well…"

He paused, and Carson waited until Bryce continued, "I guess I have to admit that I had some anger issues back in those days. Shawna was afraid of me, and that's probably the reason she never came back. But you wouldn't think a mother would leave her baby with a man who had fits of temper, would you?"

Carson shook his head. "No, I wouldn't. But you said 'back in those days.' Does that mean you don't have anger issues anymore?"

"Well, you can imagine that my wife leaving me with a six-month-old baby would get my attention, can't you? I got anger management counseling and learned to control my rages. I still get angry, but I don't take it out on other people anymore."

"Is Lilli afraid of you?"

Bryce smiled. "No, she never saw that side of me. It's not so hard with someone who's not present 24/7. Lilli and I are best buds."

"And Royal. Is he afraid of you?" asked Carson. "He *is* around 24/7."

Bryce chuckled. "Not that one. He's not afraid of anything. I remember one time when he was...oh...four or five...I went on a rampage. He got in my face and gave it right back to me. He was so like me that I cracked up. We both fell over laughing. When we got over it, we went to MacDonald's for burgers." Bryce smiled ruefully. "That one incident helped me almost as much as all the counseling I'd paid for. It made me realize I was taking myself too seriously."

Carson smiled and waited for Bryce to return to the present. Then he asked, "So Royal doesn't know his mother?"

Bryce shook his head. "No, all he ever had was photos."

"And you don't know what happened to her? Do you even know if she's still alive?"

Bryce shrugged. "Never heard a word from her after she left. At first, I was so mad I wouldn't lift a finger to look for her. Then, when I got past the angry stage, I couldn't find a direction to go in. It's kind of like...this with Lilli. Just waiting. And hoping. And always... looking."

Carson's eyebrows rose. "After what? Fifteen, sixteen years, you're still waiting and hoping? And looking? You still want her back?"

Bryce shook his head. "I don't know that I want her back for myself. But I want Royal to know her." Suddenly, he let out one short blast of laughter. "Even if she did name him Elroy!"

"Elroy? His name is Elroy?" Carson was surprised.

Bryce's whole countenance had lightened. "Right, but you'd better not mention it to him. He might knock your block off."

Carson laughed, too. "Can't say that I'd blame him. But let's get back to you and Anna. What's the big secret? If you're willing to pay child support and help take care of Lilli, why aren't you willing to let people know she's your daughter?"

Bryce sighed. "I *am* willing. That part of the story is Anna's. You'll need to talk to her about it."

"I'd like to talk to her," said Carson. "But she's in the hospital sedated. I couldn't even get close to her this morning."

"Not anymore. When her daughters got here this afternoon, they took her home."

Carson was surprised again. "Her daughters? You don't mean Lilli...?"

"No. Irene, Judith, and Karon. They're long since grown and gone, but they've come back to help with the search. And to support their mother." Bryce smiled fondly at the thought of Anna's daughters. "They dote on their baby sister, of course, but they won't stay long unless Anna collapses completely. That whole family is driven by a work ethic. Or a success ethic. Or something powerful. They'll be chomping at the bit to get back to their families and their jobs before this week is over."

"Do they know you're Lilli's father?"

Bryce shook his head. "Doubt it. Anna may have told them along the way, but I would be surprised if she did."

As Carson left the Douglas farmhouse, he checked his watch. It was early evening. It would be unforgivable of him not to visit Anna Park and offer what comfort and support he could now that he knew she was out of the hospital. They didn't have to let him in if the timing was bad. He would just go back tomorrow. But he didn't want it said that he hadn't stopped by.

Painted daisy yellow with white trim, the Park home was small and cheerful.

It was located next to a neighborhood park where Lilli had undoubtedly spent many happy hours in her younger years. Carson knew the little park had been searched repeatedly in the past two days, but it was still all he could do to keep from looking again. He forced himself to stride up to the front door and ring the bell instead of detouring through the park.

The porch light came on, and Carson could feel eyes examining him, assessing the advisability of opening the door to this stranger. He smiled and tried to look harmless.

Finally, the door opened a few inches, and a woman of about 35 peered around it. "Yes?"

"Ma'am, I'm Police Detective Caleb Carson. I would like to speak to Anna Park, but I don't want to upset her any more than necessary. Would you ask her if she's up to talking to me?"

The woman studied him another moment, then disappeared into the house. A few minutes later, she returned and unlatched the screen door. "Come in," she said, holding out her hand to shake. "I'm Irene, the oldest daughter. Mom said she would like to see you."

Carson followed her into a den decorated in greens and golds. It was a warm, comfortable room. Anna Park was resting in a recliner, looking frailer than she had ever looked in her life.

"Detective Carson," she said eagerly, her hand extended, "have you found Lilli?"

Carson took her hand and shook his head sadly. "No, Ma'am, I'm so sorry - I don't have any news." He looked around. "May I sit down?"

"Yes, please," said Anna, indicating the comfortable armchair closest to her recliner.

"I just left Bryce Douglas," Carson said after he was seated. "He's the one who told me you were home now."

He didn't miss the flash of wariness in Anna's eyes. "You talked to Bryce?" He nodded.

She studied him, then turned to her daughters. All three of them were in the den now, watching Carson alertly. "Girls, why don't you go on and finish what you were doing? I would like to talk to the detective privately."

"Mother, I don't think that's such a good idea," said Irene. "Why can't we stay?"

Carson looked up at the three women and did a double-take. "Whoa!" he exclaimed. "A blonde, a brunette, and a redhead. That's pretty amazing, Mrs. Park. How did you pull it off?"

Irene smiled. "It comes out of a bottle. Or," she glanced around, "out of three bottles. The redhead is Judith - she's in the middle. And Karon, the brunette, was the baby until Lilli came along. We started dying our hair in high school and got attached to our colors." She grinned suddenly. "Someday, we're all going to dye our hair the same color."

"Probably when we start turning gray," giggled the brunette, Karon.

Judith smiled. "Or not. We'll never agree on blond, brunette, or red."

Carson stood and shook hands with Judith and Karon, murmuring to each, "Pleased to meet you. I'm Caleb Carson."

Then, as he was returning to his chair, all three women faded into another room without another word. It was as if they operated with one mind. "You have a lovely family," Carson told Anna.

"Yes, and you haven't even met the grandchildren. They're angels."

"I'm sure they are. Look, I know it has been a long, long day for you, so let's get right down to business, then I'll get out of here." He led Anna through the story of the disappearance again, although he had heard it several times.

She had nothing new to add, so he moved on to a new topic. "Bryce said most people don't know he's Lilli's father." He glanced toward the doorway through which Irene, Judith, and Karon had exited. "I'm guessing *they* don't know either?"

Anna nodded and looked embarrassed. "I'm terribly ashamed of myself now. At the time, I felt *so* pressured that I made an expedient but faulty decision."

Carson waited.

"Malcolm, my ex-husband, got assigned to a job in the Middle East. He was excited, couldn't wait to leave. I didn't want to go. We argued, and the disagreement grew so sharp that we ended up in divorce court. I was devastated, but after he was gone, I learned that a woman from his office had gone with him. They married in short order and now have two sons."

Anna paused to deal with her tears. When she seemed calmer, he asked, "What kind of work does your…does Malcolm do?"

"He's a petrochemical engineer. He's brilliant and very well paid." She gave Carson a sad little smile. "I don't guess I'm ever going to get over him."

"You mean you still love him?"

Anna nodded. "Afraid so. Anyway, I was working for a pediatrician then. He was Royal's doctor, and Bryce was - still is - extremely attractive. I let myself get drawn into a disgraceful affair with him. Lilli was the result."

She paused and dabbed at a few more tears before she continued. "Of course, that was bad enough, but here's the really shameful part. I let Malcolm believe Lilli was his child and convinced him to pay for my tuition and our living expenses while I trained as a nurse practitioner, then became certified as a nurse midwife. I was already an R.N. at the time, but it still took several years. In exchange, I told Malcolm he wouldn't have to pay child support."

"Did he think that was a bargain?" Carson asked.

Anna shook her head. "I had to do some pretty fancy talking. He was willing to cancel the divorce and give our marriage another try since there was a baby involved. But I knew Lilli wasn't his child, and I was too proud to take him back, knowing he didn't want me."

Carson nodded. "I can understand how you felt," he said. It was a lie. She should have hung on to the husband she loved – his opinion. But he thought Anna needed every scintilla of support she could get right now. He wasn't going to say a single negative word to her.

"Thank you," Anna whispered.

"Do you regret your decision?" Carson asked. "It's none of my business, but I can't help wondering."

"Yes and no," said Anna. "Truth is - I regret it desperately. But I could not have lived with myself if I'd dragged him back to me over a child who wasn't even his."

Carson nodded, then said, "Actually, I had a phone call from Mr. Park yesterday." He barreled on, ignoring Anna's astonished expression. "He's the one who got the drones here so quickly. It was partly luck because they were nearby, and the rest was Mr. Park's connections."

Anna's face lit up. "Isn't he a wonderful man?" she cried. Then her expression crumpled. "But now I owe him even more. He's going to be so angry with me when he finds out Lilli's not his daughter." Tears sprang to her eyes again.

"So, you're going to tell him?" Carson asked.

"I have to, don't I?"

Carson put his hands up, palms forward. "Don't ask me." He paused. "Well, you probably should. Unless we find Lilli almost immediately, it will come out one way or the other."

Anna nodded. "Right. And it will be better if it comes from me." "I understood him to say that he'll be arriving tomorrow."

"I know," Anna said. "The girls called him the minute they heard. They were furious with me for not calling him first. But I didn't want to tell him at all, so I had been putting it off."

"Why didn't you want to tell him?"

"I knew he would come. It would be one more time that he sacrificed his time and money because of Bryce Douglas's child." She gave Carson a rueful look. "I have quite a guilt complex over that, I'm afraid."

Carson stood. "I'm going to shove off now," he said. "Have you thought of anything at all that might help us find Lilli?"

Anna shook her head, then seemed about to say something. Instead, tears were suddenly flowing down her cheeks.

"What is it?" asked Carson. He sat back down. "Please, don't hold anything back."

Anna was weeping so hard, she could barely speak. "I…I wasn't…going to ask." She paused, mopped at her eyes with her sleeve, and took two deep breaths. "But I have to know…I *have* to…"

Carson found some tissues, gave Anna a handful, and waited.

Finally, she calmed herself enough to blurt out, "I'm so terrified that some of those - what do you call them? - human traffickers got her. Or one of those online predators." She was gasping for breath through her sobs. "I can't bear the thought of her as a…a…sex slave…I just can't."

Carson took her hand in both of his. "Mrs. Park, don't even think like that. We've checked her phone and her computer. There's absolutely no evidence of anything like that. I promise. Can you hear me?"

Anna nodded. Carson waited, holding her hand, until her sobs receded. Then she said brokenly, "I checked her phone and her computer too, first thing, but I didn't know what to look for or where to look."

Carson nodded. "I know, but we have technicians at the department who know exactly where and how to look for that kind of evidence. It's not there. I promise. It was one of the first things we thought of too."

"What about that RV park south of town?" Anna asked. "What if some predator was just driving through town and saw her?"

Carson nodded. "It's January. That park doesn't get much out-of-town business this time of year. We did check the place. The manager hasn't seen any strangers lately. Not in months."

Anna released a long sobbing sigh. "Thank you," she whispered. "I've got to stop thinking that way. If I don't, I can't survive."

Still holding her hand, Carson said softly, "I understand, but I really believe you're safe in putting those ideas out of your mind. There's not even the tiniest hint of an online predator on her devices or a human trafficker in this area."

He waited a few more minutes as Anna's breathing slowed and the terror left her eyes. Then he released her hand and stood. He gave her shoulder a gentle pat. "I'll let myself out. Call me or have someone else call me if you think of anything."

"I will."

Carson was almost out of the room when he heard a soft, "Oh." Turning, he saw that Anna had thought of something.

"What?" he asked, moving back in her direction.

"I meant to tell you that all of Lilli's best friends and worst enemies are in her second-period class. It's a Mr. Fletcher, teaching World History."

"She has enemies?" Carson asked.

Anna shook her head. "No. That word is too strong. It's just that a boy named Palmer Evans has been bothering her - you might even say bullying her - for a week or so."

"Right," Carson said. "Royal told me about him. And about Mr. Fletcher's experiment. So, you don't need to explain. But that second-period class sounds interesting. I'll have to think about it."

By the time Carson got back to his desk, he had decided to visit Mr. Fletcher's second-period class the next morning. It only took one phone call. The principal approved the visit and promised to let Mr. Fletcher know Carson was coming.

Chapter 10: Hubble's Fate

Detective Carson was already seated at the back of Mr. Fletcher's classroom when the second-period bell rang Tuesday morning, and students began to arrive. Those who noticed him gave him a curious look, then glanced at their teacher. But no one spoke to him. They were, as a matter of fact, too busy talking to each other to spare the unknown man at the back of the room much attention.

When the tardy bell rang, Mr. Fletcher explained Carson's presence. "Students, I'd like you to meet Detective Caleb Carson from the Skyport Police Department. He will be with us for a few minutes this morning. He is interested in hearing any ideas you might have about Lilli's disappearance."

While Mr. Fletcher was speaking, Carson walked to the front of the room. Before he could begin, Palmer Evans blurted. "Lilli's disappearance? Why, we all - everybody in this room - we know what happened to her."

Carson and the entire class turned toward Palmer and goggled at him.

"You know where she is?" Carson gasped.

"I didn't say we know where she is," Palmer corrected. "We know what happened to her."

"Okay. What happened to her?"

"She's been abducted by space aliens. You know, just like that first woman back there hundreds of years ago."

Carson frowned. "Ginny Conner?" he asked.

"I don't know her last name," Palmer said, "but Jasmine told us all about her and ol' Gordo' the other day. How aliens carried her off, and Gordon made them name the town Skyport as a warning. I guess Lilli didn't get the warning."

Carson turned a baffled expression toward Mr. Fletcher.

The teacher, who had been seated at his desk, rose and joined Carson. He hadn't made his peace with Palmer yet, concerning the rumor about himself and Lilli. In fact, he hadn't even mentioned it to Palmer, believing the coaches would have more influence over their star quarterback than he would. But keeping a civil tone when he spoke to the boy grew harder every day.

Now, he took a deep breath and said, "Of course, Palmer isn't a wack-adoodle, but he does have an *exorbitant* imagination." He glared at Palmer meaningfully, then said to the class, "Okay, Palmer has taken care of the alien abduction theory. Let's move on. Somebody tell us what you know about Lilli. Something that might help us figure out where she is."

When he was greeted with blank stares, Mr. Fletcher asked Carson, "Can you give us some idea when she disappeared?"

"Between 3:00 A.M. and 3:00 P.M. on Saturday."

Mr. Fletcher turned back to the class. "How many of you helped search for Lilli on Sunday or Monday?"

Everybody in the room raised a hand.

"That's what I thought," said Mr. Fletcher. "So, you've probably shared your ideas with your search leaders. But Detective Carson is in charge of the whole operation, so he needs to hear any ideas you have, even if it's one you've already told an adult. Nobby, what about you? What did you think when you heard she was gone?"

"I thought she was out hunting for her zebra and got hurt," Nobby said. "Maybe she was even like little Luke, and Hubble accidentally kicked her. Or hurt her in some way."

"Her zebra?!" The screech came from Palmer, of course. "What are you talking about? Are you saying Lilli has a zebra? A *zebra?!*"

Carson answered. "Yes, it seems that a zebra wandered up to the Douglas farm a few months ago, and Lilli adopted it. But it has been missing for a couple of weeks, and she has been terribly worried about it." He turned back to Nobby. "What's its name? Hubble?"

Nobby nodded. "Yes, named after the astronomer, Edwin Hubble."

"The Douglas farm and the whole part of the county around it have been searched and searched again," said Carson. "No luck."

"How about Royal's truck?" asked Palmer. "Everybody knows it's always the boyfriend."

Carson gave Palmer a disgusted look. "What's always the boyfriend?"

"You know, the one that kills the girl."

Jasmine gasped. Nobby glared at Palmer. And Camilla gave a little shriek. "Killed?" she cried.

Now Carson's gaze was speculative. "Young man, do you know something we don't know?" he asked. "Is she dead?"

"How would I know?" Palmer growled, sinking lower in his desk. "I'm just saying - you should look at Royal. He's the most likely suspect."

Carson looked around the room. Some of the students were moving restlessly. Most of the girls looked devastated. "Mr. Fletcher," he said, "thank you for letting me come. I'll go now. I hope I haven't ruined the class for you."

"Not at all," Mr. Fletcher assured him. "In fact, perhaps you'll be kind enough to let me use you for a bit of a history lesson?"

Carson nodded, looking amused. "What do I have to do?"

"Just tell me – has anyone ever called you a 'peeler'?"

"A peeler?" Carson repeated. "Only my wife when I'm helping with dinner. I'm a potato peeler and a carrot peeler. Why do you ask?"

Some of the students smiled appreciatively. Most of them seemed to have filed Palmer's frightening suggestion and tuned in to the dialogue.

"One more question," said Mr. Fletcher. "Have you ever heard of Sir Robert Peel?"

"No, who is Sir Robert Peel?" asked Carson, feeling like the straight man in a comedy routine.

"Sir Robert Peel developed London's first organized police force in the early 1800s," said Mr. Fletcher. "People began calling the police officers 'peelers.' But since Peel was a Robert, another nickname became popular – bobbies!"

"Now, bobbies I've heard of," Carson grinned. "Thank you, Teach, for teaching me something today." He turned his attention to the class. "And thank you, students, for listening. I hope you'll be letting one of us 'peelers' know if you have any information for us."

He smiled and waved as he opened the door. Zion Johnson and Marion Rogers waved back.

When Carson got back to the police department, Judson Wheeler was sitting in his pickup in the parking lot. Carson couldn't squelch the spark of hope that leaped up at the sight of one of his search team leaders. "Have you got something?" he asked eagerly.

Wheeler shook his head sorrowfully. "Nothing that's going to help. But it is something I think you should know."

Carson nodded. "Okay. Well, come on in. Let's get some bad coffee and talk about it."

Wheeler was closing in on his sixties. He was a typical rancher, clad in a brown and white flannel shirt, jeans, and a Texas A&M University cap that covered his receding hairline. He was thick in the waist, but his work kept him strong and fit.

After both men had taken sips of their coffee and exchanged comments about the weather, Carson jumped in. "Okay, what's your story?"

Wheeler had thought it over and decided how he was going to approach his narrative. "I'm going to start at the end," he said. "I learned late yesterday about the zebra that Lilli had been hunting for the last week or so. I know what happened to it. Hubble, she called it, didn't she?"

"That's right."

"Well, Hubble stumbled up to my house a couple of weeks ago with a muzzle full of porcupine quills." Wheeler winced. "It broke my heart to see how the poor thing was suffering. I called ol' Doc Latimer, but he wouldn't touch it. So, I loaded the poor zebra into my horse trailer and took him to Canyon. I have a good friend on the faculty of the Animal Science department at West Texas A&M, and I figured helping a zebra would be a good experience for his students."

"Did he agree?" Carson asked with interest.

"Oh, sure. They were fascinated to see a wild zebra in Texas. But it was pretty hard on them, seeing how miserable he was." Wheeler paused, remembering the sad group of youngsters gathered around the suffering animal.

"How did it turn out?"

Wheeler sighed. "They couldn't save him. They tranquilized him and got the quills out, but he died the next day. Seems like he was pretty old, and his body couldn't handle the stress. I felt bad about it, but I didn't know anybody was looking for him. I had been seeing him around for a couple of years. He would wander through occasionally, but I never knew where he came from originally."

Wheeler paused, and both men thought about Hubble's sad fate. Then Carson remembered how Wheeler had started the story. "You said you were going to start at the end. Are you saying there's a beginning?"

"That's right. The beginning was last spring. I had a loser working for me. I forget his name, but he insisted that I call him Falcon…"

"Myles Dyer," Carson said.

Wheeler nodded. "Anyway, he seemed at loose ends. There's an old shack out in one of my far fields, and Falcon wanted to stay in it. It doesn't have electricity or water, but he said he could manage as long as he could get water from the hose in the yard. So, he spent part of the spring and half of June out there. During that time, he rescued a baby porcupine. Apparently, the mother had died, so he bottle-fed it for a few weeks and taught it how to find food."

"What do you put in a baby porcupine's bottle?" Carson asked.

Wheeler grinned. "Some kind of baby formula. He brought it over to the house early on because he couldn't get it to take the bottle. It was a tiny thing, and it just wanted to climb around in his long hair. So, my wife takes that bottle and holds it up to the porcupine's mouth while it's all snuggled up in Falcon's hair. And, sure enough, the little thing starts drinking. Once it found out that it liked the formula, Falcon didn't have any more trouble getting it to take the bottle."

"Did he take the porcupine with him when he moved into town?"

"No. He bundled up what few things he had and just took off. He said he'd gotten a job at a garage that paid better than I did. Plus, his elderly mother was about to move to town, so he was going to have to find a place where she could live with him. I still see him around sometimes, and he always asks about Porky. Of course, he named the thing Porky."

"Are you getting around to saying that Hubble crossed paths with Porky?" Carson guessed.

"I would bet on it," said Wheeler. "How often do you run across a porcupine? I almost never do. But Porky lost his fear of humans. So, he comes around sometimes, looking for a handout. And I would bet he's the reason Hubble got a snout full of quills."

"And if Hubble hadn't disappeared, maybe Lilli wouldn't have disappeared?"

"Who knows? But I can't help feeling that way, and it makes me want to hunt up Falcon and give him the threshing of his life." Wheeler's voice was bitter.

Carson sighed. "It's an interesting story, but I'm afraid it won't help us find Lilli. Look, Judson, I'm sure grateful you cleared up the mystery of Hubble's disappearance. That question worried me."

Wheeler nodded. "I thought it might." He stood to go. "Please let me know if there's anything else I can do to help. My wife and I are praying hard for Lilli to be found soon."

"So am I," Carson said fervently. "So are we all!"

Chapter 11: Anna and Malcolm

The discussion at noon in the teachers' lounge that day centered entirely on Lilli. Most of the teachers and their families had been on search teams the previous day. And all were discouraged by their failure to locate her.

"She's bound to be frozen to death by now," mourned Sadie Sharp.

"Unless she's been abducted," said Kip Fletcher soberly. "She may be in a warm house somewhere. We just have to figure out which warm house she's in."

"How do we do that?" asked Tulsa Grant, her voice heavy with despair. She looked around the table to see hopeless expressions on every face. She wiped a tear from her cheek.

"I guess the best thing we can do at this point is figure out what areas haven't been searched yet," said Mr. Fletcher. "We'll have a couple of hours of daylight after school today."

"I have an idea there aren't any areas like that," Mr. Josephs said. "Detective Carson and Sheriff Moreno will have search teams out all day today. We would have to check with them to find out what areas have been missed."

"Or what areas need to be searched again," said Mr. Fletcher.

There was silence as the teachers ate their lunches and tried to imagine where Lilli might be. A timid knock on the door was soft, but everyone heard it. They looked at the door, which remained shut.

"Come on in!" bellowed Mr. Fletcher.

The door opened just enough for a head to be thrust into view. Treena Wood peered in. "May we come in for just a minute and talk to you?" she asked.

"Come ahead," and "Come on in," several voices replied.

Treena Wood and Nobby Tanaka pushed the door wider and came in. They stopped just inside the room. Treena took a deep breath and said, "We - Nobby and I - want to ask you a favor. I'm Treena Wood, and this is Nobby Tanaka."

Laurel Tanner, whose room they used for prayer on Wednesdays, gave them an encouraging smile. "Come on in," she said. "We would love to hear what you have to say. Is it about Lilli?"

Nobby nodded his head violently. Treena's nod was more reserved.

Treena was the spokesperson. "We've been talking - the Harvesters' Club, I mean. And we want to do something to help find Lilli. My Dad has created a Facebook page called, 'Find Lilli,' and the Harvesters are going to monitor it."

She paused, and Nobby took over. "Somebody has to know something. They just *have* to. So, we want everybody to use the 'Find Lilli' page to report anything they know that might be helpful. And we want... We were hoping you might announce it to your classes this afternoon."

"What is the Harvesters' Club?" asked Mr. Josephs. "I don't think I've ever heard of it."

"We're a prayer group," Treena said. "There aren't many of us, so not many people know about us."

"I think a Facebook page is a wonderful idea," Mrs. Sharp said. "What exactly do you want us to tell our students?"

"We want everybody to report where they have searched. If they found anything of Lilli's or anything suspicious. Other places where we should hunt. Any ideas about where she could be. Stuff like that."

"But not anything that somebody else has already said. We need one writer per search team," Nobby added. "We don't want it to get so full that we can't keep up with it."

"I think it's a capital idea," said Mr. Fletcher. "I'll certainly tell my classes."

The other teachers nodded, eager to help.

"One more thing," said Nobby. "Could you email the other teachers in the school and ask them to announce 'Find Lilli' to their students?"

"Of course," said Mrs. Sharp. "I'll go do that right now. But I won't just tell this school. I'll email every teacher in the district so they can tell their students. We all want to do whatever we can to help."

"Oh, thank you, Mrs. Sharp," said Treena. "That's a fantastic idea."

"Find Lilli" was the buzz all around Skyport High School and the other Skyport schools that afternoon. And as soon as the last bell of the day rang, students rushed out to join the hunt or to write their Facebook posts.

A few students and adults headed straight for the drone operators. They wanted to see this exciting new technology and find out what it had revealed. The rest of the population, if they were searching in an area where a drone was flying, just watched the little air-mobiles with fascination. Or winced at the harsh clamor when the drones came close enough to the ground to jar their eardrums.

Palmer Evans was one student who didn't participate in the search or the Facebook page. He had spent his whole day Monday roaming around the countryside and now felt he had done his share. When he arrived home and headed straight to the kitchen for a snack, he was surprised to find Detective Carson seated at the kitchen table with his mother.

"Detective Carson," he sputtered. "What are you doing here?"

Carson stood and held out his hand to shake. "I was interested in what you said in class today, so I decided to come ask a few more questions."

Palmer shook the detective's hand, then looked at his mother. She nodded. "Sit down, son. If there's any way we can help find Lilli, we want to do it, don't we?"

Palmer shrugged. "Well, sure, we do, but I don't know anything. I helped search all day yesterday, but we had a team leader. Didn't the team leaders all give you their reports?"

Carson nodded and resumed his seat. "Yes, they did, but so far, nobody has reported anything helpful. You know Lilli, so you might be able to give me some insight into her disappearance."

Palmer scowled. "We're in a couple of classes together. I hardly know her. What can I tell you?"

"Well, this morning, you seemed to express the opinion that she might be dead. Where did you get that idea?"

"I got it out of thin air," said Palmer. His voice had gotten a little squeaky. "I don't have any idea what happened to Lilli."

Carson was studying his face. "I've gotten a bit of an idea that you and Lilli aren't very friendly. That maybe you don't like her so much."

"I don't like a lot of people," Palmer said sulkily, "but I don't go out and kidnap them or kill them, whatever it is you think I've done."

Carson sighed. "I'm not accusing you of anything, son. I'm just trying to find out where Lilli is. And I'm talking to everybody who knows her, hoping I'll pick up some kind of clue somewhere."

"Well, then, maybe you should be talking to Mr. Fletcher," Palmer said slyly. "You know, my World History teacher? He seems to have a thing for Lilli."

"Palmer!" Mrs. Evans gasped before Carson could speak. "Don't be making things up."

Palmer glared at his mother. "Who says I'm making things up?"

"Okay, calm down," Carson said. "Tell us why you think your teacher might be involved."

Palmer shrugged. "I saw them together one time. They couldn't take their eyes off each other. They were all involved in a cozy conversation, smiling and cooing at each other."

"Where was this?" Carson asked.

"What difference does that make?" asked Palmer. "The point is - they were hot for each other. Maybe Lilli changed her mind, and he killed her."

Carson frowned. "You certainly seem to be convinced she's dead. Why is that?"

Palmer gave an exasperated sigh. "I don't know if she's dead. But if she's alive, why doesn't she come home? She has to know the whole town is looking for her."

Carson looked sad. "Yes, why doesn't she come home?" He and Mrs. Evans exchanged long, mournful looks. Then Carson said, "Okay, thanks for the information, Palmer. If you think of anything else, please give me a call."

"No problem," said Palmer.

After Carson was gone, Palmer turned on his mother. "Why did you do that?"

"Do what?"

"Let that policeman come in and *interrogate* me without a lawyer present?"

His mother looked alarmed. "A lawyer? Palmer, what have you done?"

"I haven't done anything wrong. What are you talking about?"

"If you haven't done anything wrong, why do you want a lawyer?"

Palmer gave his mother one of those scathing looks that teenagers reserve for their dotty parents. "I'm out of here. I'm going to get Donte and go hunt for Lilli."

His mother stopped him with a grip on his elbow. "That's fine, Palmer, but I want you home before dark. It won't help Lilli if someone else gets hurt or lost."

Palmer pulled away from his mother and left without a backward glance. When the door slammed behind him, she groaned. He had been such an adorable child until he realized how well he could throw a football!

Palmer jogged the two blocks to the Rhodes home. Going to the back of the house, he burst through the kitchen door without knocking. The two boys were as much at home in each other's houses as if they were family. Donte wasn't in the kitchen, and the sound of TV led Palmer to the den.

"Hey, man!" Donte said, looking up from the recliner where he was lounging. He was holding a grape Gatorade and a bag of potato chips. "I thought you were doing your homework." He put down the potato chip bag and groped around in his chair. Locating the remote, he muted the TV set.

"Yeah, well, that was the plan," said Palmer in his most disgusted voice. "But who did I find in my house, conspiring with my mother, when I got home? That Carson cop. He thinks I killed Lilli!"

Donte's eyes widened. "You didn't, did you?"

"Of course not!" Palmer's indignation knew no bounds. "What an idiotic idea. Come on. Get your coat. We're going to go find her."

"You mean...you mean you know where she is?"

"Of course not," said Palmer. "But I have to find her to prove to the cops that I didn't do anything to hurt her."

Donte was obediently rising and pulling on the coat he had tossed onto the sofa when he got home. "So where are we going to look?"

"You know that ravine between Skyport and the Douglas farm?" Palmer asked.

"You mean that big old gully on the other side of Mr. Blanchard's farm?" Donte asked. "Sure, but that's five miles from here. How are we gonna' get there?"

"We're going to borrow your dad's old rattletrap pickup. What d'ya think?"

Donte halted all motion with the zipper on his coat only halfway pulled up. "Dad's not here. I can't take it without his permission."

"Then call him. Leave a note. Do something - we don't have all day," Palmer said impatiently.

Donte considered. Then he led the way into the kitchen, where he wrote a note and attached it to the refrigerator door with a magnet. "He's not gonna' like it," he muttered.

"Never mind. Let's go."

By the time the boys persuaded the old truck to start, put a couple of dollars worth of gasoline in the nearly empty tank, and parked beside the highway, the sun was low in the sky. "This is crazy," Donte said. "It's gonna' be pitch black around here in less than two hours. It'll take us ten minutes to get across this field to the ravine. Why do you want to hunt there, anyway?"

"I know some secret places in the ravine. You know that first summer we moved here before I knew anybody? I spent a lot of time exploring the ravine. I just want to check out some caves I found that summer."

"We're not going to find anything in the dark," Donte grumbled.

Palmer held up a couple of flashlights. "I borrowed these from the drawer while you were writing the note," he said, handing one of the devices to his friend. "Come on, let's go. It's going to be way below freezing tonight. If she's out here, we have to find her now."

Leaving the pickup behind, Palmer and Donte made it across Farmer

Blanchard's field in record time. But Donte balked when they reached the edge of the ravine and saw the muddy descent. "C'mon, Palmer, you kidding? I'm not going down there. My Mom will pound me if I come home covered with slime!"

Palmer just pushed his buddy forward. "When did you turn into a wuss?" he asked. "Let's go before it gets any darker."

The boys slid and skidded down a rock-strewn slope, picking their way carefully. Even so, both were wearing mud-spattered jeans by the time they reached the bottom. As they picked their way over rock formations and around pockets of mud in the streambed, Donte wouldn't stop whining about his mother's reaction when she saw the condition of his clothes. And besides, what was the point? This territory had probably been searched ten times already.

Ignoring his friend's complaints, Palmer had his own relentless tirade, which he inflicted on Donte. But his harangue was about his lecherous, old World History teacher, Kip Fletcher. In his mind, Palmer could see the whole panorama of the romance – Mr. Fletcher wooing Lilli; Lilli falling for the attractive teacher; Lilli leading him on, then changing her mind; and finally, Mr. Fletcher angrily choking her to death and hiding her body.

"You mark my words, Donte Rhodes," Palmer ranted, "Mr. Fletcher is the reason we're here. Look at all the trouble he's causing this town!"

"Yeah, yeah, yeah," muttered Donte. He'd heard it all before because, as it turned out, Donte was the only person Palmer could unload on about Mr. Fletcher without getting in trouble. "Will you give it a rest?"

"I will if you will," Palmer growled. So, both boys quit talking, and each fumed inwardly about his own pet gripes as they stumbled over the uneven streambed.

Traveling as fast as he could, Palmer led the way. With weeds dead and bushes bare, he had no trouble locating the caves he remembered. They were in plain sight on the ravine walls. But Lilli was not.

When they had checked out the third and final cave, Palmer sagged. "I just knew she would be here," he mourned. "What a waste!"

"You're telling me!" Donte agreed. Both boys had their flashlights on by now, and he waved his around, playing it over the walls of the ravine. "Is there a faster way out of here? I've had it with the mud and the rocks."

"Probably," Palmer said with a shrug, "but it's getting too dark to see anything. We'll be safer going back the way we came. At least, we'll know where we are."

"What? You think we're gonna' get lost down here?"

"No," Palmer explained patiently. "But there aren't a lot of places where we can find an easy trail out. We don't want to get halfway to the top and have to turn around and go back, do we?"

"No. I guess not. Come on, then," Donte said, taking the lead. "I want out of this pit."

"I know what I should have done," Palmer muttered to himself as he followed Donte in the darkness.

"What?" Donte yelled. "Speak up!"

"I was talking to myself," Palmer snapped.

"Whatever."

"I should have gotten one of the girls to say Fletcher made a move on her," Palmer continued his solo conversation. "Then I would have had proof."

Donte, who had tuned in to Palmer's mutterings, halted. "You mean, get her to lie?"

Palmer glared at his friend. "I thought you didn't want to talk about it anymore."

"Well, you're still talking," said Donte huffily. "Yeah, and you're listening."

"So, you should have gotten her to lie?" Donte repeated his question.

"Why not?"

Donte shrugged. "No reason. Just asking. You must really hate this Fletcher guy."

"Well, he shouldn't be allowed to prey on young girls," Palmer said with a noble air, forgetting that he didn't like Lilli. "Someone should put a stop to it."

"C'mon, man, you only saw them together that one time. They were in the hall of the school where anybody, including the cameras, could see as plain as day that they weren't doing anything wrong!" protested Donte.

"There weren't any cameras in his classroom. And you didn't see their faces," said Palmer. "If you had, you'd know, same as me."

Donte had no answer to that. And Palmer fell silent as he concentrated on his footing.

The boys made good time, retracing their steps. They yelled Lilli's name fairly often, but their goal was mainly forgotten in their eagerness to get back to the truck and head home for dinner.

"Is this it?" Donte asked when they reached the trail leading out of the ravine.

Palmer shone his light on the faint trail. "Looks like it. You want me to go first?"

Donte shrugged. "Yeah, go ahead."

The climb out was easier than the slippery trail down had been. Both boys were hurrying, and they were panting as they neared the top. Suddenly, they were bathed in a flood of light.

"Hey!" Palmer yelled. "Who's there? Get that light out of my eyes!" He stopped suddenly, and Donte plowed into him.

The boys halted, squinting upward. Then Palmer gasped and pointed at the crescent-shaped object hovering above them. "What's that?" he squawked.

Donte took one look, stepped backward, tripped, and rolled back down the trail into the ravine, howling as he went.

Palmer was frozen, staring at the object. It glowed red and seemed to be staring at him as hard as he was staring at it. He couldn't take his eyes off the strange airship. Until he fainted and sank to the ground.

The boys were still there when their rescuers came. Tracking signals from their cell phones, Detective Carson, a uniformed officer, and the boys' dads found them where they lay. Palmer seemed to be in a trance. Donte, his arm broken, was lying at the bottom of the trail sobbing.

★★★

About the time their rescuers delivered Palmer and Donte to the local hospital's emergency room, Malcolm Park and his three daughters pulled up in front of Anna Park's home. The women had all made the drive to Lubbock to meet their father's plane. Ever since he had moved to the "other side of the world," as they described it, they never got to see enough of him.

Over dinner, they had gently revealed to him the truth of Lilli's paternity, which Anna had shared with them the night before. "Malcolm has to know," she told them, "and I can't tell him. Will you do it for me? And please forgive me for being such a coward."

Irene, Judith, and Karon had been horrified at their mother's betrayal of their beloved father. But her condition was so fragile that they had been careful to hide their dismay. And now, they sent him in alone to see Anna while they drove to the police station to find out if there was any news from the search teams.

Anna had undergone a transformation since the previous day. She was up and about, having spent most of the day searching for Lilli. After showering and knowing her daughters were going to deliver their father, she had put on a fleecy aqua sweater and blue jeans. In spite of the lateness of the hour, she had applied makeup and carefully arranged her hair.

She was reading a medical journal when Malcolm suddenly appeared at the door of the den. "Knock, knock," he said. "The girls insisted I should just come on in."

Anna looked up with a hesitant smile. Malcolm had a temper, but he didn't lose it often. She could not guess how he would have reacted to the news that Lilli was another man's child. She rose and went to him with an outstretched hand. "Come in, Malcolm." She gave him her cool, soft hand, and he held it with both of his.

He was a big man with lots of auburn hair. Although he had gained the usual middle-age paunch, he was tall and carried his weight well. "You're as lovely as ever," he told his ex-wife.

She blushed and indicated that he should take the recliner where she usually sat. "It's kind of you to say so after what our daughters have just told you," she said shyly, seating herself in the armchair nearby.

Malcolm grimaced. "I have to admit, I was pretty angry," he said. "But then I thought about Lilli."

Anna was perplexed. "What about Lilli?"

Malcolm smiled. "Knowing Lilli is a privilege. How can I be angry when I

- when we, my family and I - have had the pleasure of knowing her?"

Anna just stared. She had not expected this reaction. "I thought you would be furious with me for lying to you," she finally stammered.

Malcolm shrugged. "I was. For a minute. But, Anna, I love Lilli. When she visited us in Italy last year, we had the best vacation of our lives. My boys adore her. How can I be angry about something that made her part of our family?"

Anna studied his face for long moments. Finally, she said wonderingly, "I always knew you were a remarkable man. What a fool I was to let you go."

"I was the fool," said Malcolm. "I should have turned down the overseas job when I saw how much you didn't want to go."

Anna chuckled suddenly. "Well, this evening is not turning out the way I expected."

"What did you expect?"

"I thought you would be furious, would call me a miserable liar, and would then storm out in a rage."

Malcolm looked hurt. "That's your opinion of me?"

Anna shook her head. "No, but my guilt was coloring all my thoughts. I know I deserve any hateful thing you might say to me. I've been dreading this conversation for 15 years."

Malcolm took her hand in both of his and gave it a soft squeeze. "Forget it, Anna. I wish I could take all that suffering away from you. But I can tell you now - give it up. I'm proud of you. I was proud of you back then, even though we were divorcing. You wanted to improve your skills and make a better life for yourself and Lilli. Kandi doesn't have a tenth of the ambition you do. But I didn't bother to find *that* out before I married her."

"Your boys are in school now, aren't they? What does she do all day?" Anna asked with interest.

"You mean besides spending money?" Malcolm asked. "She goes to the gym and the spa and the mall. She meets with her friends, and they complain about their husbands. She does every meaningless, brainless thing that strikes her fancy."

Anna winced. She knew Malcolm. He couldn't be pleased with such aimlessness in his wife. "I assume you've talked to her about it?"

Malcolm grinned. "Of course, that's what she complains about when she gets together with her girlfriends - how I think she should do something meaningful with her life and how I won't let her spend us into the poor house."

"Oh, that reminds me," Anna said. "I saved up enough money to pay you back for all the money you gave me during my training. It's invested now because I couldn't give it to you without confessing that I'd lied to you. And I never got up the courage to do that. But I'll get it now and send it to you with the interest it's earned. Will that help?"

"No, no, no!" Malcolm thundered. "Not a chance. You save that money for your retirement. Kandi and I are okay. I keep her on a tight leash. She has one credit card with a $2000 limit, and I…" He grinned suddenly. "I hide money. Shhh! Don't tell her."

Anna laughed, then sobered. "But it's not fair. You shouldn't have given me all that money when Lilli's not even your daughter."

"She may not be my bio daughter, but she's in my heart," Malcolm said simply. "I would pay it all again, if necessary, to keep her in my life." He frowned. "Speaking of which, is she still in my life? Now that I know she's not actually mine, will you still let her be part of my family?"

There were tears in Anna's eyes as she nodded. "Of course. You're in her heart, too. She loves the time she spends with you."

Malcolm released Anna's hand and leaned back in his chair with relief. "Oh good. It would break my heart to lose her." Suddenly, he sat up straight. "But have we lost her? What's the latest news?"

Anna shook her head dismally. "No news. Malcolm, I'm so scared…" Her sentence trailed off in a sob.

Without a word, Malcolm stood, took Anna's hand, and led her to the couch. He sat down and enfolded her in his arms. Neither spoke while Anna sobbed quietly into his shoulder. When Irene, Judith, and Karon came in, they found Anna sleeping in Malcolm's arms. He put a finger in front of his lips to shush them.

Chapter 12: Falcon's Story – Fact or Fiction?

The next day, Wednesday, the consuming desire of Skyport, Texas, and all the surrounding communities was still to find Lilli Park. The "Find Lilli" Facebook page had so many posts that Treena Wood and the other Harvesters wondered how they could keep up with it. Detective Carson and Sheriff Moreno each assigned staff members to monitor the site.

In spite of frenetic activity and unremitting communication, nobody said, "ten degrees," the Fahrenheit temperature of the previous night. Nobody wanted to think about a youngster lost and alone in the freezing darkness.

Detective Caleb Carson had just arrived at his desk and poured a cup of coffee when he received word that Bryce Douglas and his son Royal were there to see him. Trying to stifle a flicker of hope, Carson said eagerly, "Send them to me!"

The ravages of the hunt marked both father and son. Weariness and despair were etched as plainly as words across their faces. Carson quickly got them seated and put cups of coffee in their hands before he asked, "What's up? Have you thought of something?"

Bryce answered with a sigh. "Nothing good. It's something I should have told you immediately, but my mind has been in such an uproar that I forgot. Royal asked me this morning if I had told you about Falcon - about Myles Dyer."

Carson sat up straight, his heartbeat suddenly painful. "What about him?"

Bryce opened his mouth, but the words caught in his throat with a sob. Carson looked at Royal who looked almost as devastated. So, he waited.

Finally, Bryce cleared his throat, took a deep breath, and told Carson about Falcon's implied threat at the pizza joint and his appearance at the basketball game. "I didn't pay much attention," he finished. "Falcon is a blowhard, and his crimes have only been about getting his hands on some cash, not about violence or just plain meanness. So, I thought he was only pushing my buttons."

Carson nodded. "But kidnapping is about getting money."

"Has there been a ransom note?" Bryce asked, looking hopeful. Carson shook his head. "No, not yet."

Bryce slumped. "Falcon couldn't afford to take Lilli for ransom anyway. We would immediately know where to look. I mean, think about it - Anna and I aren't exactly rich. We don't have enough money between us to make it worth a real kidnapper's time and trouble."

"True," said Carson, "but what about Malcolm? Most people believe Malcolm is her father, and he seems to be fairly well off."

Bryce looked hopeful again. "That's true. When do you think the ransom note will come?"

Carson shook his head. "It should have already arrived. I wish I could tell you otherwise, but at this point, kidnapping seems unlikely." He turned to Royal. "What about you, son? Do you have any new thoughts? Is that why you're skipping school?"

"No ideas," Royal said. He glanced at the clock on the wall above Carson's head. "I still have time to get to school. I was hoping you might have some news for us, and I wanted to know about it before I have to go sit in a classroom all day."

Carson sighed. "I wish I had some good news for you, but so far, we don't have a clue."

"What about those drones flying around all over the place?" Royal asked. "Haven't they found anything?"

"Nothing," said Carson. "The weather has been perfect, cold and clear.

But they haven't seen anything helpful. And they're gone now. They were committed elsewhere, and they say there's no reason to think they might find anything. They've covered the territory pretty thoroughly."

"So now what?" Bryce asked.

Carson studied the devastated father with sympathy. He didn't want to answer the question. He didn't even want to say it to himself. "I've...I've requested the help of..."

He paused, and Bryce looked up with a frown. "Help of who?"

Carson closed his eyes a moment before he answered. "Tomorrow, we'll have a couple of cadaver dogs here. I'm sorry, Bryce, but it's the next best step. And look - if they don't find her, that will be encouraging!"

"Right." Bryce and Royal stood. "Okay, we'll get going so you can do your job. Thank you, Caleb, for everything."

The men shook hands. Bryce and Royal turned away, then Bryce stopped and turned back. "What about Falcon? Shall I go beat a confession out of him?"

Carson smiled. "Leave Falcon to me. If he knows anything, I'll get it out of him."

It took Carson nearly an hour to find Falcon. He wasn't at work, having been given the day off in exchange for working on Saturday. At his house, his elderly mother was the only one home. She thought he was at work. When Carson demurred, she suggested trying the YMCA where Falcon went to work out. At the Y, he was told Falcon might be at the home of DeDe Fletcher, wife of the high school Social Studies teacher, Kip Fletcher.

Sure enough, in the driveway of the Fletcher home, Falcon and DeDe both had their heads under the hood of DeDe's little red Fiat. Dressed in old shirts and jeans and decorated with grease, they were hard at work. Neither seemed to notice when Carson parked and got out of his car.

"Good morning, Falcon. Good morning, Mrs. Fletcher," Carson said as he joined them. "Is your poor car ill?"

DeDe straightened up with a startled expression on her face. She studied him a moment. Falcon sneered at him.

"Do I know you?" DeDe asked. "You look familiar."

Carson pulled out his badge and showed it to her. "You've probably seen me on TV talking about the search for Lilli Park."

"That's right," she said. Then she waved at the car. "Well, yes, my Lady Bug - that's her name - isn't as young as she used to be."

Carson looked at Falcon. "And you make house calls?"

"Sure," said Falcon, "if the price is right. What are *you* doin' here, cop-o'-the-mornin'?"

"Looking for you," said Carson. "You're not an easy person to find."

"Easier than that kid of Bryce Douglas's," Falcon said coolly.

Carson's eyes narrowed. "Funny you should mention Lilli. You wouldn't happen to know where I can find her, would you?"

Falcon's lip curled, "I knew Douglas would sic you on me. What took you so long?"

DeDe was watching Falcon with dismay. "Falcon, you don't know where Lilli is, do you?" she asked earnestly.

"Doesn't matter," Falcon said. "They're gonna' pin it on me whether I did it or not."

"Let's go back to the station and talk about that," Carson said.

"Wait!" DeDe grabbed Falcon's arm. "Look me in the eye, Falcon, and tell me the truth. I want to know."

Falcon paused and considered. Then, after a glance at Carson, he looked into DeDe's eyes and said, "I didn't touch her. I don't know where she is."

DeDe's hand dropped back to her side. "Okay. Thanks."

Under questioning, Falcon was about as helpful as Carson had expected him to be. His attitude was cocky, his answers useless.

"You want to tell me where you were this weekend?" was Carson's starting point.

"No."

Carson rolled his eyes and sighed. "Tell me anyway. Start with Friday evening."

"I took my Mama out to dinner," Falcon said with a beatific smile. "Then we went home. She went to bed. I watched a movie on the tube."

"And after the movie?"

"I went out hunting space aliens," Falcon said with a smirk. "I keep hearing how they've been hanging out around Skyport lately, and I didn't want to miss out."

Carson rolled his eyes again. "Where did you hunt for these space aliens?"

"Oh, I drove all over the county," said Falcon. "Checked out the town. Went north, south, east, west - past all the surrounding farms. I had a fine time."

"And how many aliens did you find?"

"None. That part was very disappointing."

"How many people saw you on your travels?"

Falcon shrugged. "There was lots of traffic. Probably half the town of Skyport saw me."

"So, name a few of them who can verify your story," Carson said patiently.

"Oh, I didn't see anybody I recognized," Falcon said with a smile. "It was just me and my truck enjoying a night ride."

"Did you ever go to bed Friday night?"

"Sure. I had to work Saturday. How'm I gonna' get the job done if I don't get my beauty sleep?"

Carson frowned. "I thought Calderon's was closed on Saturdays. Why were you working?"

"Well, now, I should think even a cop could figure that one out," Falcon said scornfully. "Big shot customer with a fancy car and lots of money has to have his ride repaired *right now*! Of course, Diego's not gonna' let him get away. So, I worked Saturday, and I'm off today."

"All right. What time did you go home for your beauty sleep?"

"I hit the hay around one," Falcon said.

"Can you prove it?"

"Can you prove when you went to bed Friday night?" Falcon countered.

"Then tell me about Saturday morning," said Carson.

"Left the house about eight. Stopped by the Golden Arches for breakfast. Started working at 8:45," said Falcon.

"When did you finish?"

"Oh, I finished the big, fancy car before noon. Ate my sandwich. Worked on two more cars. Went home at 2:30."

"Were you the only one working Saturday?"

"Right."

Carson studied Falcon. "You want to let me search your house?" he asked.

Falcon sat up straight. "What kind of fool do you take me for?" he roared. "You think I'm gonna' let you come in and plant your evidence in my house, then accuse me of taking that kid?"

Carson put both hands on top of his head. "I'll walk through the house just like this," he said. "I won't touch anything. You'll be right there with me. Show me you don't have Lilli Park stashed in your house somewhere, and I'll be gone."

Falcon thought it over. Finally, he said, "I don't know why I should do you any favors."

"To get me off your back, of course."

When Falcon shrugged and said, "Sure, why not?" Carson's heart sank. No way Falcon was going to let him in if Lilli was somewhere in the house.

He hid his disappointment and said, "Good. One more thing before we go - tell me about you and Mrs. Fletcher."

"What about me and Mrs. Fletcher?"

"How'd you come to be at her house today?"

"She wants to learn about cars. I'm teaching her." Falcon's tone was dismissive.

"Where'd you meet?"

"At the Y."

"And she told you she wanted to learn about cars?"

"Sure. Why not? She asked me where I work. I told her. She said she wished she wasn't so stupid about cars. I said I would teach her. So, I am."

"Does she know you're an ex-con?"

"Sure. She knows my whole life history," Falcon sneered.

"Right. Let's go."

The ramble through the small house where Falcon lived with his mother took less than ten minutes. Carson kept his eyes peeled for any hint of Lilli's presence. But he found none.

On his way back to the police station, he drove past the Fletcher home again. DeDe was inside the car now, cleaning the windows. When Carson pulled into the driveway, she hopped out and came to meet him.

"Good morning again," he said.

DeDe smiled at him. "You're back!"

"Right. Just for a few minutes. Falcon tells me you know he's an ex-con."

DeDe nodded. "That's right."

"So, how did you two get to be buddies?"

"We met at the YMCA," DeDe explained. "He's a talker, and he needed a listener. I listen."

"He says he's teaching you about cars."

"He is," said DeDe. "My husband is a novelist and a teacher. I do a lot of traveling around the state, publicizing his books while he's in school. It always made me nervous to be out on the highway, not knowing what makes my car run. Falcon is teaching me some of the basics."

"And you're not afraid of him?" "No."

"What about your husband? Is it okay with him for Falcon to be hanging around you?"

DeDe looked uncomfortable. She told Carson about Falcon's visit to Kip's classroom. "It was such a stupid thing for him to do that I don't want Kip to know I'm still seeing Falcon," she admitted. "I read Falcon the riot act, and he apologized. He said his rent was due, and he was a hundred dollars short, so he was hoping Kip would pay him to stay away from me."

She grinned wryly. "Of course, I gave him a hundred dollars. I guess I'm a bigger sucker than my husband, but Falcon had helped me more than a hundred dollars worth by then and always refused to take any money from me. So I don't feel too foolish. And I'm paying him for his help now. I insist on it.

"As for Kip…" She hesitated. "Well, I guess I'll have to tell him someday, but I'm not looking forward to it."

"Maybe it would be a good idea to tell him," Carson said. "You don't want him to find out some other way."

DeDe nodded. "You're probably right."

"Will he be angry? Or suspicious?" Carson asked, wondering what he could find out about the Fletcher marriage without appearing too nosy. Palmer's accusations against Kip Fletcher seemed unlikely, but still, Carson couldn't afford to leave a stone unturned.

"He'll be worried about me," DeDe said. "But I don't think he'll be angry or suspicious. Why would he?"

"Oh, some men would be," Carson said vaguely. Better save these questions for Mr. Fletcher. No point upsetting the wife over it in case Palmer was making up stories or exaggerating. "Okay. Last question. Did you believe Falcon when he said he doesn't know where Lilli is?"

DeDe smiled. "Yes, I did. Did you?"

Carson smiled back. "Well, not because he said it, but if he told me the truth about his whereabouts, he was at work when we believe she was abducted. So, I believe him for now. Until I check out his story."

★★★

The most animated chatter around Skyport schools that Wednesday was about two new "Find Lilli" Facebook posts that appeared during the night. One of them was written by Darron Vance, a freshman student. It read, "Some students think the Skyport PD should be investigating the love connection between Lilli and a certain SHS history teacher. It wouldn't be the first time a sleazy affair turned stinky, and a nice girl ended up paying for it."

By the time Detective Carson got wind of this posting and called the school, it had been removed. The high school administration had done some investigating of their own. When Darron found himself sequestered in a small office, surrounded by principals, he meekly admitted that Palmer Evans had persuaded him to write the post. Since Darron was in Mrs. Sharp's class, Palmer had explained, he would not be subject to retaliation by Mr. Fletcher. Darron bought it.

What neither boy had considered was that Mrs. Sharp could retaliate. And so could the school administration. The principals sentenced both boys to a minimum of three weeks in DAEP (the Disciplinary Alternative Education Program).

Upon receiving word of his punishment, Palmer's mouth shifted into

114

high gear. He complained to anyone who would listen that the school was covering up for Mr. Fletcher, so the school was just as guilty as Mr. Fletcher was.

This time, the coaches got involved. The athletic director called Palmer into his office and explained that Palmer would not be playing in the first three football games next season. And if the slanderous statements didn't stop, Palmer would be out of the athletic program altogether.

Of course, Palmer, who believed he was irreplaceable, was enraged. He fumed to himself nonstop that he was being unfairly persecuted and Mr. Fletcher was getting away with murder. But he ended his public campaign against the teacher because, bottom line, he needed football more than football needed him.

The other FB post that excited the town was written by Palmer Evans. Donte had spent half the night at the hospital, waiting to have his broken arm tended. But Palmer's stay had been much shorter. When he was released, he had gone home and written up the story of the evening's adventure. His most startling claim was that he'd heard a voice coming from the UFO. It said, "Forget Lilli. She belongs to us now."

Palmer closed the post with his firm opinion that Lilli Park had been spirited away by space aliens. Perhaps they were friendly creatures who had come to take Lilli to Hubble. Or perhaps they wanted to study her because of her superior intelligence. Either way, she was gone forever.

Readers of "Find Lilli" couldn't wait to weigh in with their opinions. Approximately half of those posting replies to Palmer's story agreed with him. The rest scoffed at the idea that he and Donte had even seen a UFO.

Treena Wood's response to Palmer's story was to explain that what he had seen had been demonic, nothing to do with aliens. She said these lying specters were determined to deceive and discourage everyone. She pleaded that readers not fall for their clever hoax.

Royal Douglas, upon reading Treena's post, was enraged. He wrote, "How dare you write such lies? You don't know anything! Demons don't exist, and you are the one trying to hoax everybody. Just like you hoaxed Lilli. You destroyed her! Why did you make her believe your stupid book?"

Treena replied, "Royal, the Bible is not a stupid book. The Bible is the only way we can know what happened in the past and what will happen in the future. And it is our only hope for a life of joy and peace. Aziz is an evil, lying spirit. I hope you will ignore his lies and give God a chance to show you the best way to live."

That evening, Royal read Treena's reply with Aziz's name written right there for the whole world to see. His rage turned to cold fury. "Treena Wood, you are too stupid to live," he wrote. "I'm through reading your crap."

He slid his phone into his pocket and pulled on his coat. "I'm going out to look for Lilli," he told his dad, stuffing his anger down and making his voice calm.

"Hey, it's late," Bryce said, glancing out the window. "It's dark out there. You know what happened to Palmer Evans last night."

"Yeah, I read it on Facebook," said Royal. "It sounds like Aziz and his crew are around here somewhere. Maybe I can contact them and see if they know anything. They should have a better view than that squadron of lame drones."

Bryce looked troubled. "Royal, you know what Lilli said about the Soterians. What if she's right? What if they're not who they say they are? What if they're not visitors from another world?"

Some of Royal's stuffed anger began to bubble up. "Dad, don't you go crazy on me, too. That Treena dame calls them demons! What an ignorant little fool! There's no such thing as a demon. Besides, did you see her last post? She actually gave Aziz's name. How did she even know his name?"

"From Lilli, I guess," Bryce said.

"Right! From Lilli. She ruined Lilli. Lilli knew the time wasn't right for people to hear about the Soterians, but she was telling everybody about them anyway. She didn't care if she wrecked our whole operation." He punched the palm of his left hand with his right fist. Suddenly, he was close to tears. "How could she do that, Dad? How could she take a chance that she would spoil everything?"

Bryce studied his son for a minute while Royal regained control. Then Bryce asked, "Royal, tell me something. When is the right time? It has been how long - over five years that they've been telling you to wait for the 'right time?' They're always talking about the right time, but when is it going to be the right time?"

Royal's eyes lit up. "It could be next year. Aziz told me that officials in Soteria are debating about the best way to proceed. They're projecting that they'll be ready to move ahead in about a year." His tone softened. "I told Lilli that. They're not mad at her, and she hasn't ruined anything. But I don't understand how she could be so reckless when the future of our whole planet is at stake."

Bryce had no interest in discussing an alien's concept of the Earth and its need to be rescued. So he replied, "I guess she just doesn't see it the same way you do, son. Okay, go on out, but I want you back before 10:00."

"No problem," said Royal. He pulled on gloves, snapped a leash on Adolf, and went out into the frigid night.

Chapter 13: Doomed Experiment

Bryce Douglas was at loose ends the next morning. He had taken the week off from work to help look for Lilli. But the barren winter landscape had been searched and searched again. Bryce could think of nowhere else to look. He had checked on Anna Park the day before and been introduced to Malcolm. And he had renewed his acquaintance with Irene, Judith, and Karon. That visit had used up maybe an hour.

Today, Thursday, was gloomy with thick, low-lying clouds and temperatures in the 40s. Bundled up in a heavy, black, hooded sweater and warm gloves, Bryce was wandering forlornly around his property, thinking about Lilli, when Sheriff Lucas Moreno pulled into the driveway. The sheriff was a small man. His dark hair under the standard Stetson hat was cut short. He took his job very seriously. In his early 30s, he was determined that no one would compare him unfavorably with the previous sheriff, who had retired at age 72.

Bryce went to greet Moreno eagerly. Of course, he always hoped for good news. But even if Moreno had no news, he might, at least, give Bryce a purpose for the day.

The men shook hands, then Moreno got down to business. "Bryce, we've got cadaver dogs here today. I need to know if you'll let them sniff out your place. Or do we need to get a search warrant?"

Bryce's amazement showed on his face. "A search warrant? Of course not. Bring them on. Bring a thousand of them. I don't care. Just get it over with!"

Moreno's smile flashed briefly. "We thought that would be your attitude. Let me tell you the plan. Since we've been unable to locate Lilli's body out in the open, we'll be taking the dogs to places where a body could be hidden. With the ground frozen, we decided our best first step would be to have the dogs sniff out abandoned cars around the county. I understand you have a fleet of rusted-out vehicles in a backfield, and some of them are locked up tight."

"That's right," Bryce said. "The kids call it the A.G., the automobile graveyard. Whenever I add a wrecked vehicle to the collection, I leave the key in the ignition if I have one. But some of them came without keys. We haven't been able to look inside the trunks of those. But, then, it would have been impossible for anyone to put…to put Lilli inside one if the key wasn't there."

"They could have taken the key away after they put her in it," Moreno said. "Do you have a record of which vehicles should have keys and which ones never had a key?"

Bryce shook his head. "Nope. Never thought I would need that kind of record."

"Too bad," Moreno said. "Okay, I'll give Detective Carson a call and let him know he can bring the dogs any time. Is that right? Any time is okay with you?"

"Sure," said Bryce, "the sooner the better." He pointed toward the back of his farm. "The A.G. is over there, behind that row of pine trees. The place is an eyesore, so I didn't want it to be visible to the highway."

"Thanks for your help," Moreno said, shaking hands with Bryce again. "When we finish, we'll let you know…how it turned out."

Bryce nodded. "I would ask if I can help, but I don't want to be there, just in case…"

"Of course not," Moreno said sadly. "I don't much want to be there myself."

★★★

The previous evening, Kip and DeDe Fletcher had made some serious decisions. Kip, disgusted and horrified at having his reputation dragged through slime by "that arrogant punk Palmer Evans," was ready to leave

Skyport. "Let's just pack up and go," he said urgently as they carried their supper dishes from the table to the sink.

DeDe, looking beyond the immediate darkness, saw what she considered a miracle. "Let's talk about it," she said.

They put their dishes in the sink, then DeDe took her husband's hand and led him into the den. It was a light room with glass patio doors opening onto the back yard where two rescue dogs – a black pit bull-lab mix and a lovable little part-beagle – were play-fighting over their toys.

DeDe seated herself on the sofa and pulled Kip down beside her. "Okay, now, Kip, I want you to think about everybody *except* Palmer. This whole community has rallied to your side. Most of the students are on your side. You told me yourself the A.D. is willing to boot Palmer out of the sports program at SHS. And the principal will expel him from school permanently if he has to. Now, you name one other place you could go where the community wouldn't jump all over this story and crucify you just because their petty little minds love a scandal. Most places – they wouldn't care if it was true or not. They would destroy you for the fun of it. Why would you want to leave this wonderful place?"

Kip nodded. "In other words, you vote for staying here?" he asked. "Well, you're probably right." Suddenly, he pursed his lips, trying not to smile. "I forgot to tell you the best part. When Palmer comes out of DAEP prison, he'll be in Mrs. Sharp's class." And now, Kip couldn't repress a grin. "Palmer is going to *hate* Mrs. Prim, Proper, and Precise!"

DeDe grinned, too. "Wouldn't you love to see his face when he gets that news flash?"

Kip began to laugh. "Yep, I would love that!" He sighed then and added, "But if we're going to be staying in Skyport, I've got a decision to make…"

He had been doing a lot of soul-searching about his grading experiment. In spite of Palmer's boorish behavior, Kip didn't want to believe the boy would have harmed Lilli just because she wasn't willing to share points with him. But he had niggling little doubts he could not banish.

He and DeDe discussed the whole situation. Then Kip made a decision. Well, he was pretty sure he had made a decision. He still vacillated. But he kept coming back to it.

After they had discussed the experiment exhaustively, DeDe confessed that her relationship with Falcon was a little deeper than she had initially told Kip. The worried expression on his face made her heart sink. She didn't want to trouble him, but his wife's friendship with the ex-con obviously distressed him.

He considered the situation and finally said, "What I told Falcon still goes. It's your decision. I just hope we won't both live to regret it."

"Look, Kip, I'll call it off if you ask me to. I don't want you to be worrying about me," DeDe said earnestly.

He gave her a feeble smile. "Thanks, but it's not my decision. You do whatever you want to."

"Well, I'll think about it some more," she decided. Then she told him about Detective Carson's visit that morning. "He seemed to think Falcon might know where Lilli is," she said.

Kip nodded. "Well, Falcon seems a more likely villain than Palmer. What do you think? Could Falcon have kidnapped her?"

DeDe sighed. "I don't think so. But I wish I could be 100 percent sure."

"Same here. About Palmer," said Kip.

Kip Fletcher wasn't in the habit of second-guessing himself. But on that Thursday morning, when he stood in front of his second-period class, he wasn't completely certain what was going to come out of his mouth. He had no first-period class, so this was the moment when he had to make his final decision.

First, he admitted that he was struggling with his decision. "I think I'm going to say something I don't want to say," he explained. "I've made a decision, but I don't know if it's the right decision."

The class sat like statues, waiting. They could tell that whatever he said was going to affect them all.

Suddenly, Mr. Fletcher made the final call. "The experiment is over," he blurted. "It's done! Kaput! Your grades have fallen. Lilli is gone, and…" His voice broke, and he had to pause to regain his composure.

After a few long moments, he said, "I feel that I'm breaching a contract I had with you, but I just don't have the heart to continue with it. Why don't you tell me what you think?"

He leaned against his desk and looked around. "Anybody? Nobby, what do you think?"

"I didn't like it," said Nobby. "I told you that the first day." Mr. Fletcher nodded. "Okay. How about you, Zion?"

Zion grinned guiltily. "Well, it sounded pretty good to me at first. I liked the idea of somebody else doing the work, and I'd get a better grade because of their work. But everybody is making lousy grades, so what good is it?"

Mr. Fletcher shrugged. "Maybe that's the problem. Everyone wants somebody else to do the work."

"I still think you were trying to show us how bad socialism is," said Camilla Rodriguez.

Mr. Fletcher smiled for the first time that day. "You are absolutely correct, Camilla. But I didn't want to say so at first, in case it spoiled the experiment for everyone to know."

Jasmine Clark raised her hand. "Yes, Jasmine?"

"Mr. Fletcher, what's so bad about socialism, anyway?"

"Great question," said Mr. Fletcher, and his teacher demeanor returned. "The most egregious part of socialism... What does egregious mean, Nobby?

"The worst or the most horrible," said Nobby.

"Right!" Mr. Fletcher gave Nobby a warm smile. He did like students who were serious about their education.

He continued. "The most egregious part of socialism is that no one prospers except the people in power and maybe their toadies. Guys, listen closely right now. The socialists will tell you that they're great humanitarians. They claim to be the heroes of the downtrodden working classes. But, in truth, they - the people in power - will be the only ones who aren't suffering. They'll be the only ones who can afford food and housing and clothes. The rest of us will be standing in lines all day to get a loaf of bread, and all the bread may be gone before we get to the front of the line."

He paused, then added with a rueful smile, "Okay, I confess. I get carried away on the subject of socialism. But it's because it's such an ignorant idea -

history has proved it's a disaster. Yet we have some power-hungry politicians in this country fighting like wild animals to shove it down our throats right now."

He looked around. "Let's do this. Everybody who thought my experiment was a good idea, raise your hand."

No hands were raised. Not a surprising response after his little diatribe. "Okay," he continued, "why not? What was wrong with it?"

"Nobody wanted to do the work," said Camilla. "When you were going to give their points away, even the smart kids didn't want to work."

"That's right!" exclaimed Mr. Fletcher. "Socialism is a grinding, corrosive system. It wears people down and destroys hope. So, nobody accomplishes anything."

Zion raised his hand. "Mr. Fletcher, what were those toadies you mentioned? Who are they?"

"Well, Zion, running a country is a huge enterprise. So, the tyrants at the top will need help. They'll get that help from the boot lickers. The foot kissers. The toadies. And those people who bow and scrape before them will be paid extra to reward them for not having a spine. They won't get as much money as the top dogs, but they won't be hurting as much as the rest of us."

Mr. Fletcher paused, and Nobby said quietly, "It sounds like socialism makes everybody either evil or miserable."

"You're absolutely right!" Mr. Fletcher said. He smiled at Nobby, then asked the class, "You know the main thing that's missing from a socialistic society?"

He waited but got no response. So, he supplied the answer. "Dignity. There's no dignity in trampling on the convictions of the masses. There's no dignity in kissing somebody's feet because it's the only way you can get a meal for your family. And there's no dignity in hard work when you're ground so deep into the dirt that you'll never see the light of day…"

He broke off. "That's enough. The experiment is over. Let's move on."

He made a gesture toward the day's learning objective on the whiteboard, then stopped. "No. I have to say one more thing. Class, I want you to remember this as long as you live. Any time you hear a politician crooning seductively about how wonderful, how caring, how adorable they are for wanting to save you through socialism or communism - any form of socialism - you must do this…"

He paused dramatically. The students waited.

"You must mentally tattoo 'liar' across their foreheads. L-I-A-R. Early socialists may have believed their own tripe, may have believed that socialism was good for everyone. Modern politicians know better. So, you can be sure of this - politicians who are campaigning for socialism are saying that you are too stupid to handle your own money and your own life. They want every citizen to turn over all the money and all the power to them. History has made it clear. No one benefits from any form of socialism except the power hogs running the show."

He paused again to let his words sink in. Then he said, "Come on. Let's practice it. Close your eyes. Think about one of those ultra-liberal politicians with a sanguine smile smeared across his or her adorable little face and mentally plaster the word 'LIAR' across his or her forehead."

He paused again and watched his students. With eyes closed, first, they seemed to be concentrating. Then smiles appeared.

Eyes flew open when Mr. Fletcher began to applaud. From the front of the classroom, he gave them a standing ovation. "Now, never forget," he said, "they are liars. They're wearing that word on their foreheads for all the world to see!"

He stopped clapping and grinned at his class. "Ten bonus points all around on the last test. And from now on, we'll do it the way it should be done. Every person standing on his or her own strong legs. All of you learning history for yourselves because you want to know. And each of you making your own grades."

Jasmine's hand was up, and Mr. Fletcher recognized her. "Yes, Jasmine?"

She grinned. "Is 'kaput' one of your historical vocabulary words?"

Mr. Fletcher laughed. "Nope, 'kaput' is from my 'global vocabulary.' Specifically, it's borrowed from the Germans." He grinned at Jasmine. "Thank you for asking."

She nodded. "My pleasure."

Mr. Fletcher turned to the lesson with a much lighter heart than he'd had when he began the class. How in the world, he often wondered, did people survive who didn't have youngsters around to brighten their lives?

★★★

Mr. Fletcher made his announcement again in the teachers' lounge at noon. "I've called off the experiment," he said. "I don't have the heart to go on now that Lilli's missing."

Of course, Sadie Sharp was smug. "Well, I don't blame you," she said. "It was always a big mistake to punish your good students for working hard."

Mr. Fletcher nodded forlornly. "Yes, I know you said that from the beginning. But I still believe it was a good idea."

"So, what are you thinking, Kip?" asked Mr. Josephs. "Are you suggesting that the experiment had something to do with Lilli's disappearance?"

"No, I don't think that," said Mr. Fletcher, "but I'm still terrified that it's a possibility."

"Why?" asked Laurel Tanner. "Do you suspect one of your students of doing something to harm Lilli?"

Mr. Fletcher shook his head. "There was some animosity developing among them. But I refuse to let myself believe my experiment caused Lilli's disappearance."

"Of course not!" exclaimed Mr. Josephs heartily. "That's ridiculous. And let's be downright honest - socialism isn't such a bad idea. Look at it. How many greedy, selfish millionaires do we have in this country who wouldn't give a crust of bread to a neighbor? It only makes sense that someone should force them to share, doesn't it?"

"Tommyrot!" Mr. Fletcher exploded. "In the first place, I never heard of a millionaire who refused to give a crust of bread to a neighbor. And in the second place, if the United States goes down the socialism rat hole, *nobody* will have a crust of bread to share. Nobody but the thugs in Washington, and they're not interested in sharing. Oh, they're generous with other people's money, but how many of them went to Washington for the sole purpose of bloating their own bank accounts? You teach history. You know this. Every form of socialism has failed. It has happened over and over and over."

Mr. Josephs laughed genially, but there was fire in his eyes. "Come on, Kip. Be honest. Most of the people in this world are in desperate need, and this country owns 90% of the wealth. Americans need to get off their thrones and help the rest of the world! We need to join the human race."

The silence following that statement was broken by Mrs. Tanner, speaking in her usual meek voice. "If socialists take over this country and destroy it - which is what socialists do - there won't be anybody in the world left to help those needy people. We can't help impoverished people by becoming impoverished ourselves. It would be a tragic mistake to elect leaders who are willing to destroy our country and crush the confidence of other countries who look to us for hope and help."

"Right!" exclaimed Mr. Fletcher. "That's what my experiment proved. By the end of the six weeks, the grade of almost every student in my classes would have been in the cellar. There wouldn't have been enough points above 70 to help bring *anybody* up to passing."

"He's right," said Mrs. Sharp. She turned a charming smile on Mr. Josephs. "Now, you be careful, Len. Don't let the socialists turn you into one of their useful idiots."

"Useful idiots!" Mr. Josephs sputtered. Then he snapped his mouth shut. His face reddened, and his eyes seemed to bulge just the teeniest bit. He took a deep, calming breath, then forced a laugh and a fake smile. "That's what I love about this place," he boomed heartily, "all you provincial, unflappable folks who know what you know. You can't be bothered with facts."

"Facts!" Mr. Fletcher roared in response. "Facts! You wouldn't know a fact if it came and bit you on your backside." He turned his glare on Mrs. Sharp. "Backside. Is that word acceptable, Madam?"

She beamed at him. "Perfectly acceptable."

Mrs. Tanner, who hated conflict, could see that both Mr. Josephs and Mr. Fletcher were on the verge of beginning a new volley of invectives. So she spoke quickly, "Sadie," she said, "give us some good news. I can tell by looking at you that you've lost some more weight. How much?"

Mrs. Sharp smiled proudly in spite of the stormy atmosphere in the room. "I've lost three more pounds, and my blood sugar is falling." She actually loved conflict, but she could see this argument was going to produce nothing but ill feelings. So, she was grateful to Mrs. Tanner for changing the subject.

"That's wonderful," Mrs. Tanner responded.

"Way to go!" said Mrs. Grant.

Mrs. Sharp looked gratified for a moment, then the present situation struck her gut like a battering ram. "I would take all the weight back if it would bring Lilli back!" she sobbed

★ ★ ★

It was early afternoon when Detective Carson and Sheriff Moreno knocked on Bryce Douglas's door. Their faces were deadly serious. Bryce's heart gave a lurch at the sight of them.

"Come in," he said, holding the door open.

"No, we're not staying," Carson said. "We just want to tell you what we found."

Bryce joined them on the porch and shut the door. "What?" he asked.

"The dogs alerted on one of the cars in your field. It's an old, rusted-out clunker, but the trunk is locked. Any chance you might have the key?" Carson asked.

Bryce shook his head. "I don't. But you can get into the trunk, can't you, with some of your equipment?"

"We can, but we thought we should check with you one more time about a key."

"No key," said Bryce. "Go ahead."

Sheriff Moreno returned alone an hour later. "Lilli wasn't in the trunk," he said quickly, seeing the dread on Bryce's face. "However, we found this. Do you know if it belongs to Lilli?" He held up a fleecy pastel green scarf in a clear evidence bag.

Bryce nodded before he staggered to a porch swing and collapsed in it. He buried his face in his hands.

The sheriff waited.

When Bryce looked up, his face was wet with tears. His voice shook when he said, "Her mother gave it to her for Christmas."

Sheriff Moreno nodded. His heart ached for Bryce and Anna. "Dear God," he thought urgently. "Please let Lilli be alive somehow."

Bryce spoke again with his broken voice. "She's dead, isn't she?"

Moreno sat down beside him. "I don't know, Bryce," he said, "but I'm afraid there's no way this thing can have a good outcome."

Bryce shook his head. "No way," he echoed.

Chapter 14: Alibis

For Lilli's family and friends, time seemed to stand still during the following week. They still searched for her and found nothing. They still read and wrote Facebook posts. They still prayed and cried. But their wheels were spinning in sludge.

Anna Park went back to work. She truly thought she might lose her mind if she didn't. Her daughters returned to their homes. Malcolm flew back to Italy. And at Skyport High School, a sense of gloom haunted the halls.

The whole town was figuratively holding their breaths, waiting for the lab report on the scarf recovered from the car in Bryce Douglas's automobile graveyard. Maybe…just maybe, some villain's DNA would be isolated from it and identified.

On the other hand, Detective Caleb Carson and Sheriff Lucas Moreno were plowing forward. Continuing their interviews with Lilli's family, friends and acquaintances, they created maps locating all the principals in the case during the Friday night and Saturday that Lilli disappeared. Both men had the maps posted on the walls behind their desks. Once the maps were complete, they began verifying every story.

They started with Lilli's family.

Anna Park had been working at the hospital the entire time. Her presence was easily verified. Of course, she was the one who established the time of Lilli's disappearance. She could have lied. But nobody suspected Lilli's devastated mom of harming her.

Bryce Douglas had been at home Friday night. An urgent situation at the prison had taken him back to work at 7:00 A.M. Saturday. After he returned home at 11:00, he spent the remainder of the day repairing fences on his property and tending his animals. Only his time at the prison could be verified.

Royal Douglas and the whole Skyport High School basketball team had spent Friday night and Saturday at the home of Morton Hooper, the team's point guard, better known as "Hyper." Their story was that they had been disappointed in their poor showing at the free throw line in Friday's game. So, they had manufactured their own weekend clinic to practice free throws.

The team's nervous student trainer, Titus Murphy, admitted Hyper had learned on Thursday that his parents would be out of town the whole weekend. The idea of holding a weekend "clinic" was born when this fact spread through the team.

"Okay, let me get this straight," Carson said. "The story I've been getting from the team is that they were unhappy with their performance in the game Friday night. So, the decision to hold a clinic was made after the game. Are you telling me the decision was made on Thursday?"

Titus nodded glumly. He felt like a traitor, going off the party line, and to a police detective, no less. "Yeah," he muttered. "We thought it sounded better to say we thought of it Friday."

"Why? Thursday, Friday night - what's the difference?"

Titus just shrugged. "I dunno'. Somebody said it sounded better, so we all went along with it."

"Somebody who?"

"I don't remember."

Carson waited, hoping Titus would add more details. But Titus stayed silent and looked miserable.

"Okay, let me see if I can help your story along," suggested Carson. "Maybe it sounded better because if the idea didn't come up until after the Friday night game, there really was a free-throw clinic. But if the idea came up on Thursday, somebody or several somebodies had plenty of time to gather up party 'refreshments' – like drugs and alcohol."

"Oh, no, sir!" Titus gasped. "We would never use drugs or alcohol. The coach would kick us off the team if we did."

Try as he might, Carson could not get Titus to deviate from the established story again. Just as the other boys had done, he insisted they had spent the weekend playing basketball, watching a movie, and gorging themselves on pizza.

"Of course, they were doing something illegal," Moreno said after he and Carson compared notes and found that all the boys told identical stories. "Probably beer, but it could have been anything."

Carson nodded. "And they'll be off the team if the coach finds out. So, they're going to guard their secret like it's the crown jewels."

"Really?" Moreno asked. "You think he would ditch his entire team?"

"Who knows?" said Carson. "He may not have a choice if the school board gets involved. But the issue for us is whether one or all of them are involved in Lilli's disappearance. Of course, Royal is our main concern. Did you get any hint that he might have been out of their sight any part of the weekend?"

"The ones I spoke to were pretty vague about their sleep time. Most of them were asleep by 3:00 A.M. and didn't wake up until noon Saturday. They didn't vouch for anybody else during that nine hours."

Carson nodded. "Same here. No wonder they're such a strong team. They stick like they've been glued together."

The two men agreed that they might have to come back to the basketball players at a later date, but for now, they would accept their story.

Palmer Evans had spent Friday night with Donte Rhodes. They had played video games until around 1:00 Saturday morning. Upon rising at 9:30, they ate breakfast, then spent the rest of the morning at the high school athletic center, lifting weights and exercising. In the afternoon, they went to the Evans's home to do homework because Mrs. Evans was able to help them with their algebra. Carson had been unable to disprove any part of their story.

Myles "Falcon" Dyer's story had been partially verified. No one could say what he was actually doing when he claimed to be driving around the countryside on Friday night or at what time he returned home and went to bed. Diego Calderon, owner of the garage where Falcon worked, confirmed that Falcon had done the work he claimed to have done. Calderon had phoned the garage around noon and talked to Falcon, but he had no way of knowing when Falcon arrived or left.

Kip Fletcher had been holed up at home the whole weekend, working on his novel. DeDe had been away in Plainview that Friday and Saturday, attending a niece's first birthday party.

After Mr. Fletcher provided his alibi, such as it was, to Detective Carson, he took the opportunity to ask his own questions. "Would you explain this to me? Apparently, according to Palmer Evans, I'm guilty of romancing Lilli. But what, exactly, did he say I've done?"

"Palmer claims he saw you and Lilli alone together one time. He thought you seemed enamored with each other," Carson explained.

Bile rose in Mr. Fletcher's throat. His eyebrows drew together, and his face reddened. It was all he could do to keep from exploding. Being accused by the police was the ultimate indignity, in his opinion. "We walked out of the school building together. That's it! The very idea that I would harm Lilli is preposterous!" he snarled.

"I thought so, too," said Carson, "but I had to check it out. I guess the bottom line is that no one can verify your whereabouts that weekend?"

Controlling his fury, Mr. Fletcher said simply, "I guess."

"Have you ever been alone with Lilli, other than walking out of the building with her one time?"

"Never," Mr. Fletcher said. He paused, then added, "Detective Carson, I adore Lilli Park. She has a brilliant mind and the gentlest spirit I've ever known. But she is a child and a student, and I am not a pervert. I cannot begin to tell you how offended I am by your accusation."

"I'm not accusing; I'm asking," said Carson. "It's my job."

He left the Fletcher home feeling a little bit dirty and a little bit foolish. But his next stop - at the Wood home - was the most ridiculous of all. It was, in fact, embarrassing. Treena had done her homework Friday evening so she could spend the day Saturday with LaDawn Hardy, running errands for some of the elderly members of the church. When Carson left her, he felt guilty that he had even asked her for an alibi.

Many of Lilli's classmates were interviewed. But they were high school freshmen, 14 or 15 years old, without a driver's license or access to a vehicle. Among Lilli's acquaintances, only Donte Rhodes, who had failed third grade, had a driver's license. And the parents of Nobby, Camilla, Jasmine, Zion, and all the rest guaranteed that their children had not sneaked off to abduct Lilli. Or to harm her in any way.

By Wednesday of that week, Detective Carson and Sheriff Moreno were beginning to look at other cases that needed their attention. And then the dam burst.

First, a preliminary report on Lilli's scarf revealed that DNA had been recovered. The odds were that the DNA belonged to Lilli or one of her family members, so Carson and Moreno would need to obtain tissue samples from them for comparison. If Lilli and her family members could be ruled out, the DNA might point to Lilli's abductor.

When Carson returned from obtaining a cheek swab from Anna Park for DNA testing, DeDe Fletcher was waiting for him. Her face was as white as her blouse.

"What's wrong? What happened?" he demanded.

"Falcon has a gun," DeDe said. "That's not allowed, is it, since he's an ex-con?"

Carson shook his head grimly. "Did he threaten you with it?" he asked.

"Oh no!" DeDe was appalled at the idea. "I found it by accident. He asked me to get a tool out of his pickup. I couldn't find the tool, and I was digging through the stuff under his seat. That's where I found the gun. On the passenger side."

"Did you bring it with you?" Carson asked. "Does he know you found it?"

"No. I left it where it was. Then, as soon as he left, I came here."

"He was at your house today?" Carson asked. "He wasn't at work?"

"Well, he works, but he's working late this afternoon, so he's allowed a late start in the morning. I had asked him to check out some work I did on Lady Bug, and he stopped by on his way to the garage," DeDe explained.

"Okay," said Carson, "what you did was exactly right. Are you very, very sure he doesn't know you found it? Your behavior didn't change at all?"

DeDe hesitated. "I don't think I changed. I tried really hard not to let on."

"Good. Great work!" said Carson, beaming at her. "Now you go on about your business, and don't worry about it."

"Easier said than done," DeDe observed. "I've betrayed his trust."

"Sometimes, we don't have a choice," Carson said soothingly. "We may never find Lilli's body unless he tells us where it is."

"Then you think he…killed her?" DeDe quavered. Carson shrugged. "He's our best candidate for now."

"And you've given up hope that she might still be alive?"

Carson studied his feet a long moment before he looked up and said sadly, "Yes."

After DeDe left, Carson spent ten minutes trying to think of a subtle way to approach Falcon. Finally, he gave up and drove to the garage. When Falcon saw Carson approaching, he actually smiled. "Afternoon, cop-meister," he said.

"Good afternoon," Carson replied. "I'm here to search your pickup."

Falcon shrugged. "It's out back. Help yourself." "Is it locked?"

"Naw."

Falcon returned to his work. Carson watched him for a full minute, then asked, "Don't you want to come with me?"

Falcon looked around in surprise. "You still here? I thought you were off hunting Easter eggs."

Carson rolled his eyes. "I would prefer for you to come with me. You know, like you said before, to make sure I don't plant anything on you."

Falcon was suddenly alert. "If you want something planted, you already did it. My pickup is never locked because one of the locks is broken." He wiped his hands on a towel. "Okay, let's go search my pickup."

Diego Calderon had come out of his office and was watching as Carson and Falcon moved toward the door. He was frowning.

"I'm borrowing Falcon for a few minutes," Carson told him.

Calderon nodded, still frowning. He followed them outside - at a distance.

"Now look what you've done," Falcon growled softly. "You've got me in trouble with my boss."

"Well then, isn't it a good thing I'm here so you can prove your innocence to both of us?" asked Carson.

Falcon snorted. He led Carson to an old black pickup and stood aside as Carson pulled on gloves. Carson started in the back, hoping he could keep Falcon from guessing that DeDe was the one who had reported him.

A large toolbox attached tight against the pickup's cab was not locked. Carson examined every inch of it and the truck bed. Then he went to the driver's side of the pickup and searched carefully under and behind the seat.

By the time Carson transferred his attention to the passenger side of the pickup, Falcon was looking smug, and Calderon was looking bored. Carson looked behind the seat first and was surprised to see a key. He held it up. "What's this for?" he asked.

Falcon stared at it, then shrugged. "Don't know. Never saw it before. Must have been in the truck when I got it."

"How long have you had the truck?"

"Two months," said Falcon. "Maybe three." He frowned, trying to remember.

Carson put the key into an evidence bag and stooped to look under the passenger seat. He pulled the pistol out with two fingers and transferred it to another evidence bag before he straightened and held it up for Falcon - and Calderon - to see.

The expression on Falcon's face was worthy of an Academy Award-winning actor. His stunned disbelief seemed too real to be phony. But his shock was momentary. In the next instant, he was in a fury. "Who told you that gun was there? He put it there, whoever it was. I never saw that gun before in my life." Falcon's face was red, and his eyes were wild.

Carson signaled to two officers who materialized out of nowhere and had handcuffs on Falcon almost before he saw them. They led him to their patrol car, sputtering threats and demanding a lawyer.

Calderon joined Carson. His expression was bleak. "Did Falcon kidnap that child?" he asked.

Carson's answer was slow in coming. "Falcon's not stupid." He studied

Calderon's face as he asked, "Why would he keep a gun in his unlocked pickup? He knows he's under suspicion."

Calderon just shook his head. "I can hardly afford to lose him. While he was incarcerated, he got some training from another inmate about the electronics in these computerized cars. I don't have anyone else on staff who can do what Falcon does. He's a magician!"

"Do you want to post his bail?" Carson asked. Calderon looked surprised. "Bail? Can he get bail?"

Carson sighed. "Ya' know, an hour ago, I thought Falcon was the answer to all my questions. But he didn't care if I searched his pickup. And he's no fool…"

Carson paused, his eyes closed, as he arranged his thoughts. Finally, he opened his eyes and shook his head. "There's no way…," he said with conviction. "Whoever put that gun in Falcon's unlocked pickup cleared him of suspicion, as far as I'm concerned. But now, the D.A. – that's another story."

He looked at Calderon with sympathy. "It hardly seems fair that both of you - Falcon and your garage - should suffer because some worthless, lowlife thug decided to abduct Lilli!" His anger was fierce. "But it's your money…"

"I don't know," Calderon said slowly. "Don't you think he might run?"

"He either has to leave his elderly mother here alone or take her with him." Carson shrugged, "I don't have an answer for you."

Then he grinned, "I'm pretty sure I know which public defender will be assigned to his case. I'll give him a call and see if he can convince his client to stick it out."

"Okay," Calderon said. "If his lawyer thinks he'll stay put, I'll pay his bail."

The two men shook hands, and Carson drove back to the police station. He had barely finished making arrangements concerning Falcon when he heard yelling in the front lobby.

"We found her! We found Lilli!" someone was shouting.

Chapter 15: End of the Search

Caleb Carson and everyone else in the building sprinted to the lobby. Carson was almost holding his breath, praying he would see a blond teenager standing with her rescuers. Instead, he only saw two dusty, middle-aged women looking disheartened and disheveled.

"Where is she?" he gasped. "Is she...is she alive?"

The women shook their heads, and he could see that both had been crying. "No," one of them said, "she's...dead. She's in that ravine out north of town. You know, where the two boys were searching, and one broke his arm..."

"And they saw a UFO," Carson finished for her. "Okay, who else knows you found her?"

"No one," said the spokeswoman. "We came straight here."

"Good." Carson glanced around at all the eager faces. "Nobody in this room breathes a word until I speak to the parents. This way, ladies." He led them back to his office.

The two women were Tandy Koch, a real estate agent, and Kasi Mann, an accountant. Kasi had wakened that morning with a sense of dread, thinking about her grandchildren. Upon making two calls and finding out that the children were fine, she called Tandy, her best friend, and suggested they spend the day hunting for Lilli. Both women were desperately sorry for Lilli's family and felt an urgency to find a way to help.

"And why did you choose to search that ravine?" Carson asked.

"Well, I'd been thinking," said Tandy, "what if those boys actually went out there to dump the body because they thought most of the searching was over with? And Kasi thought…"

"I thought," Kasi interrupted, "what if the space aliens left her body there?"

"That was good thinking!" said Carson. "Okay, that ravine is on county land, so I'm going to hook you up with the sheriff and his team. I need to get word to the parents before they hear it from someone else." He paused, considering. Then he asked, "Do you know Lilli? Are you very, very sure it's Lilli you found?"

The women exchanged looks. Then Tandy said quietly, "We never met her, but we've seen her picture all over the media. Of course, we didn't touch the body or get too close, but it's bound to be Lilli."

Carson nodded. "Okay, I'll tell Mrs. Park it's not a positive I.D. yet. Ladies, thank you so much for continuing the search." He choked up and had to pause to recover his voice. "We all wanted her to be found alive, but since that's not to be, we're grateful to you for locating her body."

He called Sheriff Moreno, explained the new development, and sent the women to Moreno's office. Moreno was to notify Bryce, and Carson would talk to Anna.

As soon as Tandy and Kasi were out of sight, the Chief of Police took one of the chairs they had vacated. "Is it Lilli?" he asked.

Carson nodded. "They've never met her, but it couldn't be anybody else."

The Chief sighed. "It doesn't seem possible that this could happen. Where did we go wrong, Caleb?"

Carson shook his head. "It's not us. There's a foul cancer hidden among us. How were we to know about it?"

"Maybe we couldn't, but I want to know where it is now. We have to hack it out before it does more harm."

"I'm working on it," Carson assured him. "In the meantime, I could use your help."

"Of course. Anything," said the Chief.

"I need you to call a Riley Wood at the Community of Faith Church and get the 'Find Lilli' Facebook page removed."

The Chief looked surprised. "Has Riley Wood broken a law?"

Carson said grimly, "No, but our killer is getting his information from the posts on that page. Someone let it out that the cadaver dogs were coming, and Lilli was taken out of that car trunk before we got there. Then the publicity Palmer Evans and Donte Rhodes generated gave the perp the idea of trying to lay the crime at their door by putting the body in the ravine they made famous."

He paused and frowned. "Of course, Evans and Rhodes could be the perps, and they thought they could throw us off the scent by drawing attention to an empty ravine before they dumped the body there. Either way, I want the Facebook page gone before it gives away any more classified information."

He smiled at his boss. "I wouldn't ask you to handle it for me, but I feel an urgency to get to Mrs. Park before she hears the news from someone else. And I want that Facebook page gone as soon as possible."

One phone call let Carson know that Anna Park was still at work. He found her in the lobby of her office building, speaking earnestly to a hugely pregnant patient. When the woman left, and Anna saw Carson, she beckoned him back to her office.

After both were seated, Anna spoke first. "You found her." It was a statement, not a question.

Carson nodded. "Actually, two ladies found her, a Tandy Koch and her friend Kasi Mann."

Anna controlled herself with an effort. "Do you know for sure it's Lilli?"

"We haven't made a positive I.D. yet. Sheriff Moreno will probably ask Bryce to make the I.D."

Anna shook her head. "If he went to work today, it will take Bryce 30 minutes or more to get back here. I want to know *now*."

"I understand that," said Carson, "but she's in that ravine north of town. It will take some time to process the scene, then to get her out of the ravine and back to the morgue."

"I see," Anna said dully. She slumped back in her chair. "I don't think I can see any more patients today." She smiled sadly. "They'll understand. They've been so sweet. Of course, most of them are mothers, so they can understand the pain of losing…"

Carson jumped into the pause. "Of course they do. Mrs. Park, this may be the worst moment in the world to ask you for a favor, but you can tell me to get lost, and I'll go."

She looked up with interest. He had an idea she was desperate for something to take her mind off the death of her beautiful child. And so, he hoped, his request would be a diversion that would give her a few moments of relief.

"What is it?" she asked.

"First, may I close the door of your office?" She nodded with a quizzical frown.

"Please don't get the wrong idea," was his lead-off appeal, "but I would like to ask you about Bryce Douglas's wife."

Her eyebrows rose.

"I haven't been able to find anyone who even remembers her. Do you?"

Anna nodded. "Yes, but only vaguely. She brought Royal to the pediatrician's office where I was working one time. All the other times, it was his dad who brought him. Bryce said she was so depressed she couldn't cope with Royal. Except, she called him…what was it?"

"Elroy," Carson supplied. "Bryce mentioned it one day."

Anna almost laughed. "Yes, Elroy. Poor kid. I think his mother must have already been suffering from postpartum depression when she named him."

Carson grinned, grateful to have lightened the mood. "Did you like her?" he asked.

Anna sighed. "I'm sure I did. My memory of her is too fuzzy to be sure. But I usually like people, and I don't remember *disliking* her."

"What do you remember about her disappearance?" Carson asked.

"Almost nothing," said Anna. "It seems to me that she had been gone for weeks before I even knew she left. Bryce mentioned it one day in passing. I do remember how sad he sounded and how my heart ached for him." She gave a soft, ladylike snort. "I guess you could say it was the first step down the road to romance for us."

"Was there an investigation?" "Not that I remember."

"Okay, Mrs. Park, again, I don't want you to get the wrong idea. This is just a question, not an accusation. Is there any possibility that Bryce may have…um…harmed her in any way?"

"Harmed her like murdering her?" Anna asked bluntly.

"Okay, yes. Is it possible?"

"The thought never entered my mind," said Anna. "Why? Do you think he murdered Lilli?"

"No, of course not," said Carson. "But I can't dismiss the possibility out of hand. Lilli was expected at his farm that day. And her body was stowed in a car on his property. Plus, he told me he got psychological help for anger management issues when Royal was small. Maybe he still has rages. Have you ever witnessed anything like that?"

Anna shook her head. "Never."

"What about Lilli? Did she ever say he yelled or threw things or harmed her in any way?"

"No," Anna said, her voice very certain. "Lilli adored Bryce. He's the one who got her interested in astronomy. They used to go out on summer nights and study the stars with a telescope he gave her. Those nights are some of her most treasured memories."

Anna leaned forward and looked Carson straight in the eyes. "Detective, you need to understand that my daughter is…was…very timid. If she had ever seen Bryce in a rage, she would have never gone back to his house."

Carson nodded. "What you're telling me is that you don't believe he had anything to do with her disappearance or her death?"

"That's what I'm telling you."

"What about Royal?"

That question took her breath away. "What about him?" she asked with a hostile tone and a mother-bear glare.

"Do you believe Royal could have been involved in her disappearance?"

Anna was shaking her head. "Why would Royal want to hurt her? They were great friends. They always got along."

"Maybe Royal wanted to be more than friends. And Lilli didn't."

"Have you *seen* Royal?" Anna asked. "Have you seen him play basketball?

The boy is gorgeous. He plays b-ball like a pro. He can have any girl he wants. He doesn't need to force himself on anyone, especially his little sister." She snorted again. "Anyway, he has too much pride for that."

"Right." Carson stood. "Okay, here's my last question. Do you know of anybody on this planet who might be acquainted with Shawna Douglas and know where she is now?"

"I'm sorry, Detective Carson," Anna said, "I don't."

She watched him leave, then put her head on her desk and bawled.

Carson did not want to ask Bryce Douglas about his missing wife. It would be an obvious accusation. He had been a young officer at the time of the JonBenét Ramsey murder, and the cops' treatment of the parents had made him consider changing careers. Now, here he was, faced with the duty to practically accuse a grieving parent of murdering his child. He didn't want to do it. But he didn't have a choice.

He stood outside Anna Park's office, considering options. It was another clear, cold day in Skyport, a day for happy thoughts and fun activities. With a sigh, Carson fired up his cell phone and called Bryce. Bryce didn't answer. But a moment later, his blue Silverado pickup rolled up to the curb and stopped.

Bryce had just come from the nameless ravine north of town where Lilli's body had been found. He had identified her. Now, he wanted to be the one to give Anna the dreadful news.

Carson greeted Bryce, shook his hand, and drove away. This was not the moment for asking questions about a long-missing wife. If Anna gave Bryce the heads-up about the detective's suspicions, so be it.

Carson glanced at his watch as he pulled away from the curb. It was almost 4:00 o'clock. He might as well tackle his next distasteful task.

When Palmer Evans arrived home from school that day, he found Detective Carson sitting in the kitchen with his mother. Again.

They were drinking coffee. And this time, there was a third person with them, a young woman with short, dark brown hair and a stern expression on her face.

Palmer knew who she was. He had seen her picture in the online newspaper. She was a defense attorney.

Palmer glared at his mother. "What's going on?"

Mrs. Evan's usual calm demeanor had deserted her. Her fingers, curling around her coffee cup, trembled. "Detective Carson has some questions for you," she said.

The young attorney stood and held out a hand to Palmer. "Hi, Palmer. I'm Peyton Starr," she said. "Your mom asked me to sit in on this interview."

Palmer reluctantly took her hand. But his eyes were on the floor, and his face was ashen. "Glad to meet you," he mumbled. Then he repeated his question. "What's going on?"

Peyton Starr resumed her seat, and Palmer stood alone, watching the group.

Carson stood then. "Here, son, take my chair. I'm going to take a stroll around the neighborhood while your attorney visits with you. When you're ready for me, she'll give me a call."

As Palmer sank into the empty chair, both women studied his face. His mother was remembering the little boy who used to climb into her lap for snacks of milk and cookies at this very table. The attorney was thinking that her tall, muscular client looked guilty.

When Starr summoned Carson back to the kitchen, he found a sullen group. No one was talking. They avoided looking at each other. And Mrs. Evans was close to tears.

"Okay, Detective Carson, ask your questions," said Starr. "My client seems to think I'm useless, but I'll try to do him some good anyway."

"Oh, he doesn't think…" Mrs. Evans began.

But Starr interrupted. "Never mind. He has lots of company." She gave Palmer a steely glare. "Anyway, he hasn't proved himself to me, either."

Carson seated himself at the table and opened his notebook. "Okay, Palmer, I guess you know by now that we have recovered Lilli's body."

Palmer nodded without looking up.

"Tell me about the last time you saw Lilli."

Palmer looked up then and glared at the detective. "I don't remember," he snarled.

"Do you ever sneak out of the house during the night?"

Palmer glanced at his mother before he returned his angry glare to Carson. "I've got nothing to say to you," he said.

"How did you know Lilli's body would be dumped in that ravine?"

Palmer stared at the floor.

"Did you put Lilli's body in the ravine?"

When Palmer's stony silence continued, Carson looked around. "I guess we'll need to adjourn to the department," he said wearily. "I was hoping..." He paused. "Well, never mind. Meet me there in thirty minutes."

Thirty minutes later, the same group, plus Mr. Evans, convened for a repeat performance of the scene in the Evans' kitchen. Starr would have cautioned her client not to answer most of the questions Carson asked, but it wasn't necessary. Palmer had nothing to say.

After a fruitless hour, Carson sent them home, warning Mr. and Mrs. Evans that Palmer was not to leave Skyport.

Chapter 16: Revised Approach

The town of Skyport went into mourning over Lilli. And parents became super over-protective of their children. An invisible monster seemed to be looming over their county. And some of the residents were terrified the monster came in a flying saucer and had supernatural powers. How could they fight such a beast?

Detective Caleb Carson, on the other hand, thought the monster was thoroughly human and - he feared - a friend or relative of Lilli's. He kept coming back to the victim. She was very intelligent and very timid. Two facts that had, so far, convinced him she had been abducted during daytime hours when she was out of the house.

But what if - just for the sake of argument - what if she had gone missing during the night? She was both too bright and too timid to leave with a stranger. No one but a close relative or trusted friend could have gotten her out of her safe home. And here, Carson hit his brick wall. What was the motive?

He thought the space monster business had something to do with it. Riley Wood's Sunday school students had pretty well covered Lilli's UFO experiences with their Facebook postings. But what did it all mean? Did it indicate a middle-of-the-night abduction? Lilli was afraid of the aliens. Would she go out to them for any reason? What if they promised to take her to Hubble? She might go then. But, even so, *what happened to her*?

Bryce Douglas or Royal Douglas happened to her. There was no other possibility. Well, unless you believed in space aliens. Carson hated this conclusion, but he couldn't find another *if* the abduction had gone down during the night. And, for now, he was going to proceed as if it had.

Assuming a daytime abduction had gotten him nowhere. Except to the silent Palmer Evans. Hopefully, forensics would connect Palmer or Donte to the body. But in the meantime, Carson set his grim sights on the two Douglas men.

Up to that point, he had been proceeding according to what he privately called the Hercule Poirot method of detective work. He visited his suspects, talked to them like an interested party, and waited for one of them to give himself away. Now that Lilli's death was confirmed, it was time to step up his investigation.

First, he instructed the department's internet guru, Peg Norman, to contact Bryce Douglas and obtain his wife's maiden name. She would also ask for contact information for Shawna's family, even if it was nearly 20 years old. Peg's ultimate goal was to find Shawna Douglas if Shawna was findable.

Next, he assigned two officers to have the key and the gun he had retrieved from Falcon's pickup processed by the lab. Then, they were to do some ballistics testing, just in case a bullet was found in Lilli's body. And they were to find out if the key was a match to the vehicle in Bryce's automobile graveyard where Lilli's body had been hidden.

Last, he assigned himself to the Skyport High School boys varsity basketball team. He intended to interrogate every boy on the team with special emphasis on those who had attended the so-called "free throw clinic" the weekend Lilli disappeared. He didn't care if each boy came alone, with a parent, or with a parent and a lawyer. He had very little hope of dragging helpful information out of them during this first round. No, his initial goal was to identify the weakest link. Once he singled out a likely candidate and focused on him, maybe… Just maybe…

★★★

Skyport High School was poorly attended that Thursday and Friday. Grief counselors were available for those who did attend. And teachers dutifully presided over their partially empty classrooms.

At noon on Thursday in the teachers' lounge, Mr. Josephs apologized for the argument he had spawned the previous week. He had been avoiding the noontime gatherings every day since then. Now, he greeted Mr. Fletcher with a rueful smile. "Kip, I'm sorry for the dust-up last week. Sometimes, I just get a bug to play devil's advocate. I couldn't resist that day. But it was in poor taste because you were upset over your failed experiment."

"The experiment didn't fail," Mr. Fletcher said. "It was succeeding beautifully until I abandoned it."

"Right. Your abandoned experiment, then. Am I forgiven?" Mr. Josephs held out a hand.

"Of course," said Mr. Fletcher, taking the hand. "I apologize, too. I probably got carried away."

The teachers ate their lunches in peace that day. But Mr. Fletcher and Mrs. Sharp exchanged meaningful looks. Both knew that Mr. Josephs had not been playing devil's advocate. He had been serious. And this loser was teaching Skyport students U.S. History!

Royal Douglas was ordered by his coaches to stay home with his family Friday night. If the Rockets lost their basketball game because he wasn't there, it wouldn't be fatal. They were undefeated for the season and led their district by a comfortable margin.

This mandate from his coaches was the reason Royal was with his dad at Anna Park's home on Friday evening. He was already in a snit because he was missing a road trip and a game. And now he had to waste time at Anna's circus. Her three daughters and their children had descended on Skyport. (Husbands would come for the funeral whenever the powers-that-be released Lilli's body.) And, naturally, the older children thought Royal should entertain them. Naturally, Royal thought not. But he did it anyway, just to relieve his boredom.

It wasn't that Royal didn't care about Anna. She was the closest thing he had to a mother. But she was stashed in her bedroom crying. After he had held her hand for a long moment and expressed his sympathy, he didn't know what else to say to her. So, he had let himself be dragged out to the neighboring park by her grandchildren.

Once it was too dark and cold to play outside, Royal and his young charges trooped back inside to feast on a banquet of meats, vegetables, salads, casseroles, and desserts. Anna's friends and acquaintances, as well as people she didn't even know, had cooked or baked their best dishes and brought them to her home. The whole county was desperate to do anything they could to comfort, or at least support, the bereft parents.

Royal filled his plate and found an empty chair in the den. The house was cozy and aromatic with the fragrances of warm rolls and vanilla candles. Royal swallowed the first bite of Fiesta Chicken Casserole, and his snit began to fade away. By the time he finished the delicious meal, he was feeling absolutely mellow. Moving carefully around children on the floor, he went to check out the deserts.

He had just returned to his chair and taken the first bite of a luscious chocolate cake when his cell phone dinged with a text message. Being a teenager, he decided to check the message before finishing the cake. The message read, "Elroy, I'm your mother. May I call you?"

His mouth dropped open. Shawna wanted to call *him*? He texted back, "y."

He had gobbled down the cake and just pulled on his coat when the call came through. He accepted the call, said, "Wait," and went to find Bryce.

"Dad, I'm out of here," he said. "I have an important call." He held up his cell phone.

Bryce frowned. "Important?"

"Tell you later," said Royal. And he was gone.

Safe in his pickup with doors and windows closed, Royal spoke into his phone. "Hello?"

"Hello, Elroy. Are you okay?"

"My name is Royal. I mean, I go by Royal. And, yes, I'm okay. Why are you calling?"

The woman's voice was soft and sweet. He liked it immediately. "Someone from your police department phoned me today. She said she just wanted to know if I was alive and well."

"Alive and well?" Royal repeated stupidly.

"That's what she said."

"The police department?" Royal couldn't seem to do anything except echo her words.

"That's right. I asked her if you were all right, and she said you were. But I was worried about you. I couldn't understand why it was the police calling me instead of your dad. So, I asked her for your number."

"Suddenly, you're worried about me?" Royal asked, and sarcasm laced his voice more than he had intended.

Shawna sighed. "Do you want me to hang up?" she asked.

"No!" Royal cried. "Where are you?"

"Austin."

Austin. Still in Texas.

Royal couldn't think what to say. He had a mother. He had a flesh-and-blood mother. Not just the wedding photograph that had stood on his dresser all his life. What does a person say to a mother?

"Royal, are you still there?" He loved her voice!

"Yes, but I don't know what to say to you. I'll call you back." He cut the connection and started his engine.

"I have a mother." He said it out loud with wonder in his voice. "How does a person with a mother behave?" he asked himself. "A mother!"

Royal put his pickup in gear and drove home to shoot baskets. What else would he do when he was confused? And excited? And worried?

After 15 minutes of dribbling and shooting baskets, Royal had forgotten Lilli and Anna and his mother. He was hot tonight! He couldn't miss! Why, oh why, hadn't the coaches let him go to the game? He might have set a school record for points scored!

Next to the concrete slab, Adolf suddenly stood and growled. His attention seemed to be on the barn. Or past the barn.

"What is it, boy?" Royal asked, peering into the darkness beyond the barn.

The hair rose on the back of Adolf's neck. Royal knelt down and called him. "Come here, Dolf. What's wrong?"

A blast followed, and a bullet whistled past Royal's head. Royal's first thought was for the safety of his pet. He crossed the concrete slab in two bounds, grabbed Adolf's collar, and dragged him into the pickup as a bullet pinged against the bumper. Royal scrambled into the driver's seat, turned the key, and backed up fast. In a matter of seconds, he had turned, reached the highway, and disappeared into the night.

★★★

Detective Carson's Thursday and Friday had been productive. He had met with every member of the boys' varsity basketball team except Royal whom he was saving for last. The principal at the high school had provided a vacant classroom in order to speed up the process.

Carson had served the town of Skyport faithfully and well for many years. Parents trusted him. So, although most of them were present when he questioned their sons, not one of them brought a lawyer. In fact, Carson was able to recruit some of them to his side, assuring them that he only wanted to find out what happened the weekend Lilli disappeared. He wasn't looking to arrest anyone or get them booted off the basketball team for using alcohol or drugs. As a result, he was gratified that many of the parents pleaded with their sons to be honest about the activities of the weekend.

Unfortunately, none of the boys admitted to doing anything except eating, practicing free throws, watching movies, and playing video games. But Carson had identified the player he wanted to interrogate again. The boy was in Riley Wood's Sunday school class. It was obvious that his Christian faith was important to him. Carson was almost certain the boy was longing to go beyond the party line and give him the information he needed.

"Kent Spencer." Carson looked at the name written in his notebook on a page all by itself. Kent Spencer. Surprisingly, he was a senior. Carson had expected that one of the younger boys would be more likely to "crack." Most likely the student trainer, Titus Murphy. But he was going to try Kent first. Right after he had another talk with Royal Douglas.

It was Saturday morning. A preliminary report from the coroner stated that no obvious cause of death had been identified. Until an autopsy was done, COD was unknown.

What Carson did know was that the key recovered from Falcon's pickup was a fit for the trunk of the car where Lilli had been placed by the perp. The gun, on the other hand, was a mystery. Falcon insisted he had never seen it before. If that was true, where did it come from? And why had it been planted in Falcon's truck?

Carson heaved a deep sigh. He wanted to know what had caused Lilli's death. Never in all his years on the police force had he wished so fervently that forensic work could be speeded up. He sighed and picked up his phone.

Bryce answered the call by saying, "Douglas here." It was how he answered at the prison, and he was too distracted at the moment to think about phone etiquette.

"Bryce, it's Caleb. I'd like a formal interview with Royal today as soon as possible. Is he handy?"

"Handy! He's not even here," Bryce said urgently. "I don't know where he is. When I got up this morning, I realized he never came home last night. He's not answering his phone. His friends haven't seen him. His dog is gone. I'm about to lose my mind. First Lilli, now…"

"Hang tight," Carson said. "I'm on the way."

Bryce was pacing around the yard when Carson pulled in next to his pickup and parked. He led the distraught father into the house and poured him a cup of coffee. "Sit down and take some deep breaths," Carson ordered.

Bryce obeyed, and when he seemed calmer, Carson said, "We're tracing Royal's phone. And I've put out a BOLO throughout the state for his pickup. That's the good thing about this deal. We can look for a phone and a pickup. With Lilli, it was like looking for vapor."

Bryce nodded. "I'm glad there's something good about it." He didn't sound glad.

"Look, Bryce, I've got something to tell you. I'm sorry I didn't tell you the moment I heard, but I've been swamped."

"I understand," said Bryce listlessly.

"It's about your wife. It's about Shawna. She's your wife, not your ex-wife, right?"

Bryce's eyes flashed. "Shawna? Yes, she's still my wife. At least, as far as I know, she is. What about her? One of your officers called Thursday, asking a lot of questions about her."

"Yes, Peg Norman." Carson paused to think. But how could he decide? He would let Bryce decide. "Look, Bryce, do you want me to sugarcoat this or just lay it out?"

Bryce sat up straighter. "Lay it out."

"Okay." Carson nodded. "I decided to take the tentative position that either you or Royal was involved in Lilli's disappearance. If Shawna could not be located and might, therefore, be dead, I had to consider the possibility that you were responsible. And if you were responsible for Shawna's death, it didn't prove your involvement in Lilli's disappearance, but it did say something about your character."

Bryce was studying Carson's face intently. "And?" he asked.

"Officer Norman was able to locate Shawna. Her last name is Atkins now, and she lives in Austin."

Bryce's excitement was obvious. "And Officer Norman told Royal about his mother?"

"No," Carson said. "I was going to tell you and let you tell Royal. However, Shawna asked for Royal's phone number, and Peg gave it to her."

"The important call!" Bryce exclaimed.

"What important call?"

"Royal and I spent yesterday evening at Anna's," Bryce explained. "Right before he left, he held up his phone and said he had an important call. Then he took off, and I haven't seen him since."

"Shawna?" Carson asked.

"That's my guess," said Bryce.

"Do you think he would take off to go see her without a word to you?"

Bryce was shaking his head. "Not normally. But since he's AWOL, I'm going to hope that's where he is. Can you get me her phone number?"

It took Carson less than five minutes to call the police department and connect with someone who had the number. Fifteen seconds later, it arrived in a text. Carson held out his phone, and Bryce dialed the number.

When the call went to voice mail, Bryce said, "Shawna, it's Bryce. Royal is missing. Have you heard from him? Please call me before I lose my mind!"

Carson smiled. "That should get her attention," he said. Then he changed the subject. "Listen, Bryce, why don't you tell me about the space aliens that Royal and Lilli both reported seeing? Did you ever see them?"

"No, but I heard all about them," said Bryce. "Royal was young the first time he saw them, and I thought it was just his imagination. But when Lilli saw them too, I began to wonder."

"From what I've learned, it sounds like Royal was really excited about them," said Carson. "Would you agree?"

Bryce nodded. "Yes, he has some pretty bizarre ideas. These aliens from the planet Soteria are going to come swooping in to save the Earth – save us from what, I don't know. In order to save us, they're going to have to take over, and he is going to be their human representative, their regent. It all sounds ridiculous, but he seems to believe it's gospel."

Bryce stopped a moment to think, and Carson waited. "It's almost like this fantasy is his religion," Bryce added. "I kept telling myself he would mature out of it, but he hasn't yet."

"Would you use the word 'fanatical' to describe his faith in those creatures?" Carson asked.

Bryce didn't answer. Carson waited.

Finally, Bryce spoke. "You think he killed Lilli for betraying the Soterians, don't you?"

Carson's answer was as slow in coming as Bryce's had been. "I don't want to believe it, but I don't have any better ideas. And now, he's on the run."

"On the run!" Bryce gasped. "You think he left because he murdered Lilli?"

"What do you think?" Carson retorted.

When Bryce didn't answer or move for two long minutes, Carson stirred. He started to rise, but Bryce's voice stopped him.

"Caleb, who's right? Royal says the creatures are aliens from another solar system. Lilli said they're demons. Who's right?"

Who's right? Why did Bryce Douglas have to ask him a question like that now? Carson took a deep breath, "Before this case, I would have said, 'Neither.' They're not aliens or demons. But if they actually exist - and we do have more than one witness - then I have to say that they're demons."

"Lilli," Bryce mumbled forlornly.

Carson's cell phone sounded then. He spoke into it for only a few moments, then turned to Bryce. "Royal's phone is in this area - maybe at the end of your road. Where is your mailbox?"

"That's ridiculous!" Bryce exclaimed. "Why would he put it there?"

"So it would be safe, and he couldn't be traced," said Carson.

Bryce brightened. "And maybe so I would know he's okay. So I would know he's making his own decisions."

"Yes!" said Carson, feeling a weight fly off his shoulders. "Let's go see."

Sure enough, the phone was in the mailbox. Bryce wanted to put it back so Royal would find it when he came home. But Carson wanted to keep it for analysis. "Phone numbers and texts might give us a clue where to look for Royal," he argued. He did not say that they might also help solve Lilli's murder.

Bryce nodded. "Go ahead," he said, "but let me know the minute you learn anything. I'm going to Anna's. I'm about to make myself crazy, hanging around here with nothing to do but worry."

"Good idea," said Carson. "I'll let you know if I learn anything. And you'll let me know if you hear from Royal or Shawna, won't you?"

"You'll be the first to know," Bryce promised.

Chapter 17: Stolen Gun

Kent Spencer sat in an interrogation room across from Detective Carson. He didn't look intimidated, but he was noticeably nervous. He had come alone. Carson and Kent's single mother, Maisie, had made the decision together that she would not accompany her son to the police department that morning.

Kent was a handsome, athletic kid with white-blond hair and hazel eyes. Carson remained silent for a few minutes, watching Kent, letting him stew. Finally, he said, "So, Kent, tell me, which is more important to you, protecting a criminal or being obedient to your God?"

Kent looked puzzled. "Are you saying God wants me to be a rat?"

Carson smiled briefly. "The Bible says we should submit to those in authority over us, as long as those authorities aren't violating God's laws."

"Oh. I guess I knew that."

Carson nodded. "Probably. Okay, son, here's the deal. Everybody involved in this fiasco knows you boys were doing something illegal - probably using alcohol or drugs. Otherwise, why would it matter that Morton's parents were out of town for the weekend?"

Kent looked confused for a moment at the unfamiliar rendering of Hyper's name. Then he shrugged. "Well, you know, we're teenagers. We like that feeling of freedom."

"Back to my first question," Carson said sternly. "Where is your allegiance - with God or man?"

Kent's lips stiffened. "I think it's unfair of you to say that your way is God's way and any other way is against God."

Carson sighed and slumped back in his chair. "Okay, Kent. If you don't care what monster is loose in this community, go home and pat yourself on the back. But don't expect your mother or me or anybody else with good sense to be proud of you. And if those teammates of yours don't care either, then they don't deserve your loyalty. Go on. Get outa' here!"

Kent didn't move. And he didn't speak for long moments. Then he said quietly. "All of us brought some cans of beer or whatever liquor we found in our houses. But nobody could bring too much because our parents would notice it was gone. So, Douglas said he had a new kind of dope. They were capsules - he called them 'flying pills.' He said they would take us into the stratosphere."

"Where did he get them?" Carson asked when Kent paused.

"He wouldn't say. He claimed he has a secret contact with connections in Dallas. This contact can get him more pills any time he wants them."

"And did you guys try them?"

Kent nodded. "Sure, we were already stupid from the booze, so we bolted them down."

Carson waited for more, and when it didn't come, he asked, "How did the flying pills affect you?"

"I don't remember much about it," said Kent. "They mainly seemed to hype us up in a happy, goofy sort of way. We wrestled around and called each other names. Then suddenly, we all dropped where we were and went to sleep."

"How did you feel when you woke up?" Carson asked.

"Great! We were full of energy and couldn't wait to get on the court."

"Did Royal take any pills?"

"Sure," Kent said, "he was the first one. He said he couldn't wait to start flying. But then, later, we couldn't wake him up. Everybody else was awake by noon. When he wasn't awake by 2:00, we started talking about calling an ambulance. But we didn't want to do that because then we would have to admit we'd used illegal drugs. Hyper said, 'Let's give him until 3:00, so we agreed. And Douglas woke up around 2:45."

"Are any of those pills left?" Carson asked.

"Doubt it," said Kent. "You can ask Douglas. He brought them in a plastic baggie, and those were all gone before the night was over."

Carson nodded. He leaned back in his chair to think. Royal had obviously palmed the real pills and swallowed something harmless. Or swallowed nothing. Then, he could have been gone for an hour or more without anyone being the wiser. Had he sneaked away and killed his sister? The thought made Carson ill. But wait! Who said Royal had even left the Hooper home? Maybe he had been right there with his teammates the whole time, sleeping it off on the floor.

"Look, Kent, do you have any idea at all where Royal could have gotten those pills?" Carson asked, suddenly coming out of his reverie.

"No idea," said Kent.

"Okay, here's what I'm going to do," said Carson. "I'm going to bring the whole basketball team to the station. I won't give a hint that you said more than anyone else. But I'm going to tell them I know about the pills and ask if anyone can tell me where Royal got them."

"Thanks, Detective Carson," Kent said huskily. "I appreciate your not giving me away."

Carson asked Kent a few more questions, then sent him home. Before he could make his first call, two of his officers approached. They had been responsible for getting the gun from Falcon's pickup fingerprinted and trying to locate its owner. They looked excited.

"Whatcha' got?" Carson asked.

"There's not a single fingerprint on the pistol, but it belongs to the varsity head basketball coach at the high school," one of the officers said. "He reported it stolen from the local shooting range last October. His name is…"

"Shad Harris," Carson finished for him. "Good work. Get him. I don't care if he's in Timbuktu. I want him here in fifteen minutes."

The officers grinned, saluted, and left.

While he waited for the coach to arrive, Carson gave orders for the whole

Skyport High School varsity basketball team to come or be brought to the police station. He barely had time to refill his coffee cup before Coach Harris arrived.

The coach was a tall, young athlete who had played basketball for Texas Tech University. Basketball was his passion, and his passion was infectious. The two men had met before and developed a mutual respect.

"Caleb, what's up?" asked Coach Harris.

Carson quickly waved the coach into a chair and got down to business. "I need the story on your gun that was stolen at the shooting range last October."

Coach Harris was surprised. "Really? I didn't think I'd ever hear of it again. Has it turned up?"

Carson nodded. "It turned up in the Lilli Park case."

"Oh no!" gasped the coach. "Where was it?"

"Look, Shad, I'm in a rush right at the moment. It will help if you'll let me ask the questions."

"Of course. Go ahead."

"I know you didn't report any suspicions at the time. But I need you to think again. Who else was around the day the gun was stolen?"

The coach looked grim. "I had three of the boys from the team with me - Royal Douglas, Hyper Hooper, and our student trainer, Titus Murphy."

"But you didn't suspect any of them?"

The coach sighed, "Well, no, not exactly. I never saw any of them do anything suspicious. But I also never saw an outsider hanging around. It seemed like it should be one of my group, but they all denied taking it."

Carson nodded. "I have an idea one of those boys took the gun."

"Do you think he murdered Lilli?"

"I'm not there yet," said Carson, "but it's a possibility."

"So, Lilli was shot?" the coach asked.

Carson shook his head. "No, she wasn't. We haven't worked out the significance of the gun yet. I will be questioning the students you named about it. And I'm going to have the whole team in here in a few minutes so I can talk to them again about the weekend Lilli disappeared. You can hang around if you want to."

The coach smiled. "I'll stay long enough to give them a pep talk about cooperating with the police."

"Thanks," said Carson. "Right now, I need all the help I can get. If you go out to the front desk, someone will direct you to the break room. You can wait there for the team."

The coach stood. "Oh hey!" he exclaimed. "I just remembered. My assistant coach, Len Josephs, was at the shooting range with us that day. You should talk to him. Maybe he saw something I didn't."

"I'll do that," Carson said, making himself a note.

Carson wanted to talk to Morton "Hyper" Hooper and Titus Murphy first, but, just his luck, they were two of the last boys to arrive. In the meantime, he took each boy into the interrogation room individually and, using his sternest demeanor, tried to find out who had supplied Royal with "flying pills."

The boys admitted taking the pills, but all denied knowing their source. Nothing Carson could say elicited so much as a guess from any of them.

Finally, Titus Murphy walked into the interrogation room. Carson almost said, "About time!"

Instead, he went through the same questions he had asked the other boys about Royal and the pills. Then he asked if Titus remembered going to the shooting range with his coach last October.

Titus brightened. "Sure, I remember," he said. "We had a blast. I'd never had a chance to shoot a real gun before."

"Did you know that Coach Harris's gun was stolen that day?"

"Well, sure, but he got it back, didn't he?" Titus asked.

"No, he never did."

Titus suddenly looked worried and uncertain.

"Titus, I have to know the truth," Carson said urgently. "Do you know what happened to the coach's gun?"

When Titus didn't answer, Carson knew he had finally gotten to the basketball player he had been looking for all afternoon. "You know Lilli's dead, don't you?" Carson asked.

Titus's head jerked up. "Lilli? What does Lilli have to do with it?"

"Please, just answer my question."

When Titus answered, his mumble was so soft that Carson couldn't understand him. "Wait!" he commanded. "Speak up. I can't make out a word you're saying."

"Coach Josephs took it," Titus said. His voice was loud now, and his words were clear. "He saw me watching him when he put it in his pocket, and he winked. I thought it was a joke and he would give it back later."

"Coach Josephs?" Carson's mouth dropped open. The assistant coach wasn't even on his radar. When he regained his powers of speech, he asked, "Who else knows that Coach Josephs took the gun?"

Titus shrugged. "Nobody, I guess." He thought a moment, then added, "Now wait. I'd forgotten, but Royal told me a few days later that Coach Josephs had given the gun back to Coach Harris. He said Coach Josephs didn't want me to think he was a thief."

"What else do you know about Coach Josephs?" Carson asked. "Is he the one who got the 'flying pills' that Royal gave you guys?"

Titus shrugged. "I have no idea. I really don't."

Carson stood. "Okay. I guess that's all for now, but be careful out there, Titus. Coach Josephs should be here by now. I don't want him to know what you told me. At least, not yet."

Titus nodded and followed Carson back to the front lobby. The lobby was empty.

"Has Coach Josephs called?" Carson asked the receptionist.

"Not a word," she said.

Carson turned to Titus. "Have you heard from Royal today? His Dad is looking for him."

"I know," Titus said. "Mr. Douglas called me. I think he called everybody on the team."

"Probably. Okay, thanks, son." He started back toward his office.

Titus's voice stopped him. "Detective Carson?"

Carson turned. "Yes?"

"If you're trying to find Coach Josephs, you should try his house. He may be real sick. He had to miss last night's game because he had some kind of 'bug.'"

"Is that so?" asked Carson. "Nobody mentioned it before. Thank you, Titus. It's good info. We should do a welfare check and make sure your coach is okay."

Titus waved and left.

Chapter 18: Coach's Story

Bryce Douglas was still at Anna's home when Treena Wood knocked on the door. Anna's oldest grandchild, six-year-old Lillianna, named after her great-grandmother, raced to the door and opened it. "Yeth ma'am?" she said politely.

Treena beamed at her. "Hello, sweetheart. I'm Treena. Do you know Anna Park?"

The child nodded solemnly. "Yeth, that's my MawMaw."

"Would you tell her that Treena Wood is here and would like to talk to her?"

Lillianna didn't answer. She just shut the door and ran to her grandmother. "There's a lady that wants to see you," she announced.

Lillianna's Aunt Judith took her hand. "Let's go let her in," she said.

When Anna saw Treena, she stood and went to her with outstretched hands. "You're the one who came looking for Lilli for church…that day," she said. "Please sit down."

Treena held out a canister she was carrying. "I heard your grandchildren were here, so I made some chocolate chip peanut butter cookies for them."

Immediately, she had the attention of all the children except the baby, who, at four months of age, hadn't developed a taste for cookies yet. Irene accepted the canister. "Let's take these into the kitchen and sample them," she said, leaving Anna and Bryce to visit with Treena in peace.

After Treena introduced herself to Lilli's mom and dad, she sat down on

162

the sofa. "I'm so sorry about Lilli," she said. "I'm going to try not to cry, but if I do…" Her voice broke.

"If you do, you'll be in good company," Anna assured her.

Treena smiled, nodded, and blew her nose. "I didn't know Lilli long, but I already loved her."

Anna laughed gently. "I'm prejudiced, but I can understand that. Lilli was a treasure."

Bryce, who had sat down on the far end of the sofa, was nodding his agreement.

"I was hoping," Treena said hesitantly, "that we could have Lilli's funeral at my church. I know you may have somewhere else you want to do it. But if you don't…"

Anna looked at Bryce, then turned back to Treena. "Well, we're not really churchgoers. As far as I'm concerned, you're very kind to make such an offer. We could do it at the funeral home, but I think Lilli would have preferred your church. What do you think, Bryce?"

Bryce scooted closer. "Yes, please, do it at the church. And Treena, I would like to hear how Lilli got - do you say 'born again'? She was so excited when it happened, but I didn't give her a chance to explain it to me. I'd like to hear about it now."

Treena didn't need any encouragement. She talked eagerly to a rapt audience of two, describing the morning in the high school library when Lilli accepted Jesus as her Savior. Then she told Anna and Bryce about the Sunday school class where Lilli was the star of Riley Wood's Bible lesson.

When she finished talking and answering questions, Bryce said, "It's almost like an alternate universe. I had no idea all that happened, and my little Chick-a-dee flew off into a whole new existence."

"But she did," agreed Treena. "That's exactly what she did - she began a whole new life. That's why we call it being born again."

Anna and Bryce were exchanging looks, and Treena could tell they wanted to talk. So, she hopped up. "I really have to go," she said. "Maybe someday you'll want to take some cookies or candies or something to somebody else, and they'll fit in my canister. Please keep it and use it when that happens.

When you have a date for the funeral, call Community of Faith Church. Dad will tell the pastor to expect your call."

Suddenly, she sank back onto the sofa. "Oh, I almost forgot. My dad will tell you himself when he sees you, but he wanted me to tell you how sorry he is about the 'Find Lilli' Facebook page."

Anna's surprise registered on her face. "He's sorry? I thought that was a wonderful thing to do, helping to find Lilli."

Treena nodded. "I thought so too, but the Chief of Police called Dad and told him to get it removed immediately before it let the perp - that's what he said, 'the perp' - know any more secrets."

Anna's mouth made an "O." "Oh no. I didn't know it was doing that." She looked at Bryce. "Did you know it was giving away secrets?"

"I wondered," said Bryce. "But, in the end, I thought it might be doing more good than harm. After all, at the time, she was only missing."

Treena rose again. "Anyway, Dad's sorry. He just wanted to help. We all wanted to help."

Anna smiled. "Tell your dad that we understand, and we're grateful for everything he did to help find our Lilli."

"Thank you," Treena said. She hugged both Anna and Bryce, then let herself out of the house.

Irene came back into the den. She was carrying two mugs of hot chocolate. Lillianna was behind her, carefully balancing two saucers, each holding two cookies. "These cookies are yummy," Irene said. "You have to try them."

Anna laughed. "All I do anymore is eat," she protested. Then she accepted one of the saucers and bit into a cookie. She was glad she did!

★★★

Before Carson got back to his desk, his phone was ringing. Hyper Hooper had finally showed up. Carson forgot everything else in his eagerness to question Hyper. It had become apparent to him through the course of his investigation that Hyper was Royal's closest friend. Maybe he could be persuaded to reveal Royal's location.

But Hyper was a huge disappointment. He had no new information for Detective Carson. He didn't know where the "flying pills" had come from.

He had no clue what had happened to Coach Harris's gun. And he had better things to do than listen to a bunch of lame questions the detective already knew he couldn't answer.

"Okay, here's one you *can* answer," said Carson. "Where is Royal now?"

"No idea," said Hyper. "I already told his dad I don't know where he is."

"When was the last time you saw him?"

"Yesterday at school. He wasn't allowed to go to the game last night because he had to hang around with his dad and mourn his little sister." Hyper's voice was scornful. Apparently, he believed a basketball game was more important than a sister.

"Have you talked to Royal today?" Carson persisted.

"No."

"Do you think he could have harmed Lilli?"

Hyper suddenly sat up straight. "Where did you get such a moronic idea?" he snarled.

"How did Royal feel about Lilli? Was she kind of a pest?"

Hyper snorted. "What little sister isn't a pest? So what? People don't murder sisters for being pests."

"So, Royal *did* think she was a pest?"

Hyper sighed and slumped back in his chair. "No, Royal did not think Lilli was a pest. Usually. She thought he was wonderful, and he liked that. Besides, she was really smart, and he was proud of her."

Carson's expression suddenly sagged. "So I've heard. It sounds like she was a pretty special kid. I'm glad to hear that her brother knows it.'

"He does," Hyper said. Suddenly he saddened too. "We all know it," he muttered almost to himself.

"Okay, that's all for now," Carson said, "but I need your promise that you'll let me know if you hear from Royal. His dad is pretty worried. So am I."

"I'll do that," said Hyper, standing and looking relieved. "But you probably don't need to be worrying. Royal is pretty tough. He can take care of himself."

Carson nodded. "Probably. Thank you for your time."

A welfare check on Coach Josephs was Carson's next order of business. He had just picked up a pen to make a few notes before he left when his phone buzzed. Coach Josephs and another man were waiting to see him.

"I'll be right there," said Carson.

Coach Josephs and his companion were seated in the lobby. Before he entered, Carson paused to observe them through one-way glass. The coach wore a light-weight red sweater over blue jeans. His gray, curly hair, held neatly with a rubber band, cascaded halfway down his back. His face was animated as he spoke to his companion.

The companion was younger. He was lean and attractive, wearing a black suit and red tie. His dark brown hair, turning white at the temples, was short and wavy. Narrow glasses with red frames rode low on his nose. Carson wondered if he had a pair of glasses to match every tie. Or did he only wear red ties?

Approaching their seats, the detective extended his hand and said, "Caleb Carson."

The older man said, "I'm Len Josephs, and this is an attorney friend of mine – Wade Lambert."

Carson's eyebrows rose, even as he shook hands with both men. "Wade Lambert," he repeated the name. "You're a little bit out of your own territory, aren't you?" The defense attorney was known but not especially liked in Texas law enforcement. He had a gift for getting guilty defendants acquitted.

Lambert nodded, smiling politely. "Well, I do practice mostly in Dallas, but Len here is an old friend of the family. When he called with an intriguing story, I couldn't resist coming to hear more."

"What intriguing story would that be?" Carson asked with a deadpan expression.

Josephs cleared his throat. "As it happens, I have some information about Lilli Park that I need to pass on to you." He glanced at Lambert. "I said that for Wade. As for me, I'm here to protect one of my basketball players."

"Royal Douglas?" Carson asked.

Josephs nodded energetically. "Yes, you see…"

"Wait!" Carson ordered, holding up a hand. "We'll need to record this interview. Let's get settled in an interrogation room, then I can't wait to hear your story."

When the three men were seated in the small room with cups of coffee handy, Carson stated the date and the names of the participants. Then he leaned back in his chair and asked, "Okay, Coach Josephs, what have you come to tell me?"

Coach Josephs leaned toward the detective and spoke earnestly. "Detective Carson, I need your guarantee that Royal Douglas will not be arrested based on anything I tell you today."

Carson didn't bother to hide his surprised expression. "You must know I can't give any such guarantee."

Josephs leaned back with a sigh. "That's what I was afraid of. And that's the reason I asked my old friend Wade to join me today. He is here to protect Royal's rights."

"He's here for Royal, not for you?" Carson asked.

"Well, the truth is that I don't need a lawyer," Josephs explained. "But I'm worried about how you're going to interpret Royal's actions. He's one of my star players, you know."

"Please start at the beginning," Carson said.

"Right. Well, what happened was that Royal's little sister – Lilli – became a Christian. That fact seemed to be unaccountably upsetting to Royal. He came to me in a state, asking me to help him set her straight."

Josephs was shaking his head sadly as he spoke. "I tried to make him see that her being a Christian couldn't possibly hurt anything. But he insisted and insisted that I had to help him make her see the light. He believed that the longer she continued in her new beliefs, the stronger they would become. Finally, I agreed to talk to her, just because I was hoping it would calm him down."

"When was this?" Carson asked.

"It must have been about a week before the child disappeared," Josephs said.

Carson's expression was grim. "And when did the interview with Lilli occur?"

"It was the night she disappeared. Royal arrived at my house in the middle of the night. He had told me he might bring her that night, but it got so late

I decided he wasn't coming."

"How late was it?" Carson asked.

"Must have been after 2:00 A.M.," Josephs admitted. "I was too tired to be much good and told Royal so. But he was determined. In the end, I brewed some coffee, made Lilli some hot chocolate, and did my best to explain to her why her decision to become a Christian was foolish. She was resistant and defiant. After an hour, I told Royal to take her home, and we would try again when I was awake."

"If all you did was give her hot chocolate and talk to her, why is she dead?" Carson asked belligerently.

Josephs's sigh was heartfelt. "I wish I knew. The last I saw of her was when she pulled on her big, fluffy, white coat and left with Royal."

"She wasn't harmed in any way at your home?" Carson asked.

"Of course not!" Josephs replied huffily. "She was tired – it was a ridiculous hour for her to be out! But she was healthy."

"What about the zebra?"

Josephs looked puzzled. "What about it?"

"Didn't the subject come up? Why would Lilli have agreed to come if she didn't think she was going to find her zebra?" Carson asked.

Josephs shrugged. "I have no idea what Royal told her to persuade her to come. And I certainly don't know where her zebra is."

"I have to ask," Lambert interrupted apologetically. "What zebra?"

Carson offered no response, so Josephs explained. "It seems she had adopted a stray zebra that wandered onto the Douglas farm. When it wandered away, she was dogged in her efforts to find it. She was, in fact, insistent that Royal should help her find the animal."

"Amazing!" said Lambert. "A zebra roaming around Texas, and nobody can be bothered to tie it up or pen it."

Josephs gave him a lopsided grin. "Well, you're a Texan. You should know how we feel about being *born free*. I guess nobody wanted to interfere with a wild animal's freedom."

Carson brought them back to the subject. "So, what happened to Lilli?"

Josephs had a helpless expression on his face. "I wish I knew. All I know is that she was well when they left my house."

"Are you telling me that you didn't ask Royal what happened to her?"

"Of course, I asked him," said Josephs indignantly. "He took her home and saw her safely inside. That's all he knows about it. That's all I know about it."

"In that case, I'm sure you wouldn't mind letting the department search your home," Carson said thoughtfully.

"Mind? Of course, I'd mind!" exclaimed Josephs. "Why would you want to search my place?"

"I can't allow that," Lambert said calmly. "You have absolutely no basis for such a search."

"Really?" Carson turned his attention to Lambert. "Looks to me like you're acting for Mr. Josephs here. I thought your presence was to benefit Royal Douglas."

"Yes, yes," Lambert said, sounding a little unsettled. "I *am* here for Royal, but I can't sit here and let you violate the rights of a good friend of mine."

Carson didn't snort his derision. He just turned back to Josephs and said, "Okay, tell me about Coach Harris's gun."

Josephs did a double take. "About what?"

"Shad's gun. The one you lifted at the shooting range last October."

Josephs frowned elaborately. Then the light dawned. "Oh, right. I had forgotten that incident. It was just a little joke. I gave it back to him, of course."

"Funny," said Carson, "he reported it missing, and today he denied ever getting it back."

Josephs's frown deepened. He was silent for half a minute. Suddenly, he snapped his fingers. "Oh, that's right. I gave it to Royal to give back to Shad. I had forgotten all about it. It was such a minor incident. Do you mean to tell me that Royal never returned it?"

"You see Shad every day at school," Carson observed. "Why wouldn't you return the gun to him yourself?"

"What! Take a gun to school?" Josephs asked. "I would be in *serious* trouble then."

Carson shrugged. "You could leave it in your car and give it to him after school."

"Of course, I could, but Royal offered to take it to him at his home, and I took him up on it."

"How did Royal know you had it?"

"I told him. The whole thing started as a silly little gag, but later, I just felt foolish. I was grateful Royal was willing to take the gun off my hands and return it to Shad."

"Except that he didn't return it to Shad," Carson said.

"Are you sure?" Josephs asked. "It's not like Royal to drop the ball like that."

"Shad told me today that he'd given up hope of ever recovering the gun."

The lawyer interrupted again. "Was Lilli shot?" he asked.

"No," said Carson.

"Then why are we talking about a gun?"

Carson heaved a sigh. "The gun was used to throw suspicion on an ex-con."

"Now, *wait a minute!*" Josephs protested, leaning forward and putting his forearms on the table. "How do you know this ex-con wasn't the one who abducted and killed Lilli?"

"How would the ex-con have gotten a pistol that was last seen in your possession?" Carson countered.

Josephs shrugged. "You'd have to ask Royal about that." He placed his hands on the table in front of him, preparing to rise. "Well, Detective Carson, that's all I came to say. I'm going to take Wade here to meet his client."

"Before you go," Carson said, "will you explain to me why I'm just hearing this story? Lilli has been missing for days. You were obviously one of the last people to see her. Why didn't you come to me immediately?"

Josephs's voice sounded contrite. "I have no excuse, Detective. Since I had no way of knowing what happened to Lilli, I just didn't manage to work a visit to the police station into my busy schedule. Of course, I apologize for my negligence." With that, Josephs and Lambert stood.

Carson remained seated. "You won't find Royal at home. He disappeared last night."

Josephs turned a stunned expression on Carson. "You don't mean to tell me that someone has abducted him, as well."

Carson stood then. "All I know is that he's gone."

"But his phone," Coach Josephs sputtered. "Can't you trace his phone?"

Carson shrugged. "We're trying." He shook hands with both men and escorted them to an outside door.

Josephs extended one final plea as he walked out. "Please believe me, Detective Carson - Royal Douglas is an exceptional young man. He is intelligent, an amazing basketball player, and a dedicated big brother. I'm begging you not to leap to any erroneous conclusions about him."

"That's my job," Carson muttered toward the receding backs of the two men, "not leaping."

Obviously, Carson's next logical step was to interrogate Royal. But Royal was gone. Bryce then. They had to figure out where Royal was.

Carson checked with his staff to see what information Royal's cell phone had provided. He was told that, besides family, most of his calls and texts were to and from members of the basketball team, including the coaches. He had received a call from his mother the previous evening, as Bryce had guessed. So far, there were no hints as to his present location unless he had gone to see his mother. But, in that case, why wouldn't he take his phone?

When Carson knocked on Anna's door, it was Bryce who opened it and led him to the den, where a cartoon was playing on the TV. Karon was seated among the children on the floor; Irene and Judith were absent. Carson later learned they were preparing supper.

When Anna saw Carson, she stood. "Come into my office," she said. "It's not very big, but it's private. And quiet."

The small room Anna used for an office had a small desk with a nice, rolling chair. The only other accommodations were folding chairs. She insisted that Carson take the desk chair. Bryce unfolded chairs for himself and Anna.

Carson's first question was, "Have you heard from Royal?" Bryce shook his head. "Nothing."

"Shawna?"

Bryce nodded. "I had just hung up with her when you knocked. She doesn't know where Royal is, and she's on her way here. She's worried.

Royal sounded upset and said he would call her back, but he never did." He looked at his watch. "She and her husband should be here in an hour or so."

"Her husband?" Carson asked. "So, you're not her husband?"

Bryce shrugged. "I guess not. She said she would explain when she gets here."

Carson studied Bryce. "How do you feel about seeing her again?"

Bryce had to think about his answer, but when it came, he sounded excited. "I'm thrilled that Royal is going to meet her. He needs her."

"And maybe she needs him too," Anna said.

"Very likely," Carson agreed. "Well, I have news too. Coach Josephs just left my office, and he brought a lawyer. For Royal."

Bryce and Anna both looked alarmed. "Why would Royal need a lawyer?" Bryce asked.

"Well, I got a strange story about how Royal brought Lilli to the coach's house in the middle of the night so the two of them could talk her out of being a Christian," Caleb explained. "According to Josephs, Royal was pretty upset about her decision."

"Why the middle of the night?" Anna asked indignantly.

"According to Josephs, that part was Royal's idea. Josephs said he was so tired he finally told them to leave and come back another time."

"And what happened to Lilli?" Anna demanded. "How did she die?"

"Josephs says he doesn't know. According to him, Royal took Lilli home and left her there…here…safe and sound."

"If that's true, why does Royal need a lawyer?" asked Bryce.

"Presumably because I'm not going to believe his story," explained Carson. "Presumably, I'm going to believe Royal is lying, and he did something that caused Lilli's death."

"*Royal* is lying?" Bryce spat the words. "Royal's not lying – Royal's not the one that told that cock-and-bull story!"

Carson nodded. "I understand that. *But* where is Royal? I have to hear his side of the story."

"Of course you do," Bryce agreed. "But now I'm getting worried again. If he had just gone to see his mother, he would have let me know. What if

Coach Josephs has done something to him so he *can't* talk?"

"That's my concern, too," said Carson. "We're keeping an eye on him."

Bryce looked hopeful. "You're watching the coach?" Carson smiled slyly. "Like a hawk."

Chapter 19: Showdown

Len Josephs treated his friend, the attorney, to dinner, then left him at a motel on the highway. He drove straight home. He couldn't wait to take a hot shower and relax with a movie. It had been a long day.

As soon as he pulled into the backyard where he always parked, he saw that the door to his house was standing open. He was momentarily horrified, assuming his home was being burglarized.

But he realized in a matter of seconds that Royal must be inside.

Well, now, who could have predicted that?

Josephs stepped into his kitchen. Royal had broken a window pane in the door in order to reach through and turn the bolt. But the storm door was intact. Josephs locked it and looked around.

Everything was in order, except that the door to the basement was open. Josephs never left it open. He had little doubt that Royal was in the basement where they usually held planning sessions with Aziz. But just in case, he went to his bedroom and took his pistol out of the nightstand drawer. He didn't have to see if it was loaded. It was always loaded.

Josephs walked cautiously down the first few stairs into the basement. He saw immediately that the lamp in the corner of the room was glowing red. And the constellations on the walls were lit. It took his eyes several seconds to adjust to the darkened room. When they did, he was amazed to see Royal seated in his own chair on the elevated platform. A huge Doberman Pinscher rested at Royal's feet.

"What's all this?" he asked, making his voice jovial.

Royal said nothing, but the dog lifted its head and snarled. Josephs could see the fur standing up on the back of its neck. He had been about to take another step. Now, he halted and aimed his gun at the dog.

Royal reached down and put his hand on the dog's head. "Quiet, Adolf," he said softly.

The dog lowered his chin to his forepaws.

Josephs continued down the stairs. "Why did you break into my house?" he asked accusingly. All the joviality had left his voice. "You're going to pay for the repairs."

Royal still said nothing. Adolf was alert but still.

Josephs stepped off the last stair. Why was Royal sitting in *his* chair? His *throne*? He should order him out of it. But what if the little punk refused to move? Josephs could hardly shoot him over it. Reluctantly, he moved across the floor and took the armchair Royal usually sat in. He did not like the lower position. It made him feel inferior. Len Josephs did not like feeling inferior.

Royal and Josephs stared at each other for long moments. Josephs had decided he wouldn't speak again until Royal did. This thug had humiliated him twice by refusing to answer his questions. Then let him say whatever he had come to say.

A full minute of silence passed before Royal asked, "Why did you shoot at me last night?"

The startled expression that appeared on Josephs's face was convincing. "What are you talking about? Somebody shot you last night?"

"No, somebody shot *at* me," Royal corrected. "You're the only person it could have been."

"That's crazy," said Josephs. "Why would I shoot at you?"

Royal smiled slowly. "Right. Why would you shoot at me *and miss*? That's what I had to figure out."

Josephs played along. "Okay. Why would I shoot at you and miss?"

"You wanted me to run so you could go to the police and blame me for

Lilli's death. It's the only reason I could come up with. You got a better reason?"

The coach gave a bored shrug. "I have no idea what you're talking about."

"Really? Then why did you take a lawyer to the police station this afternoon?" Royal's question was a guess and a bluff. As Hyper Hooper was leaving the department, he had seen Coach Josephs arriving with a stranger. Their best guess was that the stranger was a lawyer.

Josephs swallowed his surprise. How did Royal know about Lambert? "The police were demanding that I come in for questioning," he explained. "Under the circumstances, of course, I took a lawyer."

"What did you tell Detective Carson?"

"I told him what happened." Josephs's tone was matter-of-fact.

"After you spent days telling me we couldn't let him know? That we had to protect the Soterians?" Royal asked. "After we spent days pretending Lilli's disappearance was a complete mystery to us? Suddenly, you give him the whole story?"

The coach's hands were moving nervously in his lap. "It began to seem like the only thing to do," he said.

"If you told him the truth, why aren't you in jail?"

Beads of sweat popped out on the coach's upper lip. "It was an accident. They don't put people in jail for accidents."

Another silence ballooned between them. Royal sat as still as a stone Buddha. Coach Josephs squirmed restlessly in his chair.

When Royal spoke again, his voice was low and steely. "What happened to Lilli? What did you do to my sister? The *truth*!"

Apparently, Coach Josephs was unprepared for this question because he hesitated. When he spoke, his tone was pleading. "I told you. She just never woke up."

"Why didn't you call 9-1-1 and get help for her?"

"Royal, we've been through all this before. I told you - I didn't realize...I didn't know...she had died."

"You knew at some point because you took her and put her in the trunk of an old car on my father's property," Royal said accusingly. "Why didn't you take her to the hospital?"

"It was too late. I explained all this to you. Her body was already beginning to cool. There was no way to explain why she was at my house dead. You know as well as I do that we have a mission. Our mission has to be protected at all costs."

"No! Lilli's life was too great a cost." Royal's voice broke, and he struggled to regain control. "Lilli shouldn't have died. What did you put in her hot chocolate?"

"It was just something to make her more receptive. You know that."

"Then why did she die?"

The coach took a deep breath. "The dose may have been too large. She was pretty small."

"Why would you give her something that could kill her?"

"I didn't know it could," the coach admitted.

Royal closed his eyes. His excruciating pain showed on his face. Josephs slowly reached for the gun, which he had set on the arm of his chair.

Adolf growled. Josephs froze.

When Royal opened his eyes again, he was in control of his emotions. "How do I know you didn't purposely give her something that would kill her?" he asked.

Josephs snorted. "That's stupid! Why would I?"

"You hated her," said Royal. "She was interfering with our mission. She was cooperating with Mr. Fletcher's experiment, helping him prove that socialism is stupid. She wouldn't listen to you. She called Aziz a demon. Maybe you decided she needed to be stopped. Maybe you decided you were the one to stop her!"

Royal's voice had increased in both fury and volume with each statement. Now, it dropped almost to a whisper. "Or maybe Aziz told you to kill her."

Royal paused to study the coach's face. This new idea was growing in his mind. "You would do it if Aziz told you to," he said thoughtfully. "He already told you you're too old to be a regent when the time comes. Maybe you wanted to prove to him that you could take my place. After all, I couldn't get Lilli to change her mind about Jesus. You thought I was looking like a failure.

Maybe you thought killing Lilli would make you look worthy, *Lieutenant Josephs!*"

Coach Josephs snatched up the gun, aimed at Royal, and fired. At the same time, Adolf leaped for his throat. The bullet struck the majestic animal. Adolf fell, whimpering, at the coach's feet. In a matter of seconds, four more shots roared out and reverberated around the room. Then, four more.

Coach Josephs ducked and covered his head. When the sound and the smoke cleared, he looked up to see four of the school's varsity basketball players crouching behind the stage, aiming rifles at him.

"Drop the gun," Royal commanded. "Next time, they won't miss."

Josephs dropped the pistol and raised his hands.

"Kent, get help," Royal said urgently, seeming to speak into thin air. "Coach shot Adolph." Then he bent down, plucked a cell phone off the floor, unmuted it, and put it on speaker. "Did you get that, Kent?"

"Loud and clear," Kent replied. "Help for Adolph is on the way, and the police have been here for about three minutes, listening. Unlock the door and let them in."

Hyper Hooper bounded up the stairs to open the door for the police. When Detective Carson started down the stairs into the basement, he met Royal, carrying Adolph out of the darkness. The detective didn't hesitate. "Come on, son," he said. "We'll put him in my cruiser. I'll get you to Doc Latimer's in about half a minute."

Royal was crying, and Adolf was moaning softly. "He's bleeding," Royal warned.

Carson smiled. "Heroes are welcome to bleed all over my cruiser any time," he said.

★★★

By the time Doc Latimer had grumbled and growled and repaired Adolph's abdomen, Royal had been hugged within an inch of his life by Bryce and Anna. And he had met his mother.

Shawna Atkins was a tall, slender woman with short, sandy hair. She wore an expensive-looking gold sweater and dark brown slacks. Mason Atkins was half an inch shorter than Shawna. His dark hair was short and neatly combed. He wore a crisp white shirt and dark blue dress slacks.

"Looks like a politician," Royal thought upon meeting Mason. He was still surprised later when he learned that Mason Atkins actually *was* a Texas state senator.

After the introductions had been made, the group seated themselves in the deserted lobby of the veterinary clinic. Then, the apologies began. Shawna apologized to Royal for abandoning him and to Bryce for marrying Mason without first divorcing Bryce. Bryce apologized to Shawna for being the reason she left. And Royal apologized to the whole group for worrying them.

Everyone in the room wanted to hear Royal's story, but he wanted to wait and tell it only once in Detective Carson's hearing. So, Shawna told her story instead.

"When I left here, I was so depressed I could barely breathe," she told them. "I went home to Mom and Dad. Dad's company transferred him to Fort Worth a month later." She gave Bryce a sad smile. "I was afraid of you and didn't want you to find me. I think the fear on top of the postpartum depression made me a little bit crazy. I couldn't think straight and wasn't making good decisions. Otherwise, I could never have left my baby. Anyway, I started calling myself Smith again. I thought being a Smith would make me practically invisible."

"It did," Bryce confirmed. He looked penitent. "It took me a while to start looking for you because I was so angry that you left. Especially that you left Royal."

Shawna nodded. "I hated leaving him, but I couldn't take care of him. I just couldn't." She looked at Royal. "I'm so sorry, son. I did love you then, and I still do."

"I know, Mom," Royal said. "That's why you're here, even though you had to tell Mason you're still married to Dad."

Shawna continued her story. "Anyway, I missed Elr...Royal... so much that I found a job at a daycare center. Mason's wife, Molly, was in charge of the center, and we got to be good friends. When she developed breast cancer, we grew even closer. And when she died, Mason and I used to cry together. Then we began to date. By that time, I barely remembered that I was still married to another man. Skyport was a distant memory."

She paused to clear her throat and gather her thoughts. She was coming to the most embarrassing part. "Mason and I got married eight years ago. He was a businessman, but he became a Christian about that time and felt that God wanted him to try to do something to help our country. So, he ran for state senator in his hometown and won. After that, I was terrified of his finding out he had married a bigamist. His constituency is pretty conservative."

She stopped and looked at Mason. "I guess we can get a divorce after Bryce and I get a divorce. Do you think the voters will forgive you if you divorce me?"

Mason laughed and reached for her hand. "After you and Bryce get a divorce, we'll get married for real. And I'll 'divorce' the voters if I need to. You're more important to me than they are."

"Even if your job is God's will for you?" she asked.

"Even if," he said decisively. "If it's God's will for me, He'll find a way."

They shared a private smile, then Shawna continued her story. "When we moved to Austin, I got a job as a veterinarian's assistant. So Royal, if you want to bring Adolf home tonight, I know how to take care of him. I'll be happy to stay around a few days to help you."

"Thanks, Mom," Royal said. It had felt funny at first, saying "Mom." But he liked it better every time he said it.

"Mason and Molly had three children," Shawna added. "They're all in their teens now, and the oldest is about ready to fly the coop. I love them dearly, but I was terrified of having another baby myself. I was sure that horrible depression would come back." She looked at Royal again. "So, I'm lousy as the mother of a baby, but I'm not so bad with older children. I hope you'll come see us sometimes, Royal. We want to get to know you."

"That goes for me, too," Mason said heartily.

Royal nodded. "I'd like that," he said, "but I don't exactly know how to act around a mother."

Shawna laughed. "I don't believe that. Bryce told me Anna has been like a mother to you."

Royal suddenly had tears in his eyes. "She has," he agreed, "and I love her." He smiled at Anna, "But I always knew she wasn't really my mother, and it wasn't exactly the same. At least, that's what I thought."

Doc appeared at the door then. "Okay, Adolf is sound asleep," he said grumpily. "Now, you should all do the same."

"Will he be okay?" Royal asked urgently.

Doc glared at Bryce. "Will you get this insulting pup out of my clinic?" he scolded. He turned and headed down the hall to the clinic's back door. "Last one out, lock the front door," he yelled over his shoulder.

"Doc Latimer?" Royal blurted after him.

Without looking back, Doc waved an arm for Royal to follow him. "Just one quick look, young man, then you're out of here. The dog is asleep. He's not going to wake up just to satisfy you."

Royal watched Adolf's chest rise and fall a few times. Then he held out a hand to the vet. "Thanks, Doc," he said.

Latimer shook the proffered hand. "You're welcome, son," he said. "That is a beautiful animal."

Then he switched off the light and walked out the back door.

Royal returned to the lobby, where his family was waiting for him.

★★★

While Doc was working on Adolf, Detective Carson interviewed the basketball team. Again. This time, they had plenty to say. And the dialogue recorded on Kent's phone verified their stories.

The last of the basketball players had just left when Royal, Bryce, Anna, Shawna, and Mason arrived. Detective Carson was waiting for them.

Peyton Starr was there, too. As soon as Bryce heard about Wade Lambert, he had called Starr and asked her to represent Royal. She said she was willing, but she first had to clarify her position with Mr. and Mrs. Evans and Palmer.

Seeing her, Bryce hurried to shake hands and ask, "You won't be representing Palmer, then?"

Starr grinned. "Nope. Palmer said I'm fired. He doesn't need an attorney, and if he did, he sure wouldn't have a *girl* attorney."

After introductions were made, Carson led Royal, Bryce, and Peyton Starr into the interrogation room. Anna, Shawna, and Mason watched and listened from an observation room.

Carson began by asking, "How do you want to start, Royal? Do you want to tell us where you've been the past 24 hours? Or do you want to start at the beginning?"

"At the beginning," Royal said. "Okay. Where does this story begin?"

Royal looked at his dad. Then he took a deep breath and said, "I guess it started when I was about ten." He described his first encounters with Aziz and the Soterians. He tried to explain how deeply the dream about Tojo had impacted his life. "I guess I was having delusions of grandeur," he admitted, "but I wanted so much to do something heroic for Earth. I wanted to help make this planet a garden planet like the one in my dream."

In the outer room, Mason said softly to Shawna, "Sounds like he has the same dream God does – to bring Eden to our world."

Next, Royal explained how he and Coach Josephs had learned they were both in contact with a space alien named Aziz. "The coach has a transponder implanted in his throat," Royal said. "He can use it to communicate with Aziz any time. A few times, he let me come to the sessions when he was talking to Aziz. I loved knowing Coach could connect me with Aziz anytime I needed him to."

He glanced around and saw the skeptical expressions on the faces of his audience. "You don't understand," he said urgently. "It's true. It wasn't just the coach pretending – he has a soft, kind of smooth voice. But when Aziz used the transponder to talk to us, it was loud and rough. It was a completely different voice."

"Okay, let's go on from there," Carson said. "We'll have to agree to disagree on this point."

Royal nodded and described the plans the Soterians had for planet Earth. They were certain they could take it over and reverse the damage humans have been doing to the planet for decades. And they were going to make him an important part of the operation. "It was my dream coming true!" he said excitedly.

"And what did Lilli think about your dream?" Carson asked.

"She didn't get it. In fact, she was afraid of the Soterians. And when she became a Christian and began telling people that they're demons, Aziz was furious. He was calm about it at first. He said I had to prove myself by getting her to change her mind. But a few days later, he went ballistic when I told him I couldn't get her to listen. He said I had to make her understand that it was critical for her to renounce her faith in God and pledge her allegiance to him and the Soterians."

Royal paused and sighed deeply. He had a haunted expression on his face. "After Aziz got so angry, I called Lilli and tried again to explain things to her. She was sweet to me, like always. But she wouldn't even listen. She said she would rather be wrong believing in a God who loved her than be right believing in a monster who wanted to take over the world. I just couldn't make her understand that Aziz is no monster. He's a hero!"

Carson and Bryce exchanged looks. Lilli had spunk. That was for sure.

"Of course, I didn't let on to Lilli that Aziz was furious," Royal continued. "That would have driven her further away. So, I picked her up after school that Thursday and told her everything was cool - that Aziz had it on good authority that nothing was going to happen for at least a year. I said that Aziz understood she was young and had to make her own mistakes, but he was certain she would see the importance of our work and be ready to join us when the time came." He shrugged and shook his head as he recalled the sense of hopelessness he had felt when Lilli stubbornly refused to listen to him.

"So that part was a lie?" Carson asked. "The part about Aziz being calm and understanding?"

Royal nodded. "Right. I put on quite a performance – all excited and smiling like nothing was wrong. But it didn't work. She wasn't interested."

"So, what did you do?"

"Well, Aziz was busy. He said Coach Josephs would have to be the one to help me persuade Lilli. So, I begged Coach to think of something. I was afraid the longer Lilli kept going to that church and listening to Treena Wood, the harder it would be to make her understand the truth about Aziz and the Soterians.

"The coach has a hothouse where he grows all kinds of plants. He also has a lab in his basement where he experiments with them. He said he could give Lilli a drug he developed that would make her more receptive. She would be more able to listen and understand. Plus, if we woke her up in the middle of the night and gave her the drug when she was still sleepy, she would be even more impressionable."

"Are you saying it was the coach's idea to do this in the middle of the night?" Carson asked.

"Sure," said Royal, "it was his show - the whole thing. Of course, Aziz said it was my job, but I wasn't getting anywhere. Once Coach took over, I just did what he said."

Carson nodded. "Go on."

"We tricked Lilli into coming out that night," Royal said. He looked miserable, and his voice was mournful. "It was a lousy thing to do, but I thought it was for a good cause. So we shined a red light outside her window like the spaceship was there and played a recording of Aziz's voice. It said that Hubble needed her and she should hurry. It even said that Hubble could die."

"And that's why she left her house in the middle of the night?" Carson asked.

Royal nodded sorrowfully. "Yeah, she came rushing out in just a few minutes."

Bryce interrupted the flow of the story. "How did you get a recording of Aziz's voice?"

"Oh, it wasn't really Aziz. It was just Coach pretending to be Aziz. He used his own voice. Aziz's voice would have scared Lilli."

Bryce nodded. "That makes sense."

"What happened next?" Carson asked.

"Coach went home to get ready for us. We saw that Anna's car wasn't there, so I was going to call Lilli or knock on the door if she didn't come out. But she came. I told her Aziz had sent me for her. Then I took her to Coach Josephs's house. She didn't like it, but..." Royal's voice broke. "...but she trusted me. So she went inside with me."

Royal had to pause a few moments to clear his throat. Then he continued, "She loved the coach's basement when she first saw it. Half of the basement is a laboratory, and I've never seen that room. The other room is like a planetarium with constellations shining in the night sky. She was fascinated at first. But she studied it and said it was fake. The constellations weren't in the right places. Coach said she was wrong, that the lights represented the constellations in the Soterians' galaxy. So, of course, they wouldn't match the constellations in the Milky Way.

"I don't think Lilli liked Coach. She gave him a sour look and said that was stupid. Why would another galaxy have the same constellations we do? And how did he know what their constellations looked like, anyway?"

Royal paused and thought. Finally, he said, "I can't remember everything we said, but we tried to explain to Lilli how important it is to cooperate with the Soterians. Lilli just wanted to talk about Hubble. She asked if Aziz knew where Hubble was, and I had to admit that he didn't.

"When Coach saw we weren't getting anywhere, he said we should summon Aziz and let him try to explain it to Lilli. I didn't want to do that because Aziz gave me the assignment of convincing Lilli. I didn't want him to know I couldn't do it. I was afraid he would replace me. Lilli said we *should* get Aziz in there. She wanted to tell him she knew he was a demon and that he had to leave 'in Jesus' name.' She sounded really excited like she wanted to see Aziz. She never wanted to see him before."

Shawna and Mason exchanged smiles. Too bad Lilli didn't get a chance to put this Aziz character in his place.

Royal went on. "Coach was getting angry. I could tell by the way his little eyes were bulging. He went upstairs to make some hot chocolate, and I knew he was going to put his secret formula in it, the one that was supposed to make Lilli believe us. I don't know if Lilli would have drunk it, except that the basement was chilly. And Coach loaded it down with marshmallows. She really liked marshmallows."

Outside the interrogation room, Anna gasped and put a hand over her mouth as she tried not to weep. Shawna reached over and squeezed her other hand.

"Coach brought a couple of beers for us and a cup of hot chocolate for Lilli. We sat around like three old friends, talking about where Hubble could have gone. Then, when Lilli finished the hot chocolate, I started in on her again. I told her that I loved her, and I couldn't bear to see her throwing her life away. I tried to make her see what a wonderful future we had together, working with the Soterians to create a better world.

"She just kept yawning. Whatever Coach put in her hot chocolate seemed to make her sleepy. Finally, she nodded off, and there we were. She was asleep, and we'd gotten nowhere. It was getting toward morning, and I needed to get back to the Hoopers. I didn't want anyone to know I had left." He looked embarrassed. "I guess I really knew I was doing a stupid thing all along because I didn't want the guys to know about it. Coach gave me some kind of dope to give them that would hype them up, then throw them into a deep sleep, so I figured I would be okay. But I was ready to call the whole thing off and take Lilli home."

He paused again and looked as if he were about to cry. "If only I had taken her…" He pulled the back of his hand across his eyes. "I should have. But Coach said to leave her. He said she wouldn't sleep long, and she would be even more susceptible when she woke up. He thought he would be able to make some progress with her. If all else failed, he was going to call for Aziz and let Lilli talk to him. He said Aziz would convince her for sure. Then he would take her home.

"I thought it would be okay to leave her there because Anna was at work. I went back to the Hoopers' and slept so hard I didn't wake up until nearly 3:00 in the afternoon. I assumed Lilli was home by then. I nearly went crazy on Sunday when I found out she had disappeared.

"Of course, I went straight to the coach's house and screamed at him, asking him where she was. He tried to tell me he had taken her home and had no idea what happened to her. But when I kept screaming at him, he admitted he fell asleep. When he woke up, she was dead."

Royal stopped talking. His distress was obvious. Finally, Bryce asked, "Where was she?"

Royal did start crying then. "He put her in the trunk of one of the old cars in the A.G."

Royal couldn't go on, so Bryce said, "The coach bought a radiator from the A.G. for his car one time. I guess he remembered it and thought it was a good place…to…" He stopped then, unable to finish the sentence.

"What's the A.G.?" Mason asked Anna.

"It's a bunch of worn out, broken down old vehicles in one of Bryce's back fields," Anna explained. "The kids call it the A.G., the automobile graveyard." She should have been bawling harder than Royal was, but she had cried so many times over Lilli's body in that old car that she couldn't bear to let herself imagine it again. She was grateful Mason had distracted her so she didn't break down for the hundredth time.

Peyton Starr, who had been very quiet up to that point, said, "I'm going to have to stop Royal here. I need to speak to him privately before I can let him continue the story."

Detective Carson nodded. "Okay, then, let's find out about last night. Royal, why did you suddenly disappear?"

Royal straightened up in his chair, took a deep breath, and spoke. "After Mom called me last night, I was so confused I went home and shot some baskets. Adolf was with me, and I was really hot. I was getting angry that I hadn't gotten to go to the game. I thought I might have set a school record because I couldn't miss a basket. Then, someone shot a rifle at me. I grabbed Adolf's collar and pushed him into the pickup. Before I could get in, a bullet hit the bumper. I screeched out of there as fast as I could and went to Hyper's.

"By the time I got there, I'd figured out it had to be Coach Josephs shooting at me. First, I thought he wanted to kill me, so I couldn't tell the cops what he did to Lilli. Then, I realized that if he'd wanted to kill me, I'd be dead. Coach Josephs never misses his target. So, I started wondering why he was shooting at me."

Royal frowned. "I can't be sure, but I finally decided he wanted me to run for the hills. That would make me look guilty, and he could tell some kind of story that would make it look like I had taken off because I was responsible for Lilli's death.

"Coach thinks Spencer and I – that's Kent Spencer – he thinks we're mortal enemies. So Hyper and I took my pickup to his house. His mom said it was okay to park it in the back of the house overnight. I didn't really think Coach would come looking for me, but I wasn't sure, so I didn't want to be driving around in it.

"Hyper and I went to Walmart. He went in and bought a burner phone for me, then we took my phone and put it in Dad's mailbox. I didn't want to be traced, but I wanted Dad to know I was safe. It takes a key to open the box, so I thought Dad would know I was okay if my phone was in the mailbox."

Royal gave Bryce a questioning look. Bryce nodded and smiled.

Finding that phone *had* settled his nerves a lot.

"I wanted to be alone so I could figure out what to do," Royal continued. "I was pretty sure what Coach was up to, and I needed to think of a way to make him tell the truth. But I was afraid Dad would stop me if he got wind of my plan."

Royal gave his dad an apologetic look before he continued. "We took Adolf to Titus's house and left him overnight. Titus is crazy about Dolf, and so is his little pug, Bugsy. I guess Titus fed his folks some story about why I needed him to keep Dolf. He was sure they wouldn't mind.

"Then Hyper smuggled me into his house and put me in their guest room. He shut the door and went away so I could come up with a plan. I stewed over it for a couple of hours, then fell asleep. This morning…" He glanced at the clock on the wall. "…or yesterday morning, we worked out the details."

Royal described the plan he and his teammates had devised. First, they would find a way into Coach Josephs's house while the coach was out. Royal and four others would enter the house. When Josephs returned, he would find Royal seated in his chair. What he wouldn't know was that four members of the basketball team would be hidden under the stage, listening and armed with deer rifles.

Kent Spencer and the rest of the team would be hidden outside. Kent, whose phone was equipped to record conversations, would call Royal when Coach Josephs approached. Then, the boys would leave their phones connected, and Kent would record the conversation. If things didn't go as hoped, the outside group could go for help or storm the house.

"I have Kent's phone," said Carson. "I've listened to the call. Pretty slick trick, getting a confession out of him like that."

Royal shrugged. "Thanks." Then he looked at his dad. "The cops are probably going to keep Kent's phone. I guess I'd better buy him a new one."

"He'll get it back eventually," Carson said.

"Right. And what's he supposed to do in the meantime?" asked Royal. "He came through for me. I can't let him get stuck without a phone."

"Priorities, Detective," Bryce said. "We have to keep our priorities straight."

Chapter 20: Final Farewell

While Doc Latimer was operating on Adolf that Saturday night, Coach Josephs demanded to see his attorney. Wade Lambert went to the county jail and spent an hour with his client. Five hours later, in the dead of night, the coach's house and hothouse burned to the ground.

A police officer had been assigned to guard the house, but three men wearing dark clothes and balaclavas had taken him captive at gunpoint. They had tied, gagged, and blindfolded him, then left him in the back seat of his police cruiser. When fire engines arrived at the inferno, and he was freed, less than 30 minutes had passed.

Later, the fire inspector reported that the blaze had multiple points of origin. Both the house and the hothouse had been consumed quickly. Len Josephs and his attorney, Wade Lambert, denied knowing anything about the fire.

On Sunday morning, when Royal met privately with Peyton Starr, she assured him that what all the TV lawyers say is true – whatever he told her would be confidential. She could not repeat it to anyone except his defense team.

As a result, Royal told her frankly what he and Coach Josephs had done to cover up their connection to Lilli's death. First, hoping to implicate Falcon, Royal had driven around town - when he was supposed to be searching for Lilli – until he spotted Falcon's old rattletrap pickup. He had managed to follow Falcon to work one day. Then he gave the coach Falcon's home and work addresses. The coach had planted the gun and the key in the pickup.

"I didn't know about the gun," Royal told his attorney. "I thought Coach was only going to put the key in Falcon's pickup. When Coach told me he had left the gun there, too, I started worrying. I was afraid it would lead back to us. I couldn't understand why the coach would take such a risk.

"Of course, he had an explanation. He said someone might accidentally find the gun, but there was no chance of anyone accidentally finding something as small as a key. Besides, they wouldn't think anything of it if they did find it. They would just throw it away. And if it wasn't discovered accidentally, he said we would have to make an anonymous call, and he didn't like doing that. He said anonymous calls are suspicious.

"I thought Falcon would be the one to find the gun, and he would just throw it away, so what was the point? Besides, Coach Harris's gun would be gone forever then. But Coach Josephs said it was too late to give it back to him anyway, so it didn't matter."

"Why did Josephs steal the gun in the first place?" Starr asked.

Royal shrugged. "He said he knew it might be useful sometime, so when he saw the opportunity, he took it."

"I don't see how it could be useful since two people knew he had it. If he ever tried to use it to put the blame on Coach Harris for something, the two of you would just put the blame back on Josephs."

"I can see that," Royal agreed, "but Coach Josephs thinks he owns us. He thinks if he tells us to keep our mouths shut, we will. See, he's been coaching my basketball team, off and on, for five years now, and we're all pretty close to him. Besides, he figures any adult would believe him instead of a couple of teenagers."

Starr nodded thoughtfully. "Pretty arrogant attitude, but it might work for him. Is he that arrogant, or is he just stupid?"

"He's not stupid," Royal said.

"Arrogant, then," Starr said. "Well, go on."

"When Coach took a couple of potshots at me Friday night, everything changed for me. I finally realized he might be setting the stage to claim I was the one who stole the gun and killed Lilli. I didn't want to believe it, but what choice did I have?"

Starr shook her head soberly, hating the idea that a trusted teacher and coach could betray the youngsters who believed in him. "Okay," she said, changing the subject, "how did Lilli's body get in that ravine?"

Royal explained that when he learned cadaver dogs were going to be used, he removed Lilli's body from the trunk of the clunker car and rolled it into the ravine. He didn't want Lilli's body to be discovered on his dad's land. Plus, putting it in the ravine might implicate Palmer and Donte.

At the conclusion of these confidences, Starr gave a low whistle. "You are in big trouble, mister," she said. "So, here's the deal. You keep your mouth shut. Do you understand that? You don't tell anyone, including your dad, what you just told me."

Royal nodded miserably. "I'm sorry I was so stupid." He laughed softly. "I knew Lilli was smart. I should have been listening to her instead of trying to make her listen to me. Stupid! I'm stupid!"

"Okay, don't go overboard," Starr counseled. "The first thing I'll try to do is get an exchange – your testimony at the coach's trial in exchange for a full acquittal for you. We have a couple of things working in our favor: your age and your… Well, I'm not going to say you're crazy, but your story isn't exactly sane. That could help us."

The miserable look on Royal's face deepened. "It's not sane? You mean, people won't believe the Soterians are real?"

"C'mon, Royal. Think about it. You didn't tell your friends about the Soterians, and you didn't want Lilli to tell anyone, either. That shows me you knew it didn't sound quite rational."

"No!" Royal's hand came down hard on the table in front of him. "No, I didn't tell anyone because Aziz ordered me not to. Not yet."

"Okay, okay," Starr said. "You believe that if you need to. It can only help."

"My own stupid fault," Royal muttered to himself. "It's all my own stupid fault."

Starr ignored his mutterings. "Now, Royal," she said, "you accused Coach Josephs of murdering Lilli. You said he might have given her a poisonous drug on purpose. Are you standing by that statement?"

Royal shrugged. "It occurred to me right at that moment. I never would have believed it about him until he turned on me. Now, I can't help wondering."

"I've got an assignment for you, then," said Starr. "I want you to review everything you know about the coach. If we convince the D.A. that you can help him convict the coach of first-degree murder, we have a better chance of getting a good deal for you."

Royal nodded. "I'll try."

For the rest of the day, Royal did nothing except try to think about Coach Josephs. But every thought led him to Aziz. For Royal was certain that if Aziz had said to the coach, "Kill Lilli Park," Josephs would have killed Lilli Park. Then Josephs would genuinely be guilty of premeditated murder.

So, Royal asked himself over and over, did Aziz say to Coach Josephs, "Kill Lilli Park"? If he did, he was a monster. Only a monster could want a sweet, shy kid like Lilli murdered.

But the idea that Aziz, Royal's childhood idol, might be such a monumental fiend was unthinkable. The very idea was monstrous! And besides, who did Royal Douglas think he was, presuming to judge Aziz? Aziz was the heroic alien commander who had crossed an eternity of space just to help rescue Earth from certain ruin. How did a 16-year-old kid from a backwater town in Texas have the chutzpah to criticize such nobility?

He didn't. Not easily.

By the time Bryce arrived the next day to pay Royal's bail, Royal wasn't yet ready to forsake his faith in Aziz and the Soterians. But corrosive doubts circulating through his mind were vultures. They chipped away at the pedestal that bore all his hopes and dreams. It would take time, but a day would come when he would realize he not only could, but he *must* question Aziz's character. His motives. Even his existence.

Coach Josephs was denied bail. Emphatically. The destruction of his home and hothouse convinced the D.A. and the judge that Josephs was a flight risk. Not even his famous attorney was able to change their minds.

On Tuesday, the autopsy report on Lilli's body was delivered to Detective

Carson. It stated that she had been a healthy 14-year-old girl. Some destructive changes at the cellular level were noted in the heart and lungs. The toxicology report showed no evidence of the usual prescription or street drugs. Since the conflagration at the coach's residence had destroyed any samples that might have become available for comparison, it did not seem likely that the offending substance would ever be identified.

Bryce, Anna, and Royal met at the police department to hear the results of the autopsy. "There's no telling what that monster was growing in his hothouse," Carson told them. "And we may never know what toxic substance caused Lilli's death, which brings me to another issue. What if the D.A. offers Josephs a reduced sentence in exchange for information about the poison he used on Lilli? How would you feel about that?"

Lilli's family members exchanged long looks. Then Bryce spoke for all three. "It's a lousy idea. Josephs should be locked up until Lilli comes back to us."

Carson nodded. "In other words, give him the maximum sentence possible?"

Anna, Bryce, and Royal all nodded solemnly.

"Yes," said Anna softly, "lock him up for as long as you can."

Carson escorted them to the door and watched them drive away – Bryce and Royal in their pickups and Anna in a little white economy car. His case drove away with them. It belonged to the D.A.'s office now. All that remained for him was to join the community in telling Lilli goodbye.

★★★

The funeral was set for Saturday afternoon at the Community of Faith Church. Anna and Bryce asked Riley Wood to preside at the funeral.

Malcolm and Kandi Park arrived from Italy with their sons, Kolton and Kraig, on Friday. Anna insisted that they be included at the funeral dinner provided by the church at noon on Saturday and be seated with the family at the funeral. Kandi thanked her sweetly. Kolton and Kraig hugged her. "I miss Lilli," 10-year-old Kolton said simply. "Me too," said eight-year-old Kraig. "Me three," said Anna with a smile and a tear.

Lilli's best friends were also invited to the dinner. Nobby Tanaka, Jasmine

Clark, Zion Johnson, and Camilla Rodriguez were all present, dressed in their best clothes. Along with the other guests, they alternately laughed and cried as they talked about Lilli and remembered the good times they had shared.

As the meal was ending, two of the ladies from the church approached Royal carrying a huge sheet cake decorated in the Skyport High School colors - red, white, and blue. Right in the middle of the cake was a basketball made of orange icing. Seventeen lit candles were positioned around the edges.

"Happy birthday, Royal," they said, putting it down in front of him.

"How did you know?" he gasped, barely knowing what to say. "Little birdie told us," they smiled.

By the time the diners had enjoyed Royal's birthday cake or one of the other desserts, it was time to go into the sanctuary. It was time to say "Goodbye" to Lilli for the last time.

The Skyport High School choir director led the congregation in singing "Amazing Grace" to open the service. Then Riley Wood took his place at the podium at the front of the sanctuary. With tender smiles, he described the brief life of the lovely, loving, intelligent 14-year-old girl who had been taken from them. He named survivors and those previously deceased. He talked about the brilliant future Lilli might have had as an astronomer.

And then Pastor Wood held his Bible high above his head. "How many of you know what this book is about?" he asked. He paused dramatically, then said, "It is the story of a cosmic war.

"At the beginning of history, as we know it, God created the spectacularly beautiful planet that we call Earth. He chose to put a man and a woman in charge of the planet, to tend it and to rule over it. But He had also made other beings - spiritual beings. For our purposes, we'll call them angels and fallen angels or demons.

"It seems that at least one of those spiritual entities thought he should have been put in charge of this planet. He couldn't attack God for fear he would be annihilated instantly. But apparently, he felt slighted and wanted revenge. So, he turned his attention to the man and woman, Adam and Eve. He was able to pull them down from the exalted position God had given them. Then, he and his fellow malcontents initiated a war against God's representatives, human beings. You and me. That war has been going on ever since. It really is a *world* war. That is the story of the Bible. If you want to know who wins so you can get on the winning side, read the end of the book, the story told in Revelation. There's a blessing for you in reading that last book of the Bible.

"Our issue right now is that Lilli is a victim of the cosmic war. She had the good sense to be afraid of those demons who call themselves Soterians. The dark powers who oppose God are scary. They are terrifying. Lilli was wise to fear them. But don't forget, once she understood what they were, once she understood that she had authority over them in the name of Jesus, she had the courage to face them. To face them alone. Lilli was a courageous warrior in the cosmic conflict that engulfs our planet!

"Some of you here today may not believe in demons. And you may actually believe in space aliens - monsters from distant planets. You may even consider them *heroes* from another world. Whatever they are, they...are...the enemy. And they are the reason Lilli never had a chance to live out the amazing life God had planned for her.

"But here's the good news. Lilli found out how to choose the winning side. Lilli met our Lord Jesus Christ and chose to make Him her Savior. So - now folks, I don't want any of you to get depressed - but this very minute, Lilli is in a much better place than you are. I'm selfish. I wish she were still here. But I will thank God forever that He gives us a choice. And we can make the choice Lilli made. We can choose Heaven as our eternal Home.

"My daughter Treena and I have been having a debate this week. I say 'The Battle Hymn of the Republic' is Lilli's song. It's perfect for her! Treena has another choice, and I'll let her tell you about it later. Right now, let me explain my viewpoint.

"One of the verses reads: 'He has sounded forth the trumpet that shall never call retreat; He is sifting out the hearts of men before His judgment seat; Oh, be swift, my soul, to answer Him! Be jubilant, my feet! Our God is marching on.'

"Lilli heard that ageless trumpet call. And when God spoke to her heart, her soul was swift to answer. Based on my daughter's description, I can assure you that Lilli's step was jubilant when she received our Lord into her life. Coming into the family of God was a powerful experience for her. And her decision to receive Christ as her Savior was proof that God is marching on.

"The following verse says: 'In the beauty of the lilies Christ was born across the sea, With a glory in His bosom that transfigures you and me. As He died to make men holy, let us die to make men free, While God is marching on.'

"This verse says Christ was born in the beauty of the lilies across the sea. Christ was also born in our beautiful Lilli right here in Skyport. She was transfigured by His glory. I believe her death will lead to some people becoming free of sin and death as they follow in her footsteps because God is still and forever marching on.

"Someone once wrote a short, simple poem entitled, 'Every Day: Christmas.' It goes like this:

'Blow your trumpet! Sound your horn!
For tonight, Jesus Christ is born.
Sing, you hills! Leap up, you Earth!
For this day, gentle Jesus has his birth.

Tonight, He's born in you;
Tomorrow, He's born in me,
And every passing day,
He sets another prisoner free.

So shake your cymbal! Strum your harp!
For every day is the Lord's birthday to someone's lonely heart.
Then, sing, you breeze! Shout, you storm!
For today, the Savior of the world is born!'

Pastor Wood looked up and suddenly smiled broadly as if he had just remembered a joke. Then he actually winked at the congregation and said,

"If you want revenge, if you're angry that the evil powers of darkness stole Lilli from us, you can make them sorry. Just make today your Christmas. Receive Jesus Christ into your heart as your Savior. There's nothing you can do that will hurt and anger those evil gangsters more than that. And there's nothing they can do about it!

"I know we live in a hostile world. Even the United States is growing more and more hostile to our Savior. It takes some courage and some conviction to choose to be on the Lord's side. But don't ever forget - God wins. If you choose to be on His side, you'll be on the winning side. I hope Lilli's wisdom and courage will be an inspiration to someone in this room. I hope you will have the audacity and the sense of adventure to join God's army and become a soldier for right and justice.

"Now, the Skyport High School choir is here to sing 'The Battle Hymn of the Republic' for you. As you listen, please think about what I said. According to the Bible, we are engaged in a great cosmic war. We all have choices to make, either for the side of good or the side of evil. If you think you're not making a choice, you just chose evil. But today can be your own personal 'Christmas.' It's your choice. This song was a Civil War song. I think you'll see how appropriate it is as a modern war song."

"The Battle Hymn of the Republic" almost always reaches the hearts of listeners. It was no different that day. The beautiful song brought tears to many eyes and pride to every heart.

When the last "Glory, glory hallelujah, God is marching on" had died away, Pastor Wood said, "If you didn't know Lilli well, you might think she was a little grasshopper of a girl. But Lilli had guts. She had heart. Lilli was a conqueror and a winner. Today, I salute Lilli's courage, her intelligence, and her amazing spirit!"

Malcolm Park couldn't stand it. He was so moved he could not contain himself. He stood and began clapping. Then his sons joined him. Then, Anna and Bryce. Suddenly, the whole room was clapping and roaring their approval and love for Lilli.

Shouts of "I love you, Lilli!" and "You go, girl!" and "Lilli, we miss you!" could be heard from around the congregation.

Every person in the room was standing except one. Royal Douglas, his arms resting on the pew in front of him and his face buried in his arms, was weeping like a five-year-old. Bryce pulled his son into his arms and held him while he regained control.

"Okay, some of Lilli's friends want to say just a few words about how much they love her and miss her," said Pastor Wood. "We'll start with Nobby Tanaka."

Nobby walked to the front of the sanctuary, and the pastor handed him the microphone. "When I was in Japan, I was at the top of my class," Nobby said. "When I came to America, Lilli was always ahead of me. It was partly because of English classes, but she beat me in Math and Science as many times as I beat her.

"Always trying to win over Lilli made me work harder and do better. I am afraid I will not work as hard since she is not here, inspiring me to do my best. But I am going to try really hard to keep doing better and better in honor of her.

"I love Lilli Park, and I am glad I am going to see her again someday."

Fighting tears, he started back toward his seat. But Anna stood and moved into his path. She put her arms around his neck and whispered, "Thank you, Nobby. Lilli loved you too."

Lilli's other friends made only brief comments. Zion Johnson said emphatically, "Lilli was the best! I'll never forget her." Camilla Rodriguez said, "Lilli always helped me when I didn't understand my Math. And she never made me feel stupid. In fact, after she helped me, I always felt smart. Those were the only times I ever felt smart!" Jasmine Clark stood before the congregation and tried to speak, but she could only blubber, "I want Lilli back." She, too, got a hug from Anna.

"Okay, we're almost done," said Pastor Wood. "I'm practically positive that you are in agreement with me about Lilli's song being 'The Battle Hymn of the Republic.' But since I promised, I have to let Treena have her say."

Treena made a face at her dad as she walked forward. Taking the microphone, she said, "My dad is right. Lilli is very special. And very brave. I think if I had ever told her she was brave, she wouldn't have believed me.

But she had the courage of her convictions. She had the courage to take a stand for the Savior she had just met. I will always admire her for that.

"Lilli wanted to be an astronomer. She was fascinated by the universe. I believe she is busy exploring the stars and the planets in our galaxy right now. She may be checking out the rings of Saturn and the moons of Jupiter. She could be strolling right through the middle of the sun! And I know she will explore our neighbor, the red planet Mars, with all its crazy craters. The fact is that the person who murdered Lilli Park launched her into an early start on her dream career.

"And that's why I say Lilli's song is 'I'll Fly Away.' When her soul left her body, she flew right into the arms of Jesus. And right into His vast, glorious universe. She left this world of strife and war and escaped to a Land where joy will never end. Someday, I'm going to fly away, too. I can't wait to see Lilli on that day and get her to show me all the wonderful worlds she has discovered in God's universe!"

The choir director led the congregation then in singing "I'll Fly Away."

Royal sat silently next to his dad as the music swelled around them. His head was bowed, his heart broken, and his spirit crushed with guilt. Tears drenched his face.

As he waited hopelessly for the music to end, a vision of Lilli appeared in his mind. Robed in light, like purity, she floated in the air. Her hair, flowing down her back, glowed golden and was crowned with a circlet of lilies of the valley. Her fresh, open face – so familiar and so dear - shone with innocence. Her soft, dark eyes sought his. And her lips curved upward in her sweet, shy smile.

"Goodbye, Lilli," he whispered. "I love you forever."

Epilogue

Peyton Starr turned out to be a bulldog of a defender. Her deep probe into the background of Coach Len Josephs revealed that he was a member of a Communist cabal located in Austin. The group's objective was to infiltrate Texas schools, glamorize Communist theory, and promote it to students. Josephs had been sent to Skyport eight years earlier, and students from every one of those eight years reported that he had maligned the United States and promoted socialism, especially in the form of Communism.

So great was the anger directed toward the teacher that at another time in history, Josephs might have been tarred and feathered. In supermarkets and cafes and churches, the patriotic community of Skyport could think of no other topic to discuss than their outrage at that "Commie pinko," Len Josephs. He had not only taught their children false and failed theories, but he had so little concern for Lilli that he had willfully or negligently caused her death.

The other players in the case were also thoroughly analyzed. Potential jurors didn't like his "fancy lawyer" from Dallas much better than they liked the defendant. When the county judge in the case granted Wade Lambert's request for a change of venue, the judge came in for his own share of venom from a community that was hungry to hang the coach. The district attorney, on the other hand, became a hero when he decided to charge Josephs with murder instead of manslaughter. And Royal, a local sports hero who wore his remorse like a garment, was mostly pitied.

At Coach Len Josephs' trial, two little-known facts were revealed. First, tracking data revealed that Lilli had taken her phone with her the night she and Royal went to the coach's house. Yet the phone was found charging in Lilli's room the next day. Second, the door key to Anna Park's home was found in the ashes of Len Josephs's house. The coach had no comment concerning these facts.

The D.A. theorized that Coach Josephs had removed Lilli's house key from her pocket and used it to return the phone to her bedroom. It was a simple way to dispose of it, and it might lead investigators to conclude that Lilli had returned home safely that night. Then Josephs had kept the key in case he wanted to enter the home again, or he had put it in his own pocket and forgotten it.

Since Lilli had admittedly been in Josephs's house on the night she died, finding her house key in the ashes after the fire proved nothing. But it *was* suggestive. And Royal's story, supported by his teammates' testimonies, was riveting. Josephs was found guilty of felony murder and sentenced to 25 years in prison.

In Royal Douglas's case, Peyton Starr used his age, his willingness to plead guilty to obstruction of justice, and Coach Josephs' undue mental and psychological influence on him to keep her client out of prison. Royal was sentenced to a year of community service and a year of psychological counseling.

The Skyport Rockets varsity basketball team did not go to state in 2020. They did win district and their playoff games. But a politicized virus named COVID-19 cancelled their hopes of bringing home a state championship.

The members of that tightly bonded team did recognize the foolish risk they had taken the weekend of their free throw clinic. Every one of them understood that experimenting with alcohol and street drugs jeopardized their team's championship dreams, and they scrupulously avoided those temptations for the rest of their high school careers. In addition, most of them found ways to let Detective Carson know they were grateful that he kept his promise to ignore the illegal activity they had engaged in that fateful night.

The friendship between Lilli's parents, Anna and Bryce, deepened. Through phone calls and visits, they helped each other cope with the loss of their beloved daughter. Both of them had been comforted by the funeral. Treena's description of Lilli enjoying an exciting new life gave them hope. And a month after Lilli's funeral both of them attended services at the Community of Faith Church. Neither had known the other would be there, but both of them found comfort in the fellowship of the church and became regular attendees.

Anna also received solace from her ex-husband, Malcolm. In previous years, their communications had been rare. Now, they began talking weekly, sharing stories about Lilli that the other had no way of knowing. When they ran out of stories, they began discussing their own lives – their work, their families, and their dreams.

Five years after Lilli's death, when Kandi fell in love with a younger man and demanded a divorce, Malcolm gave up his weekly calls to Anna. He feared that his connection to his ex-wife might be damaging his current marriage. And he understood the importance of keeping his home together for his sons' sake.

But Kandi was determined. Her new love, a native Italian, was younger and more exciting than Malcolm. He rode a motorcycle, and she delighted in riding behind him, holding on to his waist and feeling the flow of the wind around her body.

Although Kandi had no interest in finding a job or developing a career, she was weary of her petty pastimes. An adventurous new life with a young lover captured her imagination. Enchanting new fantasies thrilled her. They sparkled. They cajoled and bewitched her. No wise counsel and no reality check could reach her. She was through with her old life. Period!

When Malcolm realized his wife was lost to him, he imposed some stiff stipulations upon their divorce agreement. First, he would pay alimony for no more than a year. Even though Kandi had a new love, the word "marriage" was glaringly absent in every conversation. Malcolm had no intention of supporting Kandi and her new fellow for the rest of his life. Second, he demanded that he be awarded custody of their sons at least 50 percent of the time. Kandi tossed her head and said he could have full custody. She would see her boys when she had time. After all, they were 13 and 15 now – practically grown.

The ink on the divorce papers wasn't dry before Malcolm was calling Anna. He said he would move back to Skyport if she would marry him. She said if they got married, she would move to Italy or Saudi Arabia or Siberia, wherever he needed to be. Kolton and Kraig didn't need to be half a world away from their mother. And she needed to escape from the lonely memories of Lilli that haunted her at every turn.

So, on a brilliant April Sunday, on the lawn of the little yellow and white house where Lilli had grown up, Anna and Malcolm married again. Their children and grandchildren cheered. So did Bryce and Royal. And Anna wondered if Lilli might be watching from some lofty position and cheering too.

Bryce Douglas had dated occasionally throughout the years after Shawna left him. But he had never allowed himself to fall in love again. Once his divorce was final, he began to look at the single women in and around Skyport with new eyes. It wasn't long before he was courting a lovely woman he met at Community of Faith Church.

Lilli was never forgotten by her family and classmates. In the ten years after her death, no fewer than five "Lillis" were born to her relatives and friends. Lilli's half-sister Karon got pregnant so that she could have a little girl to name Lilli. When Kip Fletcher's next historical novel - set in the Russian Revolution of 1917 - was published, it was dedicated to the memory of Lilli Park.

Lilli's adored big brother, Royal, did his community service on the YMCA basketball court. He worked with younger boys and girls, teaching them how to dribble and feint and sink baskets. In the summer, he did his community service, as usual, then put in more hours, working around the YMCA wherever he was needed so he could begin paying his dad back for veterinary, legal, and counseling costs he had incurred.

Royal's senior year, the Rockets did go to state, but they did not win the final game. Kent Spencer had graduated the previous year. Without him, the team didn't quite have the scoring power to put them over the top against the best team in the state.

After high school, Royal played basketball for Baylor University in Waco. While there, he spent many happy weekends and holidays with his mother and her family in Austin. It wasn't the same as having a mother in the home during his childhood, but the Atkins family added a richness to his life that he treasured as long as he lived.

After college, he was drafted into the National Basketball Association and played for fifteen years. About the time Royal was ready to retire from the NBA, Bryce began talking about selling the farm and moving into town. Royal packed up his family and moved them to Skyport.

Royal and his family converted the Douglas farm into Lilli Land the following summer. They made it a place where city children could get a taste of farm life. Of course, they charged admission, but once inside, children could gather eggs and take some home. They could learn to milk cows. They could harvest tomatoes and peppers and corn; strawberries and peaches and apples; whatever was growing there. These treasures were theirs to take home and enjoy with their families.

Lilies were one of the highlights of Lilli Land. Beds and borders of the colorful flowers delighted visitors. And Bryce and Royal erected a hothouse where exquisite exotic varieties of the lily family flourished. A local florist purchased many of these for gifts, bridal bouquets, and banquet decorations. Lilies were the most popular flowers in Skyport!

Bryce had gotten rid of the old A.G. – the automobile graveyard - 15 years earlier. The thought of Lilli's body locked in one of those old car trunks literally made him ill. Now, that field became an orchard. The Douglas family delighted in experimenting with fruit trees, learning which apples and peaches and plums grew best in the area. Once the field was full and exploding every year with colorful, delicious fruits, Royal's youngest child - his daughter Lilli - named the orchard "Candy Land."

The renovated farm was far from the garden planet of young Royal's dreams. But it did satisfy a deep longing in him to bring beauty and nourishment to his small corner of the world.

The second year Lilli Land existed, Royal located a pair of exceptionally docile zebras that needed a home. He named them Hubble, Jr., and Sputnik and put them in the pasture with the cattle. Soon, they were the stars of Lilli Land. Everyone who visited the farm wanted to see the zebras and pet them.

Royal, on the other hand, tried not to look at the zebras. He had gotten them to remind everyone of Lilli, but he had not known his heart would stab him every time he saw the little black and white ponies. For Royal had gladly done his community service as what he considered grossly inadequate payback for his crime. His counseling sessions had delivered him from faith in Aziz and the Soterians or any alien. But nothing could make him forget the part he had played in the death of his only sibling.

No, Hubble, Jr., and Sputnik only brought him pain. But when the pain and loss of Lilli hit him the hardest, it was usually the dead of night. Then, he would go outside into the farm she had loved. He would look up, up, up into the night sky full of constellations. UFOs would not even enter his mind. Instead, he would remember the words Treena Wood had spoken at Lilli's funeral.

She had said Lilli was out there already, exploring that vast universe. She might be riding the rings of Saturn or strolling through fiery stars. She could be documenting the craters of Mars or cruising through some galaxy on a comet. Treena said Lilli had been launched into her dream career. He would never forget those words.

And Treena had closed by saying that someday, Lilli would show her all the wondrous worlds she had discovered. That was Treena's hope. It was Royal's hope, too. He wanted to see Lilli again. He wanted to hear her voice and experience her enthusiasm.

Yes, Royal believed that Lilli had flown away. He agreed with Treena – Lilli's song was "I'll Fly Away." And Lilli's song was his hope. Someday, he wanted to fly away, too. Someday, he wanted to meet Lilli in the sky. Because, somehow, he knew in his heart that she had forgiven him. The mysterious God she had embraced in the last days of her life had given her the power to forgive even the betrayal that led to her death.

So, on those dark nights, searching the sky for he knew not what, Royal would softly sing to himself, "I'll Fly Away." He would imagine meeting Lilli on a fluffy, white cloud and saying, "Hello, Lilli. I love you forever."

The End

Author's Note to the Reader

I have written the Epilogue to this story as if the world will continue for another 15-20 years without any epic changes. However, I'm not sure that assumption is valid. According to Bible prophecy, many changes in our world signal the possibility that the Rapture, the Great Tribulation, and the Second Coming of Christ may be very near. The arrival of these events would render my Epilogue impossible. End times events will impact every person on Earth in ways we cannot completely predict today.

Time, as we know it, may be very short. Here's hoping I'll meet you one day in the clouds as we go to meet the Lord in the air. Maranatha!

You Have the Power!

If you make online purchases, you know the power of reviews. Most of us don't buy a product unless glowing reviews support it. So you have great power to influence future readers!

If you liked *Lilli's Song*, I'd be so grateful if you would share your thoughts in a review. Don't make it difficult - just write a sentence or two to tell the world what you liked about the book. Your feedback helps other readers discover the book and supports my writing journey. Warmest thanks, and happy sleuthing!

Scan the QR code to go to my review page:

Acknowledgments

It is with deep gratitude that I acknowledge those wise and wonderful folks who have helped make this novel possible. I heartily endorse the program and the books named below (numbers 5-7). I believe any reader who is interested in the topics would enjoy and/or benefit from listening to or reading them.

Personal:

1. Terri Johansen. My wonderful sister-in-law is my content editor. She has read three drafts of this novel carefully and thoughtfully, then pointed out some major changes that needed to be made. If you enjoyed the story and understood it, you can thank her. I certainly do - thank you, Terri!
2. Linda Battle. My dear friend Linda is my copy editor. She did an amazing job of catching little boo-boos and humbly asking me if I didn't want to change them. I always did. Thank you, Linda!
3. Jack Tonn. Thanks to my amazing colleague, Jack Tonn, for his baby porcupine story!
4. Family and friends. I am ever and eternally grateful to my family and friends whose support and encouragement are the gasoline in my engine!

Respected Christian figures:

1. Radio hostess: Jan Markell's weekly "Understanding the Times" radio ministry is a window to our times and our place in Bible prophecy. It was while listening to an "Understanding the Times" program that the idea for this book germinated. Then, as I was writing the story, I got bogged down at one point. It was another "Understanding the Times" program that gave me the idea I needed to continue. Website: olivetreeviews.org/

2. Author: Billy Crone. Jan Markell's program featuring Billy Crone and his book, *UFO's: The Great Last Days Deception*, sparked the idea for *Lilli's Song*. Also, studying his book helped me present the UFO appearances in a somewhat realistic manner.

3. Author: Michael Keiser. Michael Keiser's books *Supernatural* and The *Unseen Realm* reinforced and expanded my understanding of the supernatural forces at work in our world. (Please do not leap to the conclusion that Keiser promoted the idea of demons impersonating space aliens. That topic was not the subject of either book.)

You:

1. Readers. Thank you for reading *Lilli's Song*. I hope you enjoyed it and that you will constantly be discovering wondrous worlds and inspiring ideas in the books you read!

www.ingramcontent.com/pod-product-compliance
Lightning Source LLC
Chambersburg PA
CBHW072051170626
46813CB00004B/1310